BOOK TWO OF THE BLUE WALLS OF HEAVEN

THE EGG MAN

Stephen Parr

Wolf at the Door
Bristol 2014

Published by Wolf at The Door, Bristol 2014
34 Cornwallis Crescent, Bristol BS84PH
Copyright ©Stephen Parr 2014
fullmoon@wolfatthedoor.org

ISBN 978-1-326-02542-7
First Edition

The author has asserted his moral right under the Copyright, Designs and Patents Act, 1988, to be identified as the author of this work.

All Rights reserved. No part of this publication may be reproduced, copied, stored in a retrieval system, or transmitted, in any form or by any means, without the prior written consent of the copyright holder, nor be otherwise circulated in any form of binding or cover other than that in which it is published and without a similar condition being imposed on the subsequent purchaser.

A CIP catalogue record for this title is available from the British Library.

For all my teachers – too numerous to mention

What you may have missed...

In *Error Message*, the first book of this trilogy, Adam Stone hears unearthly voices in his head, which turn out to belong to highly intelligent aliens from the distant Owl Nebula. The aliens intend to reconfigure human DNA with non-violent pathways and so render humanity peaceful and fit to join the cosmic community of civilized races. In what might be seen as a grossly irrational act, they choose Adam as their unlikely ambassador, on the sole basis that he believes they are sincere and don't harbour any destructive intentions towards humans. However, they reckon without human irrationality, especially in the field of Russian jokes, which they believe may hold the key to the human mind.

Adam is also desperately in love with his old friend Jack's wife Elaine, who is just about to phone Adam with a sanity-shattering announcement...

Chapter One

A phone was warbling brightly somewhere in the far off land of dawn.

Somehow I got enough of my brain's attention to reach out and answer it, though I hadn't sufficiently considered the complex problem of making coherent speech.

'Yeh?'

'Adam? It's Elaine.'

'Is it a fire?'

'No, it's just me. I'm really sorry to wake you. But I need to talk to you.'

'Elaine? What time is it?'

'Half past four. I'm very sorry. But something awful has happened.'

Slowly the old world was clapping itself back together.

'I thought you were a fire. What's up?'

'I just told Jack I'm leaving him.'

In a microsecond my brain had snapped awake and was already calculating its moves. Frankly it shocked me how quickly it could respond when it imagined it had something to gain. And this scheming schlemiel was living in my own head off the very food I was eating, and there was nothing I could do about it.

'You're leaving Jack? You can't be serious!'

'I'm afraid I'm totally serious. It's not working. We've both been denying it for months. If not years. Pretending we had the perfect marriage. Last night we had a good talk and we agreed to separate.'

'But Elaine... I can't believe this. You *have* the perfect marriage! You told me yourself at that party. And Jack said it was a marriage made in heaven... or somewhere. I mean, you *can't* just leave him.'

'We've been talking it through all night. To go on pretending we're happy together would be a travesty of all we both believe. Adam, I feel so incredibly lonely.'

'Where's Jack now?'

'In bed reading.'

'How is he?'

'Devastated, of course. It came totally out of the blue for him. He hadn't the slightest idea anything was wrong. But that's exactly the problem: he had no idea what I was feeling. Adam, I've realized we're completely incompatible.'

'But what about all that you were telling me at Kew? That stuff about working through differences? You convinced me you were right.'

'Oh, I was doing what I always do: denying how deep feelings go. There are some differences that seem to be unbridgable no matter how you try to work with them.'

My brain was desperately trying to reclaim my attention. Knowing me pretty well, it could see where I was going with this line of argument, and was throwing up all ten thousand of its prissy little hands in horror. It thought I was playing a double bluff: arguing that Elaine and Jack should stay together and resolve their differences so she would trust me and believe I had entirely abandoned my designs on her blissful body, and would consequently agree to go away with me. You have simply no idea how painful it is having a brain that doesn't trust you. But I admit I was getting pretty good at ignoring it.

'Look, Elaine, why don't you just not make any decisions for a few days? You know, like when you make a financial investment, you get to think about it for a week or so? You might find there's a way of resolving it without splitting up permanently.'

'Oh no, we're not doing that. All I meant was I need to go away for a few weeks to find out what I really feel. I can't imagine wanting a divorce, or anything like that. I still love him after all.'

My bluff had been called. Suddenly I felt betrayed, as though a magical fragment of paradise had been dangled before me for a brief instant. So why was she telling me how totally incompatible they were?

'I don't understand, Elaine. What is it exactly you want?'

'I need to talk to someone. Someone who's been there, who understands.' She was on the edge of tears, and I so desperately wanted to say, 'I'm your man. I've been there, I understand. Come round. Spend the night with me. We'll sort everything out.' But my brain had its ethical bloody foot in the door and wouldn't budge. It was hopeless, but I found myself saying it anyway.

'Well, you know what I want, don't you?'

'Yes, Adam. And I'd like to come with you.'

My heart gave a little whoop of triumph. 'You would?'

'Yes. On the understanding of course that it's strictly platonic. I just need to talk with a friend I trust and have some space and think things through.'

'Absolutely. No problem at all. Would you like me to sign in blood?'

'We could go to my Uncle's cabin in the Quantocks. It's completely peaceful and very pretty. If you don't mind inquisitive cows.'

'They're the things I love most in all the world.'

Chapter Two

'Early spring sun caressing a still lake. A feeling of everything opening, like finding a place that has me written into the deep heart of it. Lapping of ice-clear water, very gentle, hardly audible. Supernal calm. Do you think that's too literary? Too Eliotesque?'

'No. Not at all. Please go on.'

'Insects trying on their wings, like wobbly toddlers on Christmas morning. Coming home. And then a long blank. That's when it happened: whatever went wrong happened in that blank. A wrong message lodged somewhere. A poisoned wedge of deadness in among the rainbow voices. But no way back from here. No path home. I have to live with all the consequences, do my best to undo the ghastly mistakes. Every single one of my love affairs has been an attempt to get back onto that path and put everything right. But it doesn't work. It's like the virus has been copied into the new relationship every time, even before the first smile. Or maybe with the first smile. There's a thought.'

'And yet. There is this world: a mystery with a conundrum at its heart. There is the sleeping wildness which never explains itself, but just goes on being different, as if that was its sole appointed task. There are secret forests where the gods still walk in the morning, if you look in the right way. There are sunrises that redeem all the horror for a few moments. And there's music. Thank heaven for music: a tiny, left-open gateway. And beyond it the faint silver track through the forest. And the gifts that come when they come, and go when they go, and leave no instructions. Like the Cube. Some gift that was. We're still paying for it.'

'No.' said Elaine. 'I don't like that.'

'What's wrong with it?'

'Oh I don't know. It feels too – self-conscious. Why don't you just say what happened?'

'Because Clare said I was to put my feelings into it.'

Clare was my angel-voiced ex-psychotherapist, mistress of all I'd forgotten.

'Yes, but I don't think you have done. It's like it's coming from a separate personality. It's too distant. Too... safe.'

It was our second day at the cabin and it was every bit as charming as I'd imagined. We slept in separate beds against opposite walls, with two small flowery-curtained windows facing south. Elaine seemed understandably self-absorbed, and I didn't press her to talk about Jack. Reading my therapeutic memoir to her seemed a good way to encourage her into a different space.

'Would you like to hear some more?'

'Sure.'

'This is a later bit, about my Dad. "He was a wanderer. He'd get restless and then one day he'd be off somewhere without warning, and a week or two later we'd get a postcard from him in Brazil or Morocco: 'Weather unbelievable: please send socks and razor blades'. It used to drive Mum perfectly crazy. She never knew whether she'd wake up in the morning alone or with a husband. It would have helped if she'd nagged him a bit less, but when he was in the house she couldn't ever leave him alone for one second without telling him off for some infringement of her all-pervasive rules. She'd treat him like a naughty child who couldn't be trusted to do anything right. 'Wash your plate up, Stan! Don't come in the house in those filthy boots! Wash you hands before you eat, they're smothered in dirt'. It's no wonder he took off at every opportunity. She'd've driven St. Francis crazy.'

I glanced at Elaine to see if she was faking interest.

'Go on, please.'

"He also used to play the violin very badly. It was his way of getting justice. He'd go up into his room, lock the door, and play for hours on end. It really was excruciating. Mum would hammer on the door for him to stop, and threaten him and abuse him, but he just blithely went on playing more out of tune than ever. In my imagination I can see him sawing away by the window with a demonic grin spread right across his face. It was a war of attrition which neither of them could hope to win. There was one day in October when it came to a head after he'd been playing non-stop for two hours in the middle of the night. She grabbed his violin and brought it down with all her considerable strength on the iron gas stove. It broke very unmusically into an amazing number of splinters. Dad didn't say one word. He just slouched straight into the garden shed and locked himself in. The next morning he was gone. He was away for two months; no postcards, no phone-calls for underpants, no communication of any kind. Mum went totally frantic. She bitterly regretted smashing his violin. I found her crying her heart out in the garden one morning, saying over and over: "I shouldn't have done it, I shouldn't have done it. I've killed him," and so on, completely overcome by remorse. True to form, Dad arrived back two days before Christmas and tried to pick up his old life where he'd left it, but something had gone out of him, some spark of energy or belief. He was never the same after that. Mum died only four years later, out of guilt I think. So I'm left with a very dodgy role-model for marriage. It's appalling what humans can do to each other when they become inseparable.'

'Mm,' said Elaine, stretching out on the couch so that the beautiful slim form of her body was revealed. 'I like it. It's much more readable than the first part. They seem so much more like real people. It makes me want to know more about them.' She picked an apple from the fruit bowl and bit into it noisily.

'That's good. There's a lot I want to say about my parents. The only thing is, it's not true.'

'What do you mean, it's not true?'

'Well, I'm afraid I made it up. Some of it anyway. The bit about my Mum smashing Dad's violin and then dying four years later – she didn't. She just banished him to the garden shed and died nine years later in an old people's home.'

'But why? I mean, what does it achieve? You're supposed to be writing about your life in order to understand your feelings, right?'

'I know. But it bores me. My life is the most boring thing I can imagine. I want to make it interesting.'

'But isn't that missing the point?' She bit so deeply into her apple that a section flew off and skidded across the floor. 'Presumably the point of writing is to be true to what happened. Isn't that interesting enough?'

'You're beginning to sound like my therapist.'

'I'm sorry. Obviously it's your writing and you can write in any way you like.'

'Now you're being patronizing.'

'Ok. I'll just shut up then.' She flung what remained of the apple core through the partly open doorway.

'No. Please don't. I'm just nervous about getting it wrong. The truth is, I don't know what I'm supposed to be doing. I can write about my life in so many ways. Record the events. Record my feelings about the events. Comment on them. Philosophize. Write about what I should have done. Invent things. What's the right way?'

'It probably doesn't matter. So long as you write. You're not writing for an audience. So what does it matter? I expect the truth will pop out at some point. What do you say to macaroni cheese?'

Chapter Three

Elaine's efficiency in the kitchen startled me. In less than half an hour she had a saucepan of macaroni and fresh vegetables steaming on the table. I discovered I was ravenously hungry and ate without pausing for conversation. Outside the cabin the night was clear and calm, lit by a young crescent moon glowing like an elvish ship above the trees.

I said: 'I think it's time to break out that wine, don't you? It looked quite a good one.'

'It is. I feel a bit guilty about it. Jack bought it to celebrate some occasion and then forgot about it.' She went to fetch the bottle.

'Tell me about you and Jack. I mean, he clearly still cares for you a lot. What's happened between you?'

She frowned, as though guiltily remembering what she'd come here for.

'As I said, we've both been pretending to each other for months, if not years. The bottom line, I'm afraid, is Jack's only love is astrophysics. He doesn't know how to relate on the human plane, through emotions. That's really important to me. It's what makes life worthwhile. But I still love him dearly. That won't change. And I know he cares deeply for me. There's nothing – absolutely nothing – he wouldn't do to make me happy. But he can't change the single thing that really matters: how he is in himself.'

Rain had begun to fall, making a soft animal pattering on the felt roof. Elaine glanced through the window, as though speaking of Jack so intimately might evoke his presence. Then she continued:

'I don't think he feels any need to change. From his point of view everything's perfect. Perfect job. Perfect partner. Perfect security. Beautiful daughter. Why change anything? Why can't it all just go rolling along and being perfect?'

'Maybe because his perfect world depends on a lot of imperfect people always doing the right thing.'

'Anyway, I realized it wasn't perfect for me. I was ignoring a whole part of myself, and you can't go on doing that indefinitely without something snapping.'

'So what's this all about? I mean, how does your coming here fit in? And how does Jack feel about it?'

'I think Jack feels if I must go away with someone he'd much rather it was you than anyone else.'

'Really?'

'Of course. He's known you a long time. He feels you're a soul-friend. You can be trusted to act from your principles.'

'But what have I done to make him trust me?'

'Oh you don't have to do anything, you nut! You are who you are, and Jack trusts who you are. It's really very simple.'

'Well, I don't trust myself, so I don't see why anyone else should.'

She smiled. 'Shall I give you one reason? You've been completely honest with me the whole time we've known each other. I'd say your deepest instinct is to be truthful.'

'Elaine: I have to be truthful: you're wrong.'

She giggled in that girlish way that had never failed to captivate me.

'You've just proved the truth of my intuition.'

It made my heart lift to see such pleasure in her features, though I couldn't begin to tell her the depths of her misperception.

'Truth is important, you're right. The only problem is I find it damn near impossible to speak it. There's something in me that believes if I tell the truth I'll be exposed to all the evil in the universe, with no protection.'

'But don't you see? You're telling me the truth now, aren't you?'

'I think so.'

'And nothing awful's happened to you?'

'Apparently not. At least I haven't heard about it yet.'

The giggle threatened to take over her voice entirely. 'Well then: that's why I trust you. You're completely honest about your experience. Even when your experience doesn't make sense, you're open to all its contradictions. And that's a valuable gift to give someone.'

'Really?'

'Of course! You care to get at the truth, even if it's uncomfortable or disturbing. Not many people have that much integrity.'

Her conviction seemed so misplaced I was genuinely baffled. 'Why?'

'Well because – because it makes me feel there's a real mind there to test my own feelings and ideas against. There's something that cares more for the truth than to be thought well of, or to be popular or attractive.'

'I can't help feeling there's a good deal of fantasy in that observation. I do care for the truth it's true, but I care even more about being thought attractive. If I felt you didn't find me attractive I'm not sure I'd want your company for very long.'

'I don't believe that for a moment. That isn't my experience of you. And Jack's often said you're an inspiration to him. Someone who lives his principles regardless of the cost.'

'I'm finding all this praise hard to take. How about we change the subject? Tell me why you think Jack can't give you what you need.'

'Well, for one, he's never interested in spending any time with me. He thinks time spent talking about feelings is time stolen from work. And he doesn't have any needs beyond discovering the next anomaly in some incredibly distant radio source. And third, he doesn't understand art: he thinks it's just a huge distraction from reality. And fourthly' – she came to a halt as though she'd run out of reasons. 'This is hard for me to say Adam. It feels like betraying him.' She stared at her hand holding the wine glass, as if willing it not to crush it. 'He has no sexual interest in me any more. I exist only as a mind to try his theories out on.'

I strongly suspected this last reason was the clincher. I tried a stab at her own tactic.

'I don't believe that for a moment. No man in his right mind could fail to be interested.' She coloured slightly, but went on:

'But it's true. He makes excuses all the time. His mind is perpetually on other things. I could accept that for short periods, if he was tackling a difficult project or something. But he just doesn't want to go there. I feel I'm no more than a social prop for him.'

'But you love him.' I said it as a statement, in order to trigger some faint hint of ambiguity. But she glided over it with ease.

'It's hard to accept that he's changed permanently. I'm always hoping one morning he'll come out of it and be his old self. But it's been like this for over two years now. I'm becoming resentful of him, and I so hate that.'

'Have you thought of counselling?'

'He wouldn't go for that. He'd think it was an invasion of his privacy.'

'It might be worth asking. If he knows how unhappy you are.'

'I think we've gone beyond that.'

'So maybe you have to accept it and move on.'

Her eyes quickly darkened. 'What do you mean, "move on"?'

'Consider what situation will supply your needs.'

'Oh, needs!' There was a shocking vehemenence in her response. 'How do I know what my needs are? They're so dependent on circumstances. I mean, over and above food, shelter and connectedness can you define an absolute need?'

'I'd say love was an absolute need, wouldn't you?'

'I'm not sure. If you're secure, well-fed and middle-class it may be more of a priority than if you're starving, homeless and sick.'

'I don't buy that view. I think love is fundamental. Without it we're less than human.'

The rain had stopped and a wakeful silence brooded over the cabin. I became aware of the secret life embedded in the landscape all around us. I wanted more than anything to take Elaine to bed and make gentle love to her, but it was clear that that was far from her mind. We undressed facing opposite walls and slipped quickly into our separate beds like children untroubled by adult concerns. Yet as I lay bathed in the nurturing silence my mind was a bedlam of anxieties about how long I'd be able to maintain my pretence of avuncular equanimity.

Elaine's trust in me was gratifying and terrifying in equal measure; gratifying because to be trusted absolutely by a beautiful woman gave my self-esteem an enormous boost, and terrifying because of course there was one crucial fact about me that couldn't fail to fatally undermine her trust: that I was a murderer. And if we were ever to have an intimate relationship I would have to confess that to her and take the consequences.

But then in the darkness my brain got working on the problem. 'Maybe,' it murmured, 'you wouldn't need to confess that particular item, because in a way you didn't kill Rachel did you? Because you came back later – or was that earlier? – and she was seated at the table looking the perfect party guest – as cool and radiant as ever and commenting on the quality of your cooking – not exactly the actions of someone who'd recently been brutally strangled and sexually assaulted, wouldn't you agree? And if she did die on that occasion, why wasn't there a police investigation into her disappearance? Why in over two years did you never see anything about her on TV or in the papers? It's inconceivable that no one would have missed her in all that time. Surely the answer is that you didn't in fact strangle her at all, and your memory of doing so is a kind of hallucination brought on by your chronic sense of guilt that has dogged you every moment of what you like to call your life: in other words, rationalizing your feelings by providing evidence of an act of sufficient evil to justify them. In which case what would it serve to confess this false memory to Elaine? Would it enhance her respect for you, or would it sow the seeds of future doubt and disharmony between you? Surely the best policy is to keep quiet about things that need never intrude on your relationship: "keep the dog far hence that's friend to Man'". Thus spoke the captain of my soul.

Somehow in the midst of this turbulence I must have found sleep, for the next thing I was conscious of was warm sunlight resting on my head, and sheep gargling muddily to each other outside the window.

Elaine wanted to show me something she'd found.

'There's this room full of ladders. I can't imagine why he wants them.'

We shuffled along a corridor at the back of the cabin and Elaine unlocked a door with the biggest key I'd ever seen. It didn't seem to go with the rest of the cottage, to say the least.

The room was much taller than any of the other rooms, and completely unfurnished – apart, of course, from the ladders. Most were arranged against the walls, but there were several lying flat on the ground, as though a colossal game of snakes and ladders had been in progress the moment before we entered. I made my way across the room, stepping gingerly between the rungs.

'What on earth is all this for? Did your uncle ever mention that he collected ladders?'

'Never. But it doesn't surprise me. He's always been secretive. To be honest I'm just grateful not to find anything worse here.'

I tried picking one up, but Elaine stopped me. 'I wouldn't move anything Adam. It might all be carefully arranged. I mean it might be a coded message, or part of an art installation or something.'

'Is your uncle an artist?'

'No. But as I said, he's secretive. And he has quite a temper if anything's changed. I'd rather not have to explain we've messed up his prize project. Shall we go back? I feel a bit guilty being in here.'

'This room seems to have been built as an afterthought. As though it was made for a specific purpose after he'd moved in. Do you know what he was into at that time? I mean, was he obsessive about anything?'

'I've no idea. As I said, I hardly knew him when I was a girl. He has the reputation of being a loner and not taking kindly to visitors. Most of the family just avoids him.'

We went into the conservatory for breakfast. I was fascinated by this grey eminence gradually taking form in my mind. Elaine suddenly said:

'I've just remembered something. He wrote a book.'

'What about?'

'I don't remember. Ah, wait. It was about astronomy. He used to have a telescope. I don't know if he brought it here. I think he discovered something. I don't know what. It was a long time ago.'

'So that would explain all the ladders.'

'How?'

'It was a joke.'

Elaine smiled gracefully. 'I don't know Adam. I'm as mystified as you.'

It felt very odd staying in a cottage with a room containing nothing but ladders. As though we were sharing the place with a third person who never revealed himself. I wandered around the building trying to find anything that might offer a clue to the mystery. But there was nothing: no library, no telescope, no instruments of any kind. I put it to the back of my mind and concentrated on my journal.

Chapter Four

On the fifth day of unbroken fine weather Elaine suggested we explore further afield. There was a sense that a change was coming: the humidity had been gradually building, and that usually presaged a storm before long.

We made an early breakfast and started out about nine, making for Longstone Hill and the ancient trackway that led westwards towards Quantoxhead, where we planned to stop for lunch. The skylarks were in full song as they had been every morning, making full use of the air currents as the sun heated the atmosphere and burned off early mist. It seemed a moment of sublime tranquility, and yet I was apprehensive: my obsessive thoughts of the past night reasserted themselves. How could I possibly tell Elaine how wrong she was about my integrity; that she'd elected to spend two weeks alone in an isolated cottage with a rapist and murderer? (Or more accurately, with someone who suspects he might be, but in a parallel world. And is it the emotion, my lords, which makes the murderer? The intention, or the outcome of the intention?) Yet confess was exactly what I now longed to do, above even sleeping with her I craved understanding, if not forgiveness.

We found a hollow out of the breeze and lay down, using our coats as pillows. It was still before noon, but the strong sun was heating the air and sending the birds gliding for cover in the nearby coombs. There seemed to be an almost mystical peace among the hills: an active presence which pervaded every branch and every rock. And yet I had an equal sense of impending crisis; something seemingly innocent that would nevertheless alter the whole pattern of my life from that moment on – though it was probably nothing more than an air pressure change occasioned by the approaching storm.

Elaine lay on her back and carefully positioned her hat over her eyes. I moved closer to her. She closed her eyes but didn't withdraw. The sunlight seemed to intensify, as though someone was holding an invisible lens over our bodies. She stretched herself out, shook her head so that her fine flaxen hair fell in all directions like rivers in spate, eloquent under the generous light.

I began to see her not as a sophisticated and ambitious scientist in charge of complex research programmes but as a vulnerable girl longing for contact and affection, and afraid to ask for it. It brought out a fatherly need in me to protect and nurture her. As though sensing this she leaned back gently so that her tresses fell unkempt against me, their scent mingling tantalisingly with my breath. I clasped my hands around her waist.

'Did Jack ever do this?'

'That's an unfair question. He's a wonderful man.'

'But?'

'There is no but.'

'So why are you here?'

'Because you wouldn't stop pestering me until I agreed to come for the sake of a quiet life!'

'Oh. That's a bit of a spin on the truth! Is that the real reason?'

'Well, no. Not entirely.'

'So?'

She gently shook herself free, looking pained, as if I'd pressed her into revealing someone's intimate secret.

'I need to get a handle on what's happened. Talk things through with someone who's opinion I respect. This has really knocked me sideways, you know: Jack and I have been very close for so long. He's shaped my life. I can't accept it's over, just like that.'

'I know. You become part of each other.'

'Yes. That's it exactly. So how can I leave him without killing a part of myself? You must have gone through the same thing with Cora? I mean, there's no way to separate without that pain of tearing out a part of yourself, is there?'

'That's the exact question I'm struggling with. I think you're probably right, but you have to balance it against the pain of staying together when there's no communication and no sharing. Sometimes you have to bite the bullet and take the way of least damage.'

'But if I left Jack he'd be simply hopeless on his own. He can't even boil an egg without some disaster happening.'

'But is that your responsibility? Maybe on his own he'd learn to boil an egg, and that would be beneficial for his survival.'

'He'd feel I'd betrayed him. I don't think I could bear that.'

'Well, he has the option of changing what he feels. Why not let him choose? He can learn to communicate and keep you, or remain in his own world where he doesn't need you. Not a bad position, really, is it?'

'Or maybe I should learn to be more self-reliant. Not have so many needs.'

She stared into the distance. The sunlight was changing: a pale haze had crept up the hillside and now hovered just below us among the clusters of gorse, throwing them into disturbing relief. I could sense her heart responding, betraying the stoic poverty of her words. Her living warmth felt infinitely sweet and life-affirming. Yet the struggle in her mind was palpable. I'd led her into areas she'd probably never ventured into before, where duty, loyalty, desire and passion had come together, like contending beasts, in the same arena. For a second she seemed paralysed by the extremity of the conflict. Then in an instant she twisted away like a wild creature alerted to danger. She got to her feet and brushed down her dress.

'The weather's changing. We ought to be getting down, don't you think?'

By the time we reached Quantoxhead lunchtime was history, and we settled for afternoon tea in a quiet cafe in a short cul-de-sac run by two thin elderly women who by their looks and demeanour must surely have been sisters. The only other customer was a skeletal old man in a corner reading a local newspaper. A plump, grey long-haired cat lay snoozing in the window. We were hungry and ordered several rounds of toasted teacakes well smothered in butter. We were served almost without a word being spoken. Only the cat looked up and met our eyes for a moment, in expectation of some interesting tidbits coming his way, before losing interest.

Elaine suddenly asked me again about my father.

'Well, as I told you he lived for music. After my mother banished him to the garden shed his character changed. He became more solitary, and refused to discuss anything with her. He took up solitary interests, like birdwatching and astronomy. Anything that didn't involve mixing with people. It was the beginning of his decline into old age. I really hated to see him brooding. There used to be so much humour and childlike energy in him.'

'Why did he go? I mean, what was he afraid of?'

'He just hated any kind of argument. I never once heard him argue with her. He'd just mumble something and slink off to his shed.'

'It sounds completely awful.'

'Then he started going off on his journeys. He suddenly discovered he had lots of long-lost relatives in far-flung corners of the country who urgently needed his help. They seemed to grow more numerous and more needy as he got older. Usefully they never seemed to die: they just got crazier. I could never work out why my mother didn't cotton on what he was up to. But I suppose she knew the score really: if he'd stayed home she'd probably have either poisoned him or burned the house down in frustration. The tragedy is they were both fundamentally good people at heart. But they were too alike to have any chance of understanding one another. Something deep inside them never got heard.'

'What do you mean?'

'Well, just look around here. Nobody communicates. It's like living among the dead. Just rituals and habits and bitterness. That's not life. That cat's more alive than any of these people.'

'It's just the world, Adam. And you might be surprised if you made the effort to get inside people's lives. You might find something really alive after all, behind all those rituals.'

'But that's exactly the point! Why is it so hard to find it?'

'The English believe in privacy as though it's the holy grail. You just don't show what's really going on to anyone. But it doesn't follow that nothing is going on. Just read George Eliot or Charlotte Brönte.'

'But that's exactly what's so bizarre. Why should we need to read novels to find out what your neighbour's really thinking about you?'

She smiled. 'As Iris Murdoch said, it is difficult to analyse human frailty.'

Eventually, sated with teacakes, we paid our bill (again in silence) and set out homeward.

The track eastward was drenched in richly textured late afternoon sunlight. Miraculously the storm had kept away, the breeze had dropped and most of the birds had fallen silent. Elaine too was mostly lost in her own thoughts. We descended the combe as the sun kissed the horizon; the trees mobbed around us, plunging us instantly into a domain of obstacles and ambiguity, causing us to slow down and pick our way with frequent halts and course changes.

As we crossed the stream at the bottom of the track to the chalet, she looked up and stopped again.

'Adam, look.'

I followed her glance. There was a battered-looking green Ford Estate parked discretely by the gate. I was sure it hadn't been there when we'd set out.

'That's odd.'

We climbed the track and presently came within view of the chalet. The front door was open.

'Did we leave the door open?' Elaine asked.

'No, of course not.'

'Looks like we've got visitors.'

Chapter Five

Two men were seated on the bench immediately inside the front door. The shorter of the two clasped a minute and well-worn notebook, from which he was reading aloud. The other had his eyes closed in an expression of rapt concentration. We stood at the open door and stared at them in disbelief. My first thought was that they were a couple of tramps who'd wandered in in search of food or shelter. Indeed one of them did look as though he'd been sleeping rough for a few days: he was tall, thin, unshaven, and wore a loose dark-green pullover liberally augmented with moth-holes. The two stood up in perfect unison as soon as they saw us.

'I hope you will both forgive us,' the moth-holed one began, 'for greeting you in this, er, peremptory fashion. But as you see, the door was open —'.

'And you would be?' I asked.

'Detective Inspector Rose, and this is my assistant, Sergeant Howard Horse.' He performed a shy bow of his head as though he were about to begin some dramatic monologue at a party. 'We'd appreciate the favour of allowing us to put a few simple questions to you. If it's convenient, of course.'

It must have been obvious from our expressions that it was not at all convenient, but they conspired not to notice.

'Would it make any difference if it wasn't?' I asked.

'Not a lot, frankly sir,' said Howard, with a blatantly inappropriate grin on his face.

'Then I suppose we are at your disposal. I'm Adam Stone and this is Elaine. Would you like a drink?'

As soon as I'd told our names, the man called Horse laboriously wrote them down in his ragged notebook, as though practising joined-up writing.

'Not while we're on official business, thank you all the same.' Rose and Howard exchanged complicated smiles which managed to disturb me more than their words, as no doubt they were meant to.

Elaine slowly sat down on the spare bed, threw her hair back and eyed the visitors impassively, as one might regard particularly inept doorstep salesmen or politicians.

'And what exactly is your business? Someone been murdered?' she asked.

'Oh dear, I most earnestly hope not,' Rose said, with an expression of mock horror. 'We're merely investigating a report of a sadly missing person. We were wondering if by any slight chance you might have had occasion to come across the lady recently?'

'It's a female missing person we're talking about then?' I asked.

Rose planted his feet some eighteen inches apart, as though demonstrating for my benefit the classic stance of an officer in charge of possibly extended investigations. 'Yes, we are talking about ay female person, as you so delicately put it. A student at Dundee University. May I ask as to the nature of your business, Mr. Wood?'

'Stone. Well, I'm sort of retired from business at the moment. I used to be a software developer. Then I taught classes in creative writing.'

'Unusual combination wouldn't you say, sir? Software and – writing?'

'Not really. They're both language.'

'Ah!' said Howard, suddenly unfolding himself from his book. 'Creative writing!' His eyes and the extremities of his thin mouth wrenched themselves upward in a searing parody of inspiration. 'Do say if you feel this is out of place to mention,' he said, staring at the window and affecting embarrassment, 'but as it happens I have with me something that may just conceivably interest you, being fortuitously in your own line of preoccupation, as it were.'

'What's that?' I asked.

'A novel.' Howard at last allowed his horriferous smile full rein, which made his face resemble an image sometimes seen in halls of distorting mirrors in seaside towns.

'I'd certainly be interested to see it, if it isn't too long.'

'Long? No sir, long is not an adjective I could ever apply to my little creation. In fact, if I may presume to make a claim in your presence, in terms of terrestrial dimensions it is conceivably the smallest novel in existence. With your leave sir.' He glanced at Rose, who bobbed his head and beamed like a proud and indulgent father.

He fumbled deep in an inside pocket of his overcoat, and then, finding what he wanted, drew out a tiny packet, wrapped in silver foil, about the size of a matchbox. He laid it in the centre of the table, and gazed benignly at each of us in turn.

'That's your novel?' I asked incredulously.

'Indeed it is. Complete to the last insufferable detail. Hand-tooled binding, watermarked endpapers, authentic gold blocking, rubricated title page, and Caslon Antique decorated running heads. Oh, and not to forget the Belgian floral colophon, as used by Caxton no less, in his second edition of the Canterbury Tales.'

'It must have very small type.'

'One might call it small, indeed one might. So small that the font had to be made using a specially adapted stereoscopic microscope. No small achievement, if you'll excuse the unintended pun, sir. Would you care to see it?'

'I'd be honoured,' I said, entering into the spirit of the occasion. Howard then proceeded laboriously to unpeel the layers of foil, each layer revealing a further one beneath, until at length he arrived at a tiny white box about three centimeters tall. He then delved into his coat pocket again and extracted a magnifying glass which he offered me with a slight bow of his head. 'Please,' he said, nodding beatifically towards the box like a magician demonstrating his most mind-boggling trick.

Elaine, now touched despite herself with curiosity, came over and stood beside me. I took the glass and inspected the object on the table. It did indeed appear to be a printed book, complete with title page, running heads, chapters and a delicate red and black design on the last page. Even with the magnifying glass however I was unable to make out one word of the text.

'You really made this yourself? It's quite remarkable.'

'Thank you,' he beamed. 'I will admit its unusual smallness is gratifying. But it is only the first. My aim is to make a book that can only be seen under the most powerful microscope.'

'What? The entire book?'

'Indeed. Why not? It may take many years, it may take the rest of my poor unworthy life, but what is time when one is inspired?'

'But why go to such lengths?'

He lowered his voice as though afraid of being overheard by rival miniaturists. 'I have a theory that a point will come when I will break through a critical barrier. When the writing achieves a certain wonderful smallness the universe itself will take over! I will no longer need to write anything at all! It will connect spontaneously with the inherent creativity of the cosmic mind! You see, all these books we produce in normal space are bound to fail, because there is a fundamental gap between the language and the thought impulses that give rise to it. But beyond the omega threshold – as I venture to call it – there is no gap! The words connect instantly and completely with the immediate progenitive impulse. Imagine that! It would mean the total transformation of all literature! We will have achieved absolute literature! Language that is connected directly with the life-pulse of the universe! What do you say to that Mr. Gate?'

To be truthful, I was dumbfounded. I merely stared at him, trying to work out if he was having me on, or if he was just dangerously out of his tree. But his expression was one of total sincerity, as though he'd just asked 'and when is Father Christmas coming?' I recovered myself enough to ask him what it was about.

'I'm very glad you asked me that, sir. The question shows consideration for a fellow traveller, if one may legitimately employ the metaphor.' He sat down delicately on the bench and clasped his hands. 'It is a curious story. A love story in fact. About a man who makes dolls'.

'What sort of dolls?' Elaine interjected.

'Dolls for children. naturally.'

'Oh,' said Elaine, not in the least enlightened.

'One must spell everything out these days, mustn't one?' Rose observed, looking vaguely past us into an empty corner. 'Otherwise...' He let the solitary word vibrate for several seconds in the intense quiet.

Howard went on. 'Well anyway, this doll-maker, a man called Fox, after practising his craft in a remote hamlet in the Black Forest for twenty years, at last is ready to embark on his master-work: he makes a doll so perfect that she seems to be alive, even conscious. Everyone who sees her is dumbstruck: they can't believe she has been made by their neighbour who, it has to be said, has a reputation in the community for being a bit of a clown, a few stools short of a bar, if you take my meaning. Anyway, after a while he gets a bit paranoid, and starts to hide the doll away, and when the villagers' children come asking to look at her, he sends them away unsatisfied, so to speak. So his life becomes ever more subject to speculation by the curious village folk. But the truth of the matter is, he has fallen hopelessly in love with her, and can't bear anyone else even to catch sight of her, in case they too fall under the spell of her entrancing beauty. He brings her up as his own daugher, calls her Ilse – meaning 'adorable' – as you doubtless will know sir – and talks to her constantly.

'But one night, he wakes up from a disturbing dream, in which he is led through a dark wood to his death by an evil spirit – goes to Ilse's room, and finds it empty! The window is open, and the little jacket and headscarf he made for her has gone too. Needless to say, Fox is distraught. He can't contemplate living without her, and so he packs a lunchbox, cuts himself a hazel wand, closes up the house, and slips out before dawn to search for her. Are you following me so far?'

'We are captivated,' said Rose, articulating each syllable. 'Bewitched even. The hazel wand is very good. Do go on.'

'Do you really think so, sir? I borrowed it from Yeats of course. The Wanderings of Aengus.' He turned to me. 'Do you know the poem?'

'Yes,' I said. 'I learnt it by heart at school without understanding a single word.'

Without prompting, as if in a dream, Howard began to recite. ' "I went out to the hazelwood, because a fire was in my head, and cut and peeled a hazel wand, and hooked a berry to a thread," – that would be the bait to attract the fish with its brightness, wouldn't it? – "And when white moths were on the wing, and moth-like stars were flickering out," – you see, he's showing you the stars there, flitting about just like the little white shapes of moths – "I dropped the berry in a stream, and caught a little silver trout," – isn't that perfection itself, sir, wouldn't you agree? "A little silver trout,"– which becomes a glimmering girl with apple blossom in her hair. Now if that isn't great poetry I'd just like to know what is, am I not right sir?'

'You are right, ultimately and contingently,' Rose replied.

'Anyhow, what happens is, the girl calls his name and then escapes, and he spends the rest of his life hopelessly searching for her: "I will find out where she has gone, and kiss her lips and take her hands; and walk among long dappled grass, and pluck til time and times are done, the silver apples of the moon, the golden apples of the sun". And they are the fruits of the imagination, the object of all poets' endeavours, what we all secretly long for in our deepest heart of hearts.'

'It's beautiful,' I found myself saying.

'I'm unspeakably touched that you appreciate it. It makes all the difference in the world, I can assure you. Its story is very close to my own, as I'm sure you'll appreciate. So I felt justified in borrowing the hazel wand. Wouldn't you agree?'

'I'm sure Yeats would have allowed it,' I said, wondering if the novel – if that was what it was – was ever going to get to its point.

'So off goes Fox on his horse of sorrow – I thought that an apt metaphor, "horse of sorrow" – meaning that his sorrow is what carries him onwards in his quest – not, needless to say, that he set off mounted on a sad horse. That would be a banal reading.'

'Indeed it would. One could hardly support it!'

'Anyway, he wanders alone for many days without sight of her. But just when he's on the point of giving up and going home defeated to his old life making tired, lifeless dolls for the local children, he catches a glimpse of a figure under the trees beyond the smoke of his fire, and starting towards her, realises it is Ilse. She smiles at him, and his old world-weary heart leaps again with renewed life. All is not lost: the life he once created out of his imagination is still there! Don't you think that's wonderful, after all that time, to re-discover your secret inner soul, at the very point when you were despairing of ever finding it?'

'I imagine so,' I said, despairing of his story ever finding an ending.

'Well anyway, to conclude. He is overcome with joy, and races after her. But she is frightened by his sudden motion, imagining that he intends to capture her and take her back to the village – as indeed he might well have intended. We will sadly never know if this is the case, because in his headlong flight, he doesn't see that right in his path is a deep black pit, a vast bowl of darkness like the very maw of hell itself! But of course it is not hell: only a derelict quarry. Ilse flies over the edge of the cliff and disappears from sight. Fox just manages to pull himself to a stop at the very brink, but realizes Ilse has plunged to her doom in the plumbless impenetrable blackness. He collapses into the heather, wishing he too had gone over the edge, because he knows his true life has really come to an end. There, that is the conclusion. What do you think? A shade too dramatic maybe? Slightly unrealistic? I'd very much appreciate your professional opinion, if it is not overstepping the threshold of propriety of course.'

'Why a quarry?' was all I could say. 'I mean, why does she fall into a quarry of all places?'

'Oh, Just a whim of mine. I was born and brought up on the edge of a quarry. So you could say it's my natural landscape. And my father, bless his heart, was a stonemason. So stone is in my blood, so to speak. Ha Ha!'

'Yes but, why did you choose a quarry?' I repeated, as though his first answer had been entirely irrelevant.

'Ah yes. I see. You mean why a quarry, when there are so many other terrible ways of dying? A good point, my friend, and one which no one but a thorough professional like yourself would ask. Well, I can only say that the logic of the story necessitated it. It has the required desolate associations. It has grandeur. It has wildness. It has the necessary elemental quality. For example, someone could be raped and suffocated to death in a boot-cupboard, in the company of expired footwear, or cans of superfluous dogfood stored up against a time of dearth, and the dramatic effect would be significantly lessened, wouldn't you say? Whereas a quarry is a suitably wild and desolate place where a body may not be found, given a certain quantity of luck, for – oh, I don't know – two or three weeks maybe. So there's an element of suspense introduced, which must be to the good.'

'I suppose so'.

Howard's face was suddenly animated as a child's catching his first sight of snow at Christmas. His intense eyes glittered. 'Oh but of course sir! Suspense is an essential factor. You couldn't write a successful story without it, I would have thought. It is, after all, the quality required to keep your reader engaged with the plot. I read that on my own fiction-writing correspondence course, by the way. Without suspense there would be no motivation on the reader's part to involve himself in the situation of the character. We want to know what his fate's going to be don't we? I mean, whether he'll be able to convince his interlocutors of his innocence, or whether he'll merely confirm them in their already well-grounded suspicions, dig a deeper pit for himself, to speak metaphorically. Or whether on the other hand, he'll succeed in coming up with some entirely original and irrefutable explanation for his actions. You see, suspense is a vital factor in all of these scenarios. And a lucrative storyteller such as yourself must be able to master all the different factors that contribute to the overall concupiscence. This is the wonder of the literary art.'

'I keep telling you, I'm not a writer! Merely an occasional teacher. A simple spectator at the feast, you could say.'

'Ah, my inveterate apologies Mr. West. 'I conflate the sower with the harvester, if you take my meaning.'

'Is that the end of your story? I mean, is that how it ends?'

'At present sir, yes. That is the currently operative termination.'

'I think it's really time you were leaving, don't you think?' Elaine said, staring directly at Rose.

'Leaving?' Howard looked from one to the other of us, with a bewildered expression on his face, like a child whose birthday party has just been irretrievably ruined.

'Yes. We weren't expecting any visitors. We're only here for two weeks.'

'Ah, of course! How stupid we've been!' Rose exclaimed, lurching backward and theatrically slapping his forehead – 'You are – visitors! Yes, that puts a different party frock on it entirely! We have been making the unwarranted assumption all this time that you are the legitimate inmates of this desirable location. Whereas the true facts of the case – em, I mean the matter at hand – is that you are merely en passant! You are birds of passage, temporary refugees from the hostile and uncaring elements, in a dwelling belonging to a totally different – and one would presume absent – party. Am I correct sir?'

I looked wearily at the fading sunlight draping the furniture. 'You are. So please can we now call it a day?'

Rose glanced at Horse and then looked quickly down in apparent embarrassement. 'Sadly there is a small matter to be attended to before we are in a position to er, call it a day, as you so succinctly put it. We have ay missing female person on our hands, and it is our unfortunate and regrettable lot to endeavour to discover what has befallen her.'

'And you need our assistance, is that it?'

'You identify our need precisely. If it isn't too much to ask, after all you've been through already.'

'What do you mean by that?' Elaine asked.

'Oh just that we've detained you, it would seem, longer than might be thought strictly necessary in the cause of duty, and for that we apologise. Don't we Howard?'

Howard grinned his imbecile grin again, put his hands together as though about to pray, then apparently thought better of it and started screwing up the bits of silver paper left over from his unwrapping ceremony.

'Does this missing lady have a name?' I asked.

'Rachel Goodman.'

My stomach immediately prepared itself for imminent freefall into the abyss.

'I see the name means something to you.'

'It's just that I happened to meet a girl of that name about a year ago. She was a student at Dundee university I think.'

'Can you describe her?'

'Fair, lightly built, full mouth, grey eyes, a very passionate way of speaking.'

'So a good looking piece would you say?'

'Pretty enough, yes.'

'Pretty enough to be a heroine perhaps?'

'What are you talking about?'

'Well sir, it's just that, well, Howard with his literary interests reads a lot of these, em, novels, strictly in his spare time of course.'

Howard grinned sheepishly. 'I have a complete collection of Colin Dexters at home. All first editions, perfect condition, most of them signed. He's good isn't he? So good on people. Do you do romance or crime?'

'I've told you. Neither. I only taught writing, and even then only part-time. I'm not an authority in any way.'

'But to teach writing,' Rose said, 'must require a certain, how shall we say, sensitivity? Un peu de savoir faire, perhaps? Culture, at the very least. A teacher must be aware of what seas his ship sails in, even if he himself cannot swim. To over-extend the metaphor perhaps.'

'Yes.'

'And all of us can learn from a little culture, wouldn't you say? It broadens the mind. And in our line of work a broad mind comes in very handy, eh, Howard?'

Howard's whole face became a vehicle for the unsavory grin that had previously been content to hang out around his mouth only.

'Howard has a theory he has evolved entirely independently of the authorities on these matters, which may yet prove seminal.' He smiled encouragingly at his colleague.

'Well, you see my theory is that everything that ever happens to us is stored somewhere in the little grey cells. It goes on swirling around in there until we're under some kind of stress, some kind of disturbance to our normal routine, and then, like it or not, out it pours, like a river of molten lava descending with implacable power upon a doomed town, or like a tornado pulverizing everything in its path, or indeed like a flood overwhelming and carrying away all objects in its vicinity. So why should writers be any different? Except that with them it usually emerges in the characters they appear to make up. That's why you get so many books about pornography and violence you see. It's because all that deeply submerged effluvium is rising remorselessly from the miasmic depths unbeknown to the writer himself!'

'That's a very impressive theory!' I said, genuinely taken aback. 'Have you thought of writing about it? I should think it would make an excellent basis for a crime novel.'

'I take that as a real compliment from a professional such as yourself,' Howard said, apparently without irony.

'So, if, as you say, you teach... writing,' Rose continued, labouring over each word, 'and we have no reason, as yet, to doubt you, perhaps you would indulge us by telling us something of your method? Something of your post propter hoc, as it were. Just so we have some small, albeit infinitely inadequate, idea of how it is done?'

This calculated stroking of my ego had its desired effect, largely due, I had to admit, to the presence of Elaine.

'Well, it hardly amounts to a method. I try to get students to write about their lives; about what really captures their imagination. Then I encourage discussion about what they've written, with a view to improving it. That's about it. Pretty basic stuff.'

'Ah,' said Rose, in a trance of satisfaction. 'Now we are progressing. Enfin we are proceeding towards an unequivocal commencement. Excellent. Are you recording all this in your book Howard? Wonderful. "Encourage discussion with view to improvement." Howard's style has much to commend it, wouldn't you say?'

Elaine was becoming increasingly exasperated.

'Do you really need to know about Adam's teaching methods?' she asked. 'I would have thought it's more important to find out where the girl was last seen, what she was wearing, whether she phoned home – that sort of practical stuff.'

'Oh dear me,' said Rose, discomfitted into addressing Elaine directly for the first time. 'I should hope we have progressed beyond such blunt instruments by now. That may have been good enough for your Monsieur Poirot, my friend. In the real world however we approach things very differently. We aim – I speak also for my inestimable colleague here – we aim to understand the totality of the character: the character as a dynamic singularity in a complex field; someone who responds in a manner that mere contingent observations cannot compute, no matter how much data is accumulated. Do you follow me?'

'No, not really,' Elaine said in her best bored voice.

'Well it is really very simple. You see, everyone is conditioned by what's happened to him, yes? If as a child you were lost in a wood and thought you'd been abandoned, then you'd be most likely to have an enduring fear of being alone in woods. They would make you nervous, cautious at the least, yes? So you might think twice before going into one alone. We look for the secret portal into a person's mind. It might be anything at all – a lost doll, an acorn, a trio by Debussy, a picture by Klee, a story by Chekhov. But once we find it we know the key signature of their lives. It may seem an insignificant heap of information, but I can assure you within a few weeks—.'

'A few weeks?' Elaine exploded, 'She'll be dead before then.'

'Oh I rather think not. I would guess she will be very much alive. And if I'm not much mistaken not too far from here.'

He glanced conspiratorially at each one of us, as though to underline the all-penetrating subtlety of his insight. But Elaine wasn't taking the bait. She walked to the door and held it open in a suggestive way.

'I think it is time you both left now. We've answered your questions very fully, when really we needn't have answered anything at all. We're both extremely tired. We need to make our supper and get some sleep. Do you follow me?

Chapter Six

'Ah' said Rose, seemingly embarrassed and crestfallen. 'I'm very much afraid we must inconvenience you still more. We have another tiny matter to attend to before we are able to contemplate leaving.'

'And that is?' I was beginning to feel desperate for them to leave, but something still impelled me to avoid confrontation, in case they had more knowledge than they were admitting to.

'The contents of the locked room.'

'You've got to be crazy! I've already told you it's not our home. And there's nothing there that would interest anyone other than junk collectors!'

Rose's eyes glinted. 'Well, how about that for a brass fish Howard? The coincidences are certainly flowering like treacle spoons today are they not? It so happens that sitting right next to me is one of the great collectors of significant ephemera of our times in the western hemisphere: Howard St John Horsebladder. Would you conceivably make an exception to your very understandable reluctance and indulge his curiosity by showing him some small fragments of your unique collection? To establish a common ground for negotiations, let us say?'

'Oh do me a favour will you? This whole conversation is getting beyond ludicrous! You've already taken over an hour of our time. I'm very sorry you've had a wasted journey. Maybe some other time?'

But Rose was still playing his game, and assumed his officious air once more. He moved closer to me and, in a quiet, mock-conspiratorial voice said: 'I find myself obliged to *insist* that you show us the room Mr. North. I have an idea we'll find something there that will throw some light on this whole unpleasant business.' He turned towards Elaine. 'If you are agreeable of course?'

Elaine was all for throwing them out without more ado, but I needed time to work out who they really were, and I judged it would do no harm to show them what they wanted. In any case I could not easily delay things much longer without planting more suspicion in the minds of these bog-brained tree dwellers. I drained my glass and stood up once more.

36

'Ok, if that's what you really want. But I have to warn you, I do this under duress. I won't be held responsible for any damage you suffer as a result.'

'That's quite alright my friend. We see many bizarre things in our line of duty. I don't expect there will be anything we haven't seen before.'

I led them in. It took them several seconds to take in the sight that met their eyes.

'Holy feathers!' Howard whispered in an outbreak of unaffected awe. 'Ladders! There must be bloody millions!'

'Thirty four to be precise.'

'Most fascinating. Most fascinating!' Rose set himself to pacing around like an art connoisseur at a private view.

'We discovered it when we arrived, exactly as you see it now.'

He surveyed the blank windowless walls as if he were a builder assessing dry-rot, then strode over to me, his eyes two glittering wells of frustration. He stood with his legs apart and his hands locked behind his back.

'Tell me Mr Woods, if you would: what would induce someone to fill a room with ladders that don't lead anywhere?'

'Search me. I'm not a world expert on ladder-fanciers. Maybe it's a work of art. Maybe it's meant to symbolize the real world: you know, full of things that appear to lead to interesting places but actually never do?'

Howard's face came alive again. 'Like eggs,' he said.

There was a silence of incomprehension from all of us. I stared at him.

Rose echoed, 'Eggs?'

'Yes. I always thought eggs were a great disappointment. They seem so full of magic. Unknown potentiality. But when you open them there's nothing but runny yellow stuff that dribbles all down your pullover.'

Rose glanced at him, as though thinking of a withering comment, then managed to suppress it. He stroked one of the ladders gingerly, like someone trying to calm a temperamental cat.

'I'm disappointed in you Mr. Forest. I somehow expected more from a writer than that. Something more... ingenious. But it interests me all the same. It presents a most captivating conundrum does it not? Is it likely that someone would go to such trouble to collect so many ladders and arrange them like this without any ulterior purpose? Apart from art, I mean. Hardly.

No. It has to have a meaning. Let us think this through. Ladders. What does one do with ladders? One climbs them! Yes! Very good. One uses them to get somewhere that is otherwise inaccessible, am I right? A roof, perhaps, or a high shelf where interesting articles might be secreted away from the general view'. Without warning he hopped onto one of the ladders and with surprising agility heaved his bulk to the top and peered about, inspecting the bare walls. Then he beamed down at us. 'Are you with me? I believe you are, yes. We are beginning to get somewhere at last. Yes. We are beginning to connect, I think. Excellent. Now, there are no shelves here at all, or skylights. No concealed alcoves or recesses where a sophisticated person of, em, elevated tastes might squirrel away material for future contemplation. No marks of erstwhile fixtures. No repairs to plasterwork. No screwholes. In short nothing at all! We have here a room full of nothing, Mr. Lane, save – ladders. Ladders without any ostensible purpose!'

Rose and Howard crept around the floor like virgin burglars, peering alternately slack-jawed and purse-lipped at the ladders as though they'd just stumbled into Dr Crippen's workshop. I watched them glide around the room as if they were in the middle of a minefield.

'What does this suggest to you Mr Field?'

Elaine intervened. 'Only that someone lived here who had more ladders than was good for him. Perhaps that was his problem. Excess Ladder Syndrome: the next European plague!'

Rose appeared not to relish anyone but him making jokes. He abruptly stood up straight.

'Or – perhaps he had exactly the *right* number of ladders!'

'What do you mean?'

'Thirty four. Think of that number for a moment. Why do you suppose he stopped at thirty four?'

'Maybe the Inland Revenue got on to him?' Elaine offered.

Rose glared silently at her, then without altering his expression turned to me. 'Mathematics, Mr. Banks! The secret harmony! Thirty four is the tenth term of the great divergent series of Fibonnacci: the prodigious mystical sequence of golden numbers! Don't you see? This whole edifice is an elegant mathematical symbol! A message to humanity! Maybe even the final message!' He paused and threw his arms out theatrically. 'The number is composed of three and four conjoined together – male and female! And what do you get when you add three and four? Why, seven! The Divine Child! The magical number par excellence! The key to innumerable mysteries down the ages. Now at last we have it! Right here in this room we have the answer to the most challenging question of all time: what is the purpose of human life on earth? What are we supposed to do with our time here? One ladder doesn't lead anywhere. Even two aren't much use. But thirty four ladders... thirty four ladders, Mr West, may lead us to heaven!' And thus rendered reckless by his discovery, Rose proceeded to caper along the ladders laid on the ground one after the other, being careful not to walk on any twice, and having done that he climbed each of the vertical ladders in turn, anticlockwise, barely pausing to mutter its number in the sequence after he had returned to the foot of each one, so that by the time he'd reached the top of the final ladder, half way along the inner wall, he was extremely out of breath, and had to cling onto the sides to recover his composure.

'Thirty three. We are short of one ladder! So. We are faced with yet another can of sardines. How do you account for that, gentlemen? What do you suppose had happened to the missing ladder?'

'Maybe my uncle needed a ladder to fix something and forgot to return it.'

Rose sniffed. 'Conceivable, I grant you. But it invites us to look deeper does it not? What we have before us here is a divine pattern with a flaw: to wit, an infra-numerary item. It invites us to contemplate a world which is perfect – and at the same time incomplete! A world which has incompleteness written into it, so to speak, at its very heart. Do you follow me?'

'On the other hand, I could have miscounted.' I said quietly.

'I do not think so,' Rose declaimed from his ladder-pulpit. 'I put it to you that you counted correctly. I think thirty-four ladders were in this room when you arrived. But at some time subsequently and contingently one ladder was quietly removed.'

'Why should anyone come here and secretly remove one ladder?'

'That my friend is precisely the question it behoves us to address. That is the next step, so to speak, on our quest. And we will take it, with your help.'

'Oh I don't think so,' I said. 'We're on holiday. And we're asking to be left alone to enjoy it – now that you've made such good progress in your investigation.'

'Oh but Mr. Root, I assure you we have barely begun! Heaven is not to be entered by a mere exhibition of gymnastics. But I see something now that I could not have seen before, from the perpetual twilight of the sublunary realm.'

Rose allowed himself to descend to a less rarefied altitude before halting again and continuing his speech. 'Beauty, Mr. Brook, Beauty! All we know on earth, and all we need to know, eh? Am I right? What do you think? Am I hot on the trail of our lapis philosophorum?'

He descended the last few steps to the ground, and then, his breath restored, wandered around the room with the air of a scientist explaining his discovery of a new fundamental particle. 'Numbers work not because they give us answers, but because they are beautiful! They have the elegant architecture of a perfect work of art. We can't see truth directly, but we can see beauty! And we can feel it in the deep heart's core, as our greatest word-master has observed. If we have beauty, if we are open to its magic, we don't need to puzzle out what it all means! We have our hot-line to truth already open!'

This peroration was beginning to get to Elaine, who had been sitting on the floor trying to take in the implications of this spontaneous manifestation of the theatre of the absurd. 'Is there a point to this lecture Mr Rose? We are desperate to get some sleep.'

Rose contemplated the bare floorboards awhile before squatting down and reverting to his oratorical mode. 'Sleep! Ah yes. A desirable state. A supremely desirable state, is it not? But alas! Not all may achieve it. Some have great burdens to carry through the vicissitudes of this world. Still, we must respect our neighbours' needs, must we not, even though we may not share them? We shall bid you goodnight, until the morrow.'

Still they made no move to depart.

Presently we went into the kitchen and began pointedly clattering around with saucepans and crockery. A few minutes later I heard Rose and Horse let themselves out of the door and glimpsed their vague figures lurching down the steep track to the road. I at once began to relax, and foolishly allowed myself the delicious sensation of hoping I'd seen the last of them.

Chapter Seven

It was a warm night and our spirits were being tested. Elaine was asleep on the far side of the room. But for me sleep was a land to be dreamed of. A half-moon haunted the sky, spilling tenuous milky rivulets across the dusty floorboards. I lay in the eye of an argument that refused either to go away or resolve itself: who were these two characters who'd crawled into our lives from the nether regions of third-rate crime fiction? What did they have to connect me with Rachel? Was it indeed the same Rachel? I had obviously nothing to fear: my Rachel had walked unharmed from my flat after that strange dinner date a year ago, and subsequently vanished out of my life. Of course it was possible she'd been abducted on the way to her brother's wedding. But there could not possibly be anything to connect me with her disappearance. So why was I so totally unmanned by Rose and Howard's appearance? Why couldn't I simply have demanded they leave? After all, they were the trespassers, not me; why did I allow them to treat me like a criminal?

The Moon was sinking gradually into the cloud-murk, its whey-coloured light stalking across the floor and sipping at Elaine's peaceful figure. I listened: her breathing was almost inaudible. Above it I could hear the usual sporadic scratchings of mice and insects, the occasional thin cry of a wakeful bird. In that suspended quiet a small thought was born: that, despite welcoming my attentions when it suited her, she did not seem to want physical intimacy; her studied coolness triggered all my latent feelings of loneliness and inadequacy. The injustice of it stung hard. I called her name quietly, then more urgently. Some subliminal change in her breathing told me she wasn't asleep. I propped myself on an elbow and watched for any slight movement, imagining the feel of her cool velvet skin under my hand, the hardening of her small nipples as she began to respond. Eventually my longing got the better of me and I sat on the edge of the bed, watching myself helplessly as I prepared to do something exceptionally stupid, even for me. Then I saw myself creep across the no man's land of lit floor and slowly lift the edge of the duvet. As I came close to her I saw that her eyes were watching me intently.

'What?' The word was slurred with incomprehension. She tried to retrieve the duvet but failed to get a hold. 'What you doing?'

'Sleeping with you.'

'No you're not. Absolutely not. Go away.'

The rejection cutting me, chilling me to the bone, slamming me abruptly into the horror story of the past.

'But what about this afternoon?'

'I don't know... please let me sleep.'

'Alright. Then let's just sleep together.'

More awake now, she opened her eyes wider and looked directly at me.

'No Adam. We had a strict agreement.'

'I can't understand your behaving like this. You were so warm towards me this afternoon.'

'Warmth is one thing. Sex is entirely another. Surely you can see that?'

'You said you found me attractive.'

She reached for her blouse and drew it very slowly around her shoulders as though hypnotised – an action that only made her seem more naked and more helpless, and drew out from me the need both to protect and seduce her at the same time.

I put my arm around her and tried to kiss her, but she turned away with that same dreamy half-conscious movement that so maddened me, as if with a part of her mind she was challenging me to overcome her resistance.

'This is ludicrous! Elaine, look at me!' She turned back, compliant but only half present. 'What do you want me to do? Challenge Jack to a duel?'

'I don't want you to do anything, except be truthful.'

'But I am: I want you in every way, physically and emotionally. I don't want anyone else. I want you to be happy, and you're not happy with Jack. That's my truth.'

'Yes, I know you believe that; but I also know that if you got half a chance you'd jump back into bed with Cora without the slightest hesitation. I don't think you understand emotional truth. You're just feeling lonely and rejected, and you see me as a way to avoid that feeling.'

'No. That's all finished. Cora and me are definitely over.'

'Well Jack and I aren't over.'

'You told me you'd decided to leave him. That he doesn't satisfy you.'

'Why are you so fixated on physical satisfaction? You reduce everything to animal gratification. It sickens me!' Completely awake now, she slipped out of bed and began wildly grabbing at clothes and dragging them on. There seemed to have come over her a complete change of mood; in the early dawn light a steely determination mastered her features.

'What are you doing?'

'Going home. I can't stay here any more. I shouldn't have come at all. It was madness to think it would work. I'm sorry.'

As she went into the bathroom I suddenly realized she was serious about leaving. I leapt after her, catching her arm before she could lock the door.

'Don't be ridiculous. It's five o'clock! You can't leave at this time.'

'I can't stay here. Not with this kind of pressure. I feel like a whore.'

She tried to gather her small collection of things from the shelf, but I dragged her back, causing everything to crash noisily onto the tiled floor. I found myself grabbing her jeans in a crazy attempt to restrain her. She wrenched herself out of my grasp and ran back to the lounge, her blouse falling to the floor like a sacrifice to appease a wild beast. I slouched back to the bedroom and threw myself back on the bed, utterly defeated, unable to think or feel, or imagine where we could possibly go from here. At that moment I wanted nothing and regretted nothing: in my exhaustion I was far away from the world of humanity, in a limbo of inscrutable and amoral forces. For a second I opened my eyes: the moon was on its back above the horizon, like a creature exiled from the world as a punishment for speaking the truth. As from a great distance there came the noise of Elaine gathering her belongings, followed by a door-latch snicking quietly. From even further away an owl screeched high and lonely, but was not answered.

When I awoke again the sun was high and the cabin utterly silent. I splashed myself with cold water, put the kettle on the gas, then wandered from room to room, half expecting to find Elaine asleep on the couch, and Rose and Horse sipping cocoa and reading poetry to each other in the morning sun. But gradually the full horror of the night came back to me, and I sat in a corner of the conservatory feeling utterly wretched.

Elaine had taken every one of her belongings with her: books, clothes, make-up, even her small collection of gemstones had gone. I felt miserably certain she would not be back; despite her distress she had taken the trouble to eliminate every shred of evidence that she had been in the cottage, for what reason I chose not to guess. In the unforgiving light of morning I felt nothing but visceral disgust for my behaviour with her, and dared not imagine what kind of madness had possessed me. Frustration and rejection were understandable; but such violence toward someone for whom I imagined I felt nothing but tenderness was beyond countenancing.

I made coffee and took it back into the conservatory. I didn't feel like staying on after what had happened: the whole place seemed infected with my madness. Elaine had taken her car, so wherever I went I would have to walk or hitch a lift. I glanced at the blue sky and the lush landscape; suddenly the idea of walking seemed attractive. I packed, made a final inspection of the cabin, then let myself out into the cool, sharp morning.

I was nearly half-way down the track when I heard the gate at the bottom of the hill clang shut, and looked up to see two figures labouring unsteadily towards me, carrying bulky travel bags. It took me no time at all to recognise them: my persecutors had returned. My blood instantly ran cold. I felt I was falling headlong into still another nightmare, a circle of Hell in which meaningless events repeated themselves forever. I put down my rucksack and struggled to claw back a degree of composure.

Rose was red in the face and sweating profusely as he reached me, but despite his labours he looked triumphant.

'My dear friend!' he beamed, 'You surely were not thinking of leaving so soon?'

'Yes, I'm afraid so.'

'But this will never do! We have so much to talk about! So many things to discover! You must at least stay to hear the culmination – for it is nothing less – of our singular adventure. Mustn't he Howard?'

Howard performed his customary wince for my benefit, and very slowly (as though unsure whether the pause would justify it) set down his own bag.

'I'm afraid I can't wait,' I said as decisively as I could manage, 'Elaine's left. I have to find her.'

Rose adopted his best avuncular manner. 'If you'll take my advice you will not try to find her. For myself I have always found it true that the impetuous act invariably comes to be regretted at leisure. Isn't that the saying Howard? Come now.' He took my shoulder and eased me round to face the cabin. 'We really must insist on your hearing the end of our fascinating story. Over some of your unparalleled Lapsang Suchong, perhaps? There are deep waters swirling around us all. Deep waters indeed. I would be sorry if, having allowed you to leave, we found you had drowned in them.'

And against all my instincts and judgement, I found myself picking up my rucksack and climbing again to the cottage.

'What a fine time we've had!' said Rose, rubbing his hands together theatrically as he waited for me to find the key. 'A time to dream about when the frigid fingers of winter close around us, eh Howard?'

Feeling defeated, helpless and very alone, I led them back into the still hot and airless interior.

Chapter Eight

'Why don't you just tell us everything, exactly as it happened?'

Rose had seated himself next to the kitchen stove, and looked like a starving bird that had at last found a safe place to roost.

'Everything? Do you know how much everything there is?'

'Well you could try the cut-down version.'

'Even so, I'd find it hard to know where to start.'

'May I suggest you start with what is most on your mind at this juncture?' Rose leant back and clasped his bony hands in the stance of a vicar preparing himself to suspend judgement (for a while) on his erring parishioners.

'What is most on my mind is getting away from here, and getting my life back again.'

'But my dear friend, do you suppose we are detaining you? You are free to go wherever you wish without let or hindrance, as the quaint phrase has it.' He sniffed and searched in his huge pockets in vain for a handkerchief. 'But before you leave, we thought you might be diverted by something we found not too far away from here.'

'Quarry,' said Horse, and pulled something bulky out of his own grubby overcoat pocket. I recognised it instantly: it was Rachel's blue silk scarf, the one she'd worn the night she'd visited me. There was absolutely no doubt about it: it was not just a similar scarf – it was the exact same one. Something instantly collapsed in the region of my heart, depriving me of coherent speech. I stared at the scarf, crumpled in Howard's ample hand, and felt the world slide vertiginously away from me.

'I see you are not entirely unacquainted with this, eh, touching item,' Rose observed.

For several moments I could do nothing but stare stupidly at it. It seemed like the laws of time and space were being scrambled before my eyes, specifically to make me lose all sense of rationality or control. I forced myself to remember that Rachel did not die on the evening of the dinner date: she left for her brother's wedding exactly as she had planned to do; ergo there was no crime committed; There was no subsequent police investigation because there was nothing to investigate. I didn't hear from Rachel again and assumed she'd forgiven me my momentary indiscretion and continued with her promising life without me in it. Fair enough: I still had Cora (as I thought then); something could be retrieved, and maybe in time something like love would prevail. So why did the sight of this garment fill me with such all-consuming dread?

'It's Rachel's scarf.'

'Ah,' said Rose. 'Please record that Howard, without deviating from the identical selfsame words that graced the original utterance, if you please.'

Howard wrote it in the same notebook that he apparently wrote his poetry in.

'So. I'd be insufferably obliged to you if you would tell me about this – Rachel. How did you meet her?'

And so I told him about my trip to Scotland, and my meeting with Rachel in the inn, and our visit to Magnus's house, and even the terrible moment when I found her enjoying bestial sex in Magnus's library. When I came to the dinner date however, I had a problem: was I incriminating myself by admitting I strangled her to death, hid her body, then went back in time and undid the act? Did I in fact undo the act by revisiting it and editing out the strangling? Or did the original remain somewhere in all its abysmal perfection regardless of what was done the second time around? If it ever came to a legal argument I was probably lost, because I was sure there was no legal concept of 'undoing' an act: in the legal world an actual act remained done, no matter how one tried to recompose the natural flow of events subsequently.

And yet my lords it remained a fact also that Rachel had walked out of my flat at ten pm on that same night alive and unharmed – if maybe slightly inebriated by cheap Californian wine. And the proof of that is that somewhere she is still walking around visible to all the world—

Except of course that, if Rose and Horse are right, she isn't.

If they are right. My entire future pivots on that slender word.

'So what happened to her?' I asked Rose.

'This is the precise and selfsame identical question that occupies the crux of our investigations. At this moment in time – at least, until the startling assertion you have just rendered us concerning this item's ownership – we are merely trying to find a person reported missing some months ago—.'

'Months ago? How many months?'

'How many months, Howard?'

'Months?'

'Since we started.'

Howard sucked his pen and appeared to address himself to the question. Then he held out his fingers and counted off. 'Five. Six. Seven. I'd say about eight. In that region. Maybe nine. Yes, nine. Absolutely. Give or take. Call it ten to be safe.'

My state of stricken dumbness suddenly flipped into outrage.

'You call that safe? A girl missing for ten months? What have the police been doing all this time? Powdering their cheeks?'

'The police, my friend, have been meticulously drawing in their web, inch by inch, nail by nail, floorboard by floorboard. Make no mistake about that. And it is a most subtle web.' He leaned across the table so I could see every erect hair on his chin in horribly surreal detail. 'What that web does not find is not to be found. Indeed, so subtle is their web that few can say with any assurance at any moment where it is and where it is not.'

'And you are part of it I assume?'

'It would be hard to deny that we are part of it, certainly. And yet, at the same time and contiguously, in the name of truth I would be obliged to deny it.' He fingered a banana lovingly, as though he expected it to burst into blossom under his stroking. 'After all, there are webs and webs, and some are of astounding, mind-harrowing subtlety, while others are of merely everyday subtlety, adequate to the job in hand, but no more.'

I said nothing, but continued watching the banana for any signs of transmogrification.

'Until seven o'clock this morning,' Rose continued, after a lengthy and contemplative pause, 'I was of the opinion that we were swimming in waters of no excessive depth. But at seven o'clock the nature of our quest changed stentoriously.' With a slow, dreamlike motion of his hand he took the scarf from Howard and stretched it across the tabletop, carefully smoothing its surface so that under the low lighting of the room it began to resemble a slow-flowing river in flood.

'Observe, if you will, this unprepossessing garment; it is its own web: see how quietly it draws us into it as it ripples and undulates from nowhere to... nowhere. I hear it asking us a question: how? How did it come here? What rare and intricate circumstances rose up like pale truffles at dawn to bring about its presence? This is what we must address our best inquisitions to if we are to solve its riddle. Does anyone have anything to offer in answer?'

A long, moist silence nuzzled close around us, only mitigated at intervals by the mist-blurred lowing of cattle and the scuttering of birds as they landed almost within touching distance on the low tarred roof. I glanced at Howard: his pen was poised above his ragged notebook, over which he frowned intently, as though faced with a particularly knotty problem of poetic syntax. As I continued looking I got the uneasy feeling that he was no longer present; there was no movement in his eyes or lips, such as one would register, at least subliminally, if someone were lost in concentration; it was as though his mind had been quietly turned off, while leaving everything else intact. I turned to Rose.

'I think Howard's ill. He seems to be having a stroke or something.'

'Oh no, he's perfectly alright, I assure you. Merely a temporary disruption.'

'Disruption? To what?'

'To nothing, my dear friend. There is quite simply nothing to be disrupted. Everything is absolutely normal. Please, pay no attention to Howard. He is a man of fits and starts, such is the creative temperament. And where would we all be without that? Now to the task in hand—.'

'Just a minute. What are you blethering about? What has been disrupted?'

'Mr. Forklove, I must insist that you co-operate with our investigations. There is little time left, and we have much to do.'

This litany of cliches was beginning to irritate me. I repeated: 'What – is – being – disrupted?'

Rose did not respond, but as I looked at his figure it seemed to jerk sideways a centimetre or two, exactly like a glitch in a digital film before the data catches up and it resumes its normal flow. And then, just as abruptly, everything was normal again: Howard's pen began curving towards his notebook, and Rose continued with his official detective rhetoric as though nothing at all had happened; the whole incident had lasted no more than a minute at most.

'This scarf, Mr. Northfoot – this scarf is the key to everything: it shows beyond all doubt that the victim – or someone who had contact with her – or someone with the facility of communicating with her – was in the vicinity within the last few days, and therefore—.'

'I couldn't conceivably have murdered her,' I said. 'For the simple reason—.'

'Please! Let us not jump through several conflagrations where one would be sufficient to kill us! We are not yet speaking of murder. We are not even speaking of assault, or gross indecency, or kidnapping or grievous innuendo for that matter. These are contingencies yet to assay our equanimity.'

He at last succeeded in peeling the banana he'd been holding and took a savage bite from it. 'Now, you have told us – categorically – that this garment – not one *like* it, but this very selfsame intrinsic item – is the one worn by your, shall we say friend, on the night of her visit to your flat for the purposes of, em, entertainment. Am I right?'

'Yes.'

'Therefore it is reasonable to assume that she was in this present vicinity within the past few days, yes? Because the garment, as you can plainly observe, is unbesmirched by weather, abrasions, extrusions, miscellaneous body fluids, etc etc?'

'A crow could have brought it,' Howard said from his corner, without enthusiasm.

Rose glared at him. 'And what is your unlikely explanation as to how this putative bird acquired the scarf?'

As though someone had flicked a switch in the back of his head, Howard became instantly fired with inspiration. His eyes shone. He cleared his throat. 'The young lady character arrives at the flat of the young male character believing she is to be a guest at his dinner party. She discovers on arrival, however, with a shiver of apprehension, that she is in fact the only guest. Unbeknown to her, her host harbours uncontrollable jealousy over her recent affair with his old friend. They enjoy their meal, talking about old times, times gone by, opportunities not taken, pleasures perverted, losses suffered, scandals endured, visions traduced, duties subverted, iniquities witnessed, treasures misprisioned, gifts abused, hopes quenched—.'

'Yes yes, Howard. Spare us the litany of human miseries, or we shall be here beyond Christmas.'

'Sorry sir. Well after a while she becomes slightly intoxicated by the wine. She says it is time for her to leave. The male character asserts his need – no, his pressing need, – for her to sleep with him. She says this is impossible: her sense of propriety does not permit it. He tells her how deep and unquenchable is his passion and respect for her, and locks the front door. She tries to phone her brother, and the male character snatches the phone from her and rips the clothes from her body in one single, but hardly graceful motion. He then throws her to the floor, whereupon she becomes unconscious. He engages in sexual union with her, and discovers that in the heat of his passion he has killed her. He then falls into a state of unconsciousness himself until the following morning.'

'Don't forget the scarf Howard, without which your exquisitely formed drama will be deprived of its climactic culmination.'

'I was about to draw in the scarf sir.' He sniffed and performed his obsequious bob of the head. 'So the next morning the young male character wakes very early and recalls what has happened. He is understandably dismayed. He is unable to act for several hours, rehearsing endlessly his insoluble dilemma. At last he musters his resolve and decides to bury the body. He gathers it up and wraps it in a blanket, then carries his burden into the garden, where he labours for an hour to dig a suitable grave. After the interment he returns to his flat and pours himself a glass of wine. While doing so he notices a window is unaccountably open, and on the sill stands a large black crow. He endeavours to shoo away the crow, but it stands its ground, cawing at him each time he approaches it. Now a crow's caw is extremely loud, being as it is employed for—.'

'The scarf Howard, for the love of God.'

'Sorry sir. So the crow holds steadfast to its vantage point in the open window, while the man does everything he can think of to induce it to leave. He tries talking to it in a kindly voice, then in a wheedling voice, then an angry voice. He tries singing a Bach aria to it. He offers it a saucer of cake crumbs, then bits of cheese, then little pieces of fried bacon—.'

'For mercy's sake Howard. Your audience is expiring with ungratified expectation.'

'After trying every strategy in his power, he lights upon the lady character's scarf—'.

'*Thank* you Howard.'

'—which is still draped delicately – if redundantly – over the back of her chair, although of course it is no longer her chair, as she is no longer, em, that is, she is no longer a person and therefore—'.

'We grasp what you are driving at Howard.'

Howard released a shy genuflection of thanks.

'The scarf is so meticulously woven that it seems to sail in the air of its own volition. Its colour resembles a lake of pure mountain water surrounded by expanses of snow under a—'.

'Howard we have no need of this unmitigated encomium when we have the item in question before our own living eyes.'

'I'm sorry, Sir. So the male character gathers up the scarf with both hands and conveys it to the crow, who to his amazement without hesitation grabs one end in his steely beak and soars triumphantly away into the west. He watches the crow until it is no more than an indeterminate speck of blackness on the far and wide horizon.'

'Howard, I have to admit that, notwithstanding your unwonted prolixity of discourse, you have excelled yourself. Remind me to mention your achievement in my final report.'

Rose sprang up from the table and began pacing across the tiny space between door and window. 'However, it has to be said, in the interests of verisimilitude, that it is unlikely that a crow would be motivated to carry such an incommodious – and more to the point inedible – item from London to Somerset, even assuming the physical capacity to perform such a task. One is obliged to ask, what end would be served?'

Howard contemplated this objection, then brightened. 'Unless the crow had a lady sweetheart waiting for him in, em, Porlock – who has asked him to bring her something as light as air itself, and as blue as the summer sea around tropic isles, and as delicate and subtle as the fugitive colours in a newborn baby's eyes. Then the crow would be motivated to seek out such an object and carry it any distance required, regardless of obstacles and contingent impediments, for it would be the means of consummating his heart's desire.'

'A commendable theory Howard, which would not be out of place among the timeless anthologies of world literature. However we are not at liberty to indulge our passions for the perennial chronicles of the heart, so we must perforce rein in our vagabond enthusiasms.' He cleared his throat at length. 'Item: one silk scarf, purported to be the property of item two, to wit, one missing female person, answering, or perhaps, eh, *not* answering, to the name of Rachel Goodman, domiciled in the county of Perthshire.'

All this time I'd been sitting almost incapable of coherent thought, stunned into silence by Howard's prescient ramblings. It need not be stated that they were all far too accurate for coincidence, and I wondered where he could conceivably have got it all from.

And then I thought of the Cube. Could it have played a part? If so, the possibilities were terrifying: it simply meant that no human thought could be secret any more; everything was potentially transparent to anyone possessed of consciousness. I decided the only possible path to safety lay in attack, and the 'glitch' that had occurred a few minutes earlier gave me an opening.

'Are you connected with the Cube?' I scrutinized Rose's eyes for any sign of reaction, but if there was one he concealed it perfectly.

'My dear fellow! Is that a serious question? You think we are agents of the, em, Visitors?'

'I've no idea who you are. But the fact is you don't feel quite right to me: that 'disruption' you spoke of earlier for instance. You avoided answering my question.'

'Well then, allow me to set your mind at rest. We have of course, like everyone else, heard of this putative artifact, but our opinion is firmly that it is a hoax created to divert attention from the West's misadventures in the Middle East. As for its reputed power to control human minds, that is self-evident hogwash. It is the governments we should be scrutinizing in that respect.'

'Of course,' said Howard, 'The crow could have been a spy for the government.'

Rose glared at him.

'Howard, we are finished with the crow; the crow is history; it no longer signifies.'

'So what did you mean by 'disruption'?

'Disruption means to interrupt the flow or continuity of a data stream or energy system such that the state of that system is significantly altered or reduced such that the system is unable to operate. In the case of complex networks, such as those supporting consciousness, the design process must allow for continued functional viability when areas of the information flow are disrupted through external agency or internal component failure.'

I stared at Rose as though he'd suddenly sprouted feathers. 'What in the name of Higgs are you talking about?'

'Methods of ensuring network viability under stress. Secondly, in the case of large-scale data disruption, fallback protocols must be present in order to preserve minimum ongoing functionality. Come my dear sir, let us not bandy circumlocutions with one another. The journey that is never begun is the longest, is that not so Howard? The journey of a thousand miles begins with the first step. He who sets out on a long journey should first lock his front door. Eh, Howard?'

Howard took this nonsense as further encouragement.

'At last the crow comes in sight of his beloved's home. He is overjoyed at the prospect of being reunited with her, and laying his bounty out in all its splendour before her feet—.'

'Sadly we appear to have lost him, let us hope temporarily.'

'However,' Howard went on oblivious of the comment, 'when the crow reached the nest, which was built precariously on the branch of a tree overhanging the sheer vertical wall of an old quarry, he was horrified to find it abandoned, with not even a note to explain where his mate had gone. Heartbroken, he searched the quarry from end to end, and then he searched the woods all around it, and then, finding nothing, searched the hills above the woods—.'

Rose constructed an indulgent smile. 'I think it would be better if we repaired to the conservatory for the rest of our discussions. I'm sure Howard will come to himself presently. The stress of unremitting creativity, you know.'

It occurred to me that I could probably leave the cabin without either of them even noticing; but then I guessed I was probably learning something of unique value by staying, now that the intricate fabric was finally revealing its weakness. I followed Rose into the conservatory, leaving Howard reciting his crow story to an empty table.   The sudden low sunlight was blinding.

Realizing I'd left my coffee behind, I went back to get it. When I returned Rose was standing gazing out onto the hills, so that all I could see of him was his skeletal silhouette. For a moment I glimpsed a faint yellow disc in the centre of his head, covering perhaps a quarter of its width; I couldn't figure out any logical reason for such a thing, until I saw it move when I moved: with a gut-loosening shock, I realized it was the sun.

Something was going seriously wrong somewhere, and I was inclined to think it was me: too much strong coffee, or the stress of Elaine's desertion, or both. It was suddenly clear that this would be a good time to leave. I gathered my things from the bedroom and cleared up as best I could.

At the kitchen table Howard was still engrossed in his fairy tale, reciting it for all the world as though he was encircled by an audience of rapt children.

'The princess was overjoyed by the gift, and blessed the crow, who became her personal advisor and perpetual companion. Wherever she went, the crow was with her to counsel her and guide her heart. But despite his good fortune in finding such a protector, he secretly longed for his lost mate, for whom he had embarked on his quest so long ago. So the Little Red Hen said, "Now, who will help me gather dry sticks to make a fire?" But everyone in the farmyard said they were far too busy, so the Little Red Hen went out into the fields by herself to gather dry sticks to make a fire. "All the better to see you with", said the Little Red Wolf.'

Howard did not so much as break his rhythm as I passed in front of him to collect my books. In the conservatory Rose still stood in the same position facing away from me, although the sun was now partly behind his right ear, and the entire side of his face had become translucent. I wondered if he was about to dissolve completely.

I'd reached the outer door when Rose's voice startled me.

'Scuttling away with our guilty secret are we?' He was unaccountably only a few feet from me, and his face had taken on the aspect of one of the demons guarding the gates of hell. 'That will not do at all. We haven't had our little talk yet, have we?'

'I'm not scuttling away, and I haven't got a guilty secret. But I have had more than enough of your insane antics. I want my life back.'

He came closer, and seemed to suddenly acquire an authority he hadn't possessed while Howard was present. It was as though a new personality was emerging from the chrysalis of the bucolic and avuncular persona he had previously cultivated.

'Wouldn't it have been wiser to consider that before you deprived Rachel of her's in a vicious unprovoked attack of infantile rage?'

'Look, I've no idea where your friend got his insane concoction from, but it's not what happened. Rachel left my flat that night alive and unharmed. You have my solemn word on that.'

'That is perfectly true of course; we were quite aware of that. But it is no less true, is it not, that previously, she tried to leave and you became uncontrollably jealous and strangled the precious living spirit out of her?'

Now suddenly the dreadful possibility stood before me that both scenarios could be true. Suppose my journey through the labyrinth had brought me out, not into the same world I'd left earlier that evening through the hatchway on the stairs, but a different one, leaving the original Rachel lying lifeless in the parody of a grave I'd dug for her? If that was the case, why hadn't there been a huge murder hunt? Maybe there was, but I was no longer in that world? And what had happened to Rachael after I'd left her? The police would have done a thorough forensic sweep of my flat without any doubt, so why hadn't they come looking for me long ago? Of course by normal logic it wasn't possible for two identical people to be created; but suppose the Cube had indeed changed the fundamental laws of the world enabling parallel worlds to co-exist and influence each other? If they could achieve that then there was simply no limit to the ways in which the world I knew could have altered. But the bizarre possibility remained that now I both was and was not a murderer, and would have to pay the price of the former case persisting, whatever had succeeded it.

I tried to stand up but found I had lost all control over my legs. Howard seemed to have recovered and was holding out a glass of water which I took from him gratefully, if shakily. Calmed slightly by the cold liquid, I considered what to do. There seemed no possibility of returning to my old life after this: I was on the outermost edge of everything normal, and facing in the wrong direction.

I glanced up at Rose. 'How did you find out about all this?'

'You are already forgetting, Adam. The world is no longer the same as it was before out little gift arrived.'

'Your gift?' The already parlous daylight took another lurch further into unreality.

'Of course. Did you really think we were just a couple of literary cliches that had stumbled out of the pages of a very bad novel? We made what you call the Cube, and the Cube made us, and now it is making you. In its own image, you might say.'

Chapter Nine

I'd been walking all day and still hadn't arrived anywhere I recognised. By sunset I was still trudging through thick woods that showed no sign of coming to an end, which was odd because by my calculation I should by now have been within sight of Bridgwater.

With my new knowledge I didn't dare take public transport in case my picture had been circulated to the police. The trouble was, I didn't know for certain which world I would find myself in when I encountered civilization: the world in which I had killed Rachel, or the one in which she was still alive; or, what would be far worse, the world in which whether I had or hadn't killed her depended on exactly where I happened to be at any given time. I had to constantly remind myself that if the Cube was now remaking the world according to its own unhuman principles, I had no means of knowing what the current laws of physics, chemistry or pyschology might be. It was even possible, I speculated, that the Cube's powers extended to altering the laws of mathematics themselves, in which case every imaginable aspect of the world, from gravity to time and the speed of light, might change catastrophically and without warning.

But in practice I thought it more likely the changes would be subtle, considering its mission, and they would happen incrementally: a little less greed, a touch less suspicion of others, more openness to different points of view, more generosity and transparency. In the days when Les regularly spoke to me he often used to say the Cube would work slowly and invisibly – and one day we'd wake up and the world would be changed. But then he also said there wouldn't be enough time: humanity would try to destroy the Cube before it could make enough difference.

I realized I probably wasn't going to get much further that day: dusk was already filling the woods with duplicitous shadow, and I was feeling disorientated and weary. After battling through tangled undergrowth for another twenty minutes I found a hollow sheltered from the wind by rocks, and at once started gathering firewood. Amazingly I'd remembered the matches, tea bags and water bottle, and there were enough scraps of food in my bag to keep me from starving. In half an hour I had a fire going and had made tea in my aluminium mug.

Within minutes of the sun setting the temperature began to drop alarmingly. I put on all the extra clothes I had with me, and cast around for dry grass and leaves to improvise a bed. Although the hot drink had revived me, I began to worry that a night in the open was going to be hard to get through; still I had no enthusiasm for further battles with the obstacles of darkness and deep undergrowth.

I lay down and dragged my coat tightly around me. There was only a thin relic of moonlight, and the thickly crowded trees effectively hid the sky from me. I started to hear sounds of small creatures foraging among the detritus of summer, and thought with anguish of the people who lived like this as a matter of necessity, with no other option open to them: alone, friendless, hungry, faced with a future of ill-health and empty of human companionship. My legs and arms began to ache, and my neck felt like it was locked in a clasp of ice. It was soon clear I would stand little chance of sleep in this place. I decided to try to re-light the fire, and stumbled off in search of more fuel. It took longer than I'd expected: the dead wood was sparse and I had to sweep a large area to collect enough to last the night.

I was turning back towards my 'camp' when I fancied I saw a dim light wavering through the trees: it was hard to say what kind of light it was because no sooner had I glimpsed it than it went out, leaving me in deeper blackness than before it had appeared. Instinctively I walked in the direction I'd seen it, hoping it had only been obscured momentarily. I was aware of the danger of losing my bearings completely, but the lure of the light – and all it promised – was too strong to resist. A minute passed, two minutes; then I saw it again, but this time to the right: a reddish glow, undoubtedly a house light, maybe the glow of a wood fire; and now that it stayed visible for seconds together I could see the vague outline of the building it was part of: a long, substantial stone structure with a steeply sloping roof and articulated Victorian chimney. But even as I was deciding what to do the light was again extinguished, and when I tried to make out the building there was no trace of it.

I was afraid of losing this new lifeline to civilization, but I also needed to collect my belongings from the hollow. Trying to fix the direction of the house in memory, I turned to retrace my steps, and realized I'd no idea at all where my camp was: everything before me was shadow interlaced with deeper shadow. My only chance was to follow what I imagined were my own footsteps in the soft ground, barely discernible in the tiny beam of my torch. After ten minutes the beam began to give out completely, and I collapsed against a beech trunk, cold, exhausted and confused. I felt torn between huge opposing pulls: to take refuge from the hostile night in the consolation and comfort of the fleetingly lit window; or stay in the wood until cold, hunger and remorse overcame me and severed me from human life forever. I must admit I was sorely tempted by the latter: a sense of justice can be a strong motivator, stronger in some cases than self-preservation; to be sure, I wanted my life back, but not on any terms; if those comedians at the cabin had indeed been 'sent' by the Cube – and it was yet an unproven thesis – I was in deeper trouble than if I'd simply been caught in the act; for there would be no way to hide from them: in one form or another they'd be with me for the rest of my life. And they would be beyond the reach of any bribe or threat that I could make. Therefore (I reasoned) what would be the point of taking refuge in comfort and human company? It would at most amount to a brief distraction from my true situation. I could always, of course, take the other false refuges so often resorted to: alcohol or drugs; but I knew the end of that road would be no different: at first, maybe, a partial mitigation of pain, a free ride through the phantasmagoria of rampant sensations; but after that respite an agonising, drawn-out decline into darker and darker hells. No: however I looked at it, it was clear as noon sunlight that the rational option was to stay where I was and freeze or starve to death: at most, given the time of year, it would take three or four days, I thought; and I could easily hurry it along with the little tablets of painkillers I'd brought with me.

But no sooner had I set myself on this path, than my suddenly panicking brain offered me a whole procession of compelling reasons for taking the alternative one, like hopeful actors auditioning for something for which they were entirely unsuited. What about Cora and Elaine? Do you really want to inflict such misery on two essentially good people? Not to mention the other people in your life – do you think they wouldn't suffer by your act of revenge? Or don't you even care? Haven't you learned one single thing about human beings in your forty-five years among them? And do you rate your own humanity so low that you really think you have nothing at all to offer the world? Do you imagine that you alone of the human race have been plucked out for this singular extreme of uselessness? Surely this is arrogance to equal that of any tyrant? And so on and so on, until I was utterly drained of all energy for constructive thought.

And then, prompted by the aching in my neck, I glanced up and there was the light again, or maybe a different one, for it seemed much nearer and more defined, and this time it glowed steadily and didn't leap around the horizon like a Jack O'Lantern on speed.

Somehow, in those last moments, I'd found my way to a decision. I trudged in the direction I imagined I'd just come from, until within two minutes I stumbled over the faintly glowing embers of my own fire. Without hesitating, I scooped up earth and threw it over the remains, and stamped all over it to make sure it didn't revive; then I shouldered my rucksack and started back the way I'd come, hoping that the elusive window would still be lit when I reached the point I'd last seen it. But there was no window: only the layered and unrelieved blackness of the wood. I have to admit I began to feel despair at that point, because it was borne in on me that what I'd seen couldn't have been a real object. Having so recently abandoned hope of regaining a place among ordinary people, and more recently still clawed back a trace of that same hope, now to have it summarily snatched away again cut me to the heart.

After a few seconds a faint scent came on the still air which it took me some further seconds to recognise: wood-smoke. Without giving myself time to hope, I got to my feet again and began following the trace, tripping over roots, crashing through tangles of undergrowth, pausing every few yards to get my breath and check my direction. And then, like a grotesque face that without warning leers out of nowhere in a hall of mirrors, a huge edifice reared above me, its grimness relieved at intervals by a few mullioned windows at different heights, from the lowest of which a dim, oddly pulsating light issued. I couldn't imagine how I'd failed to notice it for so long.

I tried to clean myself up as best I could before working my way along the wall to what seemed to be a side door, recessed a foot or more back from the facade. Summoning my best spirits I thumped twice on the solid panel, and stood back to wait. The sound of my knocking seemed to die even as my fist hit the wood, so that it was impossible to believe anyone had heard it unless they were in the room immediately beyond. Nevertheless I thought I heard faint footsteps, and doors being manhandled into reluctant motion a long way off. But then there was more silence, only marginally relieved by branches rustling in a spasmodic breeze, and the alternate calling of a couple of night birds from deep cover. I concluded I must have imagined the steps, and knocked again. Almost at once I was startled by a loud metallic clattering on the other side, as though someone had fallen over a bucket in the dark, and moments later the door was unlatched and inched open.

Chapter Ten

The figure in the doorway was in his late forties, slight, lean, shaven-headed, and gazed intently and unsmilingly at me with no sign of surprise. He took in my bedraggled appearance, my mud-streaked clothes, my obvious exhaustion, and said simply:

'You'd best come inside.'

His accent was East Yorkshire carried almost to the point of self-parody.

The first thing that struck me about the interior was how empty it was. There was a huge kitchen with a solid-fuel stove (possibly the only 'modern' appliance in the room), a dresser, sink, and a large, almost bare pine table. The floor was stone-flagged, with a large red and black chequer-patterned carpet in its centre. Two tall windows, both uncurtained, looked out onto the black outline of the forest. There didn't seem to be any electric light, for two brass oil lamps stood on the table and cast an unsteady radiance around the room. Beside one of the lamps lay a thick spiral-bound notebook and a pen.

'I'm Joe.'

'Adam. Pleased to meet you.'

Joe drew a heavy upright chair to the table.

'Have a seat.'

In the light of the lamps he seemed younger and less like a recently escaped convict, but he still had the intense directness and economy of manner and expression I'd noticed at first sight.

'I'm so thankful to find you. I hope I haven't woken you up.'

'No. I'm a regular night-bird. In fact some days I hardly see the light of day at all. Some tea?'

'Thanks.'

Joe didn't seem the least fazed by my unannounced arrival. He made the tea in a slow, considered way, as though he'd got all the time in the world to spend exactly as he wished. He also didn't seem anxious to know who I was, which, in the circumstances, surprised me.

'Do you live alone here?'

'Yes. For the past six years.'

'May I ask what you do?'

'I do experiments.'

'For a living?'

'God no. Nobody in their right mind would pay me to do these.'

'What kind of experiments?'

'You could call them mind experiments.' He slid the lamp nearer, perhaps so he could see my face more clearly. 'For example, you were puzzled just now because I hadn't asked you anything about yourself - who you are or how you arrived here, right?'

'Yes, I suppose I was now you mention it.'

'Well, I'm deliberately not asking you anything because I don't want to prejudice myself. I don't want to make any assumptions about your character. If you start telling me your background and what you do I'll inevitably be tempted to jump to some kind of judgement about you, which could get in the way of our openness with each other. That's the experiment.'

'That's very courageous. I mean, I might be a murderer. I might have just escaped from some lunatic asylum. I might have come here with some cock and bull story to win your trust, intending to rob you.'

'Yes, precisely. So why bother to ask you? Now I don't have the problem of working out whether or not to believe your story. Anyway, you'd be hard put to find anything worth stealing here.'

'I had noticed the er, spartan atmosphere. Have you always lived like this?'

He poured the tea into two squat earthenware mugs and pushed one across to me.

'Far from it. But I suggest we eat before I tell you my story. How does that sound?'

'It sounds the best thing I've heard all day!'

In fifteen minutes Joe had conjured up a delicious spicy vegetable soup and was serving it out of a black wrought iron cauldron. I quickly discovered I was ravenous, and we ate in near silence. Afterwards Joe cleared away the pots and topped up the lamps. He seemed relieved to have an audience.

'Still awake enough to hear the answer to your question?'

'Absolutely.'

'Good.' He paused for dramatic effect, or to make sure he had my attention. The unsteady light from the oil lamp threw hard black verticals from his strongly sculptured features. 'For many years I lived a pretty typical educated middle-class life. I had security and everything I needed. My Dad was in the Navy, and though he never rose to the top he had a pretty good job in the high-ish echelons of the administration. So I got quite familiar with the ways of ships. For a few years I lived on the knees of luxury. I was a submarine communications officer for eight years, then a commander for four. Everything was going, er, swimmingly. I ended up in Australia, running a successful electronics business. Married a golden-haired beauty called Adele who'd been a model in Melbourne. She didn't like city life, so we looked around and found a place out in the Dandenongs. We were very much in love, we lived in a beautiful land and life was good to us. Two years later the bottom fell out of the whole shebang.'

'How?'

'Adele got cancer of the throat. Didn't tell a soul about it until she had no choice. She thought the best way was to go quickly and quietly, so she took poison. Trouble was, no one believed it was suicide. You see, I'd had an affair about a year before: an Indonesian girl called Li who'd come to look after Adele. Her greatest advantage was that she wasn't remotely beautiful. Somehow that made her irresistible. Anyway we fell in love more or less instantly; it was one of those affairs that are so intense and non-cerebral you just have to go along with the chemistry: to resist it would have killed us both, I'm certain. The locals knew about it, inevitably, and they put two and two together and made twenty five. In their unalterable opinion I'd poisoned Adele so I could inherit her fortune and marry Li. That was what men did. I was a man. Ergo... In their eyes it was a no-brainer. Anyway, long story short, there was a trial which I won, thanks to an excellent judge who had the wisdom to see that the popular perception was based on pure prejudice. I got off technically, but remained guilty in the eyes of virtually the entire community. A whispering campaign was started, to get rid of me. It began with hate-mail, then progressed to lumps of concrete through the window, and then finally my dog was poisoned - they doubtless thought I couldn't fail to get that message.'

'So you sold up?'

'God no. How could I? It would have been tantamount to admitting I murdered Adele. No. I bought in three months' provisions, put up a strong security fence, and dug myself in. I thought in three months time the heat would be off and some of them at least would be willing to hear my side of the story. I spent weeks writing to journalists explaining exactly what had happened. Eventually I got one of them - a bloke named Tom Margrave - who worked for The Age - to believe my story and write an in-depth report on the case. He became a good friend: I'm still in touch with him. But it was tough: once the community decides you're guilty, evidence and logic go sailing out of the window. I wasn't the first to discover that. It's fear of the unknown really; a primitive survival mechanism. Anyway, once the article in the Age came out, the whole controversy was stirred up again, but this time I had a few friends out there, and that made all the difference. Tom in particular made a huge difference. in fact it's not going too far to say he probably saved my life. His word was respected over a wide area, and he carried on supporting me far beyond the call of duty. And he was persuasive: I got letters of support from complete strangers. I got invitations to give talks, which I refused. Which proved a wise decision, because there was still a small core of die-hards that had it in for me, and were just waiting their chance to get me alone. I realized that no persuasion or evidence was going to work with them: I'd murdered their queen and they wanted blood.

So I had a dilemma: sooner or later I would have to leave the house, and they'd be watching. I wasn't willing to admit guilt for something I hadn't done, and neither was I prepared to go on living like a cornered rat. I decided on a radical approach. My instinct all through the business had been to isolate myself, physically and mentally; to take refuge in a siege mentality. But this only made me more alien in their eyes: an arrogant invader on their territory, who thinks he's invulnerable. What I realized was I had to reverse that strategy: to become totally vulnerable, to see the world as they saw it. In a sense I had to stop being me. So I set to thinking how I could do that. Little did I realize then how completely I would achieve it!

I found that my mind kept imposing limitations: I'd get rid of most of my expensive furniture, but keep just one or two things that held special value for me, such as an antique writing desk that I'd bought cheap in an auction a few days after I'd moved there. Or I'd buy a gun to take with me whenever I went into town, not to use of course, except as a last resort! I made it a practice whenever these strategies emerged always to ignore them, because they were undermining the essence of my plan, which was not to protect myself, because there was no threat to protect myself from; as long as I perceived there to be a threat I would inevitably behave like one who was threatened, and my plan was bound to fail. So I spent some weeks training myself to deconstruct the narrative I'd set up, that there was a group of people who hated and feared me and wanted me out of the way. That was the hardest part of the whole thing, because essentially I believed that story.'

'But hang on: surely it was more than a story? It represented reality. I mean, there were such people out there, weren't there?'

'No. That's the strangest part: there weren't. But nevertheless that's the picture that was driving my behaviour. What in fact there were was a few people who were terrified that there was someone living amongst them who was a murderer, and who was getting away scot-free. And they weren't absolutely sure what had happened, but he always kept himself behind locked doors and security fencing so he must have done something bad. You see what I mean? When you start to unpack the images of the story the reality is much more complex and less rigid. What these people were really scared of was the unknown, represented by the interior: and the interior can be either physical territory, such as the Outback, or it can be the unconscious, the thing you can't look at directly. So anyway, after I'd worked all this out it was quite clear what I had to do: I had to go into their territory completely undefended, relaxed and open, not taking with me any trace of that fear or uneasiness that was the result of the story I'd built up on the basis of past experience. So that's what I did.

'There was a bar in town - well it was a one-bar town so there really was no choice - that I'd heard was frequented by these men. I started hanging out there in the afternoons. First three days nothing happened: I got talking to a few people who turned out to be relative newcomers like myself, and didn't know anything about the tribal feuds of the town. But the next afternoon I recognised two of the troublemakers and deliberately went over and introduced myself. The taller of the two was wearing a beige bush hat that almost hid his grey eyes. He was well built with thick arms, and fitted my long-ingrained picture of a belligerent hooligan to a T. His mate was thinner and darker, and had a narrow face with bulging eyes, which gave him the appearance of a rabbit. Together they made a daunting pair. At that moment all I saw before me was two scared kids who craved for some authority that they could rely on to tell them what to do.

'They didn't shake hands. I offered to buy them a beer. The hatted one eyed me up for a second or two and then said 'Yeh, ok.' I went over to get the drinks, walking as unhurriedly as I could. Luckily the place was nearly empty, so I didn't have to contend with people desperately trying to avoid my eyes. First hurdle negotiated, I thought, as I took the glasses back and set them down. 'You've got a blasted nerve, haven't you?' the rabbit-face said. 'I didn't kill her.' I said. 'I suppose the roos did it, is that right?' I noticed his left arm was shaking as he reached for his cigarettes. 'She poisoned herself. She had cancer of the throat.' 'You're a blasted liar!' the hatted one said, getting up without touching his drink. As he made for the door his mate stood up, made to take a sip from his glass, then threw its entire contents in my face. I was drenched from head to feet. 'Thanks for the beer,' he called over his shoulder as he followed the other outside.

'I was certain they'd be waiting for me round a corner somewhere, but I was wrong: they'd vanished like mirages in a heat-haze. I walked home, expecting a car to pull alongside at any moment and more abuse to be hurled from it. But no car came, and no one followed me. I felt I'd come through the first test pretty well.

'That night I did some hard thinking. I felt sure my intuition of the nature of the conflict had been right; I represented a threat to them in some way that had to do with my 'alienness'. But how on earth to open a dialogue about it? Talk was the last thing they wanted. Still there was one thing I was quite sure about: I had to go back to that bar the next day; if I failed to do so, it would simply convince them that I was guilty and had been scared off.

'The following afternoon was hot, and I sat at a table on the verandah of the bar and waited for the action in my very own cowboy western. Overnight I'd had a valuable insight: the encounter of the day before had failed because I was still judging them, if unconsciously, exactly as they were judging me; so I was playing the same game: they were the baddies and I was the victim. Suddenly as I sat there I felt deep down I had nothing left to defend; I no longer cared what happened: I didn't care any more about myself than about them. To use that awful cliche, I felt my heart melting, the boundaries between me and them crumbling, and I saw with a shock of clarity that all these fences that kept things separate were really constructed by fear – primarily my fear of not existing.'

'I drained my glass and enjoyed the image of the tree shadows dappling the earth, and the sound of the wattle birds chasing each other through the maze of leaves. A small child was kicking a ball in the road, and his delight in his new-found skill eased into my mind like music. Everything I looked at became pure pleasure, and it wasn't simply due to the beer: some ancient habit of perception inside me had quietly shifted.'

In the midst of this reverie a voice sneered:

'You here again? Didn't you get wet enough yesterday?'

He still wore his hat, but now he was alone.

'Can I buy you another?'

'No. I'll get my own.' He gave me an appraising glare before disappearing inside.

'I was watching the kid in the road as he discovered he could balance the ball on his foot for several seconds before losing control, when out of nowhere an articulated lorry fully laden with timber roared round the curve about fifty metres away. The boy, engrossed in his play, didn't hear it. As soon as I'd clocked the image I found myself diving headlong into the road to catch him, and reached him while the lorry was about twenty feet away. The driver stood on his brakes but at the speed he was going he hadn't a hope in hell of stopping in time. Somehow when the lorry reached us my impact with the child had shot him out of the path of the vehicle, but I wasn't so lucky: I was caught by its offside wing. I hit the road and blacked out. To this day I don't know how I wasn't killed outright. I escaped with concussion and a broken leg. The child, miraculously, was bruised but unharmed. I was in hospital about a week; I was in shock for most of that time, but later on I had the opportunity to work out the detailed sequence of events. There was absolutely no doubt that if I hadn't been there that child would be dead, because no-one in the bar would have seen the lorry at all.'

'Anyway, eventually I was fit enough to get myself home with the aid of crutches. Among the pile of letters waiting for me was a bunch of flowers and a card from one Dan Gallacher, a farm manager from a couple of kilometres south of the town. The card said simply, 'Thanks for saving the kid's life. We're all indebted to you. See you around – Dan.'

'About a week later I went down to the bar again. Dan and his sidekick were in their usual places. They bought me a drink this time, and we got talking. It emerged there had been a notorious murder case about ten years before I'd arrived, in which an 'incomer' from Europe had done away with his wife to get her money – but he was wealthy enough to nobble the judge and get off with a minimal sentence. So my coming on the scene was a bit like a Greek tragedy unfolding: this newcomer would have to pay the price of the original crime. Well, I did, in a way. Anyway was I really innocent when I arrived there? Is there ever such a thing as an innocent man? Our ideas of guilt and innocence are crudely worked out on the whole. What is certain is if I hadn't gone back after that first encounter I'd have been hunted down by those self-appointed furies.'

'That's a very impressive story,' I said. 'But what made you leave after going through all that?'

'Well, that incident had a big effect on me. It woke me up to the power of the unconscious. I got more and more interested in how we can train our minds to work in harmony with the unconscious, not to be the victim of it. This became my main work, and it was difficult to do it in a place like Australia, where there wasn't the culture to support that kind of work. I mean, you need other people prepared to work with you, to take risks with you; to meet regularly and compare ideas and experiences, or simply understand what you're trying to achieve. So I upped sticks and bought this place. Very cheaply, I may say, because it already had a bit of a reputation.'

'But I think you said you'd lived with someone a few years ago?'

'That's right, I did. I knew nobody when I arrived back in England. I'd lost contact with my old submarine crew; to be truthful I didn't particularly feel I had anything in common with them in the first place. So what I did was I advertised for people to share the house with me.'

'Wasn't that risky?'

'Of course it was. But my business is taking risks. I couldn't think of a no-risk way of acquiring a community. Anyway eventually three people – all men, as it happened – ended up making the commitment to live together on the basis I'd laid down. I'd insisted on a few ground rules: that we'd be completely open and honest with each other about what was happening between and within us; that we'd respect the work and put it foremost in our lives; that we wouldn't bring friends into the house without first checking it out with the others; and we'd contribute a certain proportion of our time each day to physical work on the property.'

'And did it work?'

'For a while, yes. The first six months were amazing. We really seemed to have a common vision. I think the work I'd done in Australia – I mean the mind experiments – did much to help the project: I was very clear about the sort of life I wanted, and I communicated this very painstakingly to everyone before they joined, so there was no room for confusion of aims. In spite of the fact that our backgrounds were very different – class, education, religion, previous lifestyles – we did manage to cement a strong friendship and cohesiveness. We spent most of our waking time together, talking, working, dealing with problems, gardening, playing games, playing music. But gradually tensions began to assert themselves; people began making excuses for not meeting or panning up on their work agreements, that sort of thing. Then someone had a serious falling out over an issue of privacy, which couldn't be resolved. One said he needed privacy for certain parts of his life, the other said this contravened the spirit of the project – and neither would budge. The interesting thing for me was that neither of them could see that what was happening was their earlier unsatisfied emotional needs were surfacing and demanding to be recognised. Even after all that time together they were unable to apply the principle that everything that happens is an opportunity to observe one's mind in action. Anyway the thing simmered away in the background for a while, which created an unpleasant atmosphere, and the mind experiments were forgotten. Over the weeks the inevitable small differences blew up into irresolvable conflicts, and I asked them both to leave. Eventually there was just me again. But I'd learned a hell of a lot in those years. I decided to stay here and try to take my experiments deeper, with a view to maybe gathering a new community together later on.'

'But you didn't.'

'No. The fact is I was moving into a very different space, much more inward. I found other people's needs and demands a distraction. I wanted to see how far I could take the experiments. I began to spend several hours each day tracing my thoughts and feelings to their source, no matter how uncomfortable they were, and watching the myriads of free-associations that every single thought and stimulus threw up, and seeing the attitudes and beliefs they crystallized into. It was a revelation. I knew I was onto something important, but I couldn't put it into a context. What I mean is, I couldn't see where it was leading, what its fruit might be.

'About that time I discovered the Roman philosopher Seneca. His writing came as a revelation. He'd clearly travelled very much the same path that I was on, only two thousand years before. He demanded total honesty and great courage in the face of isolation, ignominy, even death. I felt he was a spiritual brother to me; and he was practical too: he said you shouldn't take discipline to an extreme, because then you'll get disheartened. If you are alone predominantly then you should mix with people at intervals. That will cure you of longing for crowds. And regardless of circumstances you should keep you prime principles at the focus of your life at all times. I found this of immense help in the work I'd set myself. Anyway, after a few months I lost all desire for distraction and stimulus from the outside world. I slowed down to a virtual standstill: I'd spend an hour or more lost in wonder watching a moth or a flower. Blake was right you know: the world just as it is is infinity. And the present moment is eternity.'

'And can you honestly say you never got lonely?'

'That's a good question. The answer is no, I can't; but what was valuable was what I did with the loneliness. Which was, basically, that I simply watched it. And watched the whole process of watching, and all the reactions that desperately tried to get in on the act. It began to seem quite funny. There I was in this infinite paradise, where everything I looked at opened up into limitless beauty - and I was feeling miserable because there was no one with me!'

'I suppose you don't suddenly cease to be a human being just because you have an insight into how the world works.'

'Quite. But I eventually came to understand why we do actually need other people. Not just to fill the void, but to grow into true humans. I've come to see there are some crucial lessons we can never properly learn on our own.'

'Whereas I've come to see there are crucial lessons I'll never learn either on my own or with others.'

'That's a useful starting point. Listen, you're not going anywhere tonight, I take it. If you've finished your tea I think this would be a good moment to show you the house. It might answer some of your questions.'

The place was huge. Rather like the Tardis, there were some rooms that seemed larger than the entire building itself, and which had windows looking onto views that couldn't exist where they appeared to be. I found it impossible to orientate myself among the maze of corridors and staircases.

'The people I bought it from called themselves the "deep learning trust". They'd intended it to be a special school for children with unusual abilities, and added bits all over the place at different times. Unfortunately for them they were deserted by their benefactor at just the crucial moment, so they were forced to sell up just as I appeared on the scene. They say the devil looks after his own! I'd like you to see my memory room, if you're not too exhausted.'

'No. Actually I feel strangely revived.'

He led me along a corridor lined with Goya and Titian prints that seemed to have been unmoved for decades. There was a door marked 'games' which struck me as oddly incongruous.

Joe noticed my amusement. 'Ah yes. The truth is I'm a bit of a snooker freak on the quiet. Once in a while I need to have a blast on the old baize to get my thoughts clear. Do you play?'

'Very badly.'

'Brilliant. That's exactly what I need. It'll do my self-confidence a power of good.'

We arrived at a large doorway with a curtain across it. 'Now here's what I want to show you. This is one of the few rooms with electric light. The deep learning people turned out not to be very practical: they'd only managed to install it in a few rooms by the time they had to leave. But I rather like that: it's like living in several centuries at the same time.'

'Why do you call it a 'memory' room?'

He went over to a large display case and took out some kind of animal carving – possibly a deer – done in highly polished black wood.

'I call these active memories.' He set the little piece gently down on a low table. 'It's something I made a few years ago in a very strange state of mind. You can touch it.'

The material felt warm to the touch, and quickly drew me into its world. For a moment I was transported to a green meadow thick with scents and wild flowers. Birdsong was loud all around me, and there was a sense of fecundity and wholesomeness. The whole thing happened in a flash, and then I was back in the meagre artificial light of the room with Joe's quizzical gaze upon me.

'Did you go somewhere?'

I described the field I'd just seen.

He nodded. 'Yes. That's where I was. Southern Italy, about May, three years ago. Did you hear the bells?'

I hadn't noticed any, but when I made an effort to recall the scene I had the distinct feeling there had been cathedral bells tolling somewhere in the distance.

'Are you saying what I experienced just now was actually embedded in this object?'

'Yes. Precisely that.'

'But that's not possible. Is it?'

'It would seem so.'

'But how?'

'I can't tell you how. All I know is there's an intimate relationship between the raw material, the physical form and the state of concentration of its maker. Something of the mental state you are in when you create it gets built into the structure. And someone whose mind is open enough can detect this many years later. That's all I can say with any certainty. How much is due to the material and how much to the creating and receiving minds I wouldn't like to say. Except that I'm certain the ancient Egyptians knew about this and their major works of art embody it. Have you ever stood in the Egyptian gallery ay the British Museum and felt something pull on your mind?'

I had, of course: there was that strange afternoon I'd had the vision of the desert in one of those very galleries. The memory gave me sudden goosepimples.

'Good. Not everyone can tune in to them of course. It does need a bit of training. I'll show you more tomorrow.'

After the tour I was ready to fall asleep. Joe showed me to a small attic room with a bed in the corner ready made up.

'Were you expecting visitors tonight?' I asked as I fumbled in my rucksack.

'Expecting, no. Prepared for, yes.' His grey eyes got almost as far as twinkling. 'Visitors are always a gift. You never know what treasure they might be carrying.'

Chapter Eleven

'Imagination is the key. We grossly undervalue it in our so-called culture. We – all of us – have huge resources that we're almost totally unaware of, because we spend our lives "getting and spending, laying waste our powers."'

We were having breakfast in what Joe called 'the morning room', because it was smaller and faced the early sun, and was therefore easier to warm than the kitchen. I'd slept deeply and long – my first really peaceful night in many since leaving London. There was an atmosphere about the house that promoted calm, no doubt due to Joe's sustained mental toil. And now the warmth and quiet, together with the home-made muesli, nurtured me until I began to feel human again.

I was amazed at how much I found myself wanting to reveal all my innermost secrets to this man, and had to constantly restrain myself; after all, I thought, Joe could just as easily be an agent of the Cube as Les and Len were: I had to exercise judicious caution until I had more idea of the lie of the land. But this proved a futile strategy.

'I can see you've had some trouble Adam. I don't want to invade your privacy, and it's not my way to offer advice. But if you stay here a while you may get the help you need – though not necessarily from me. Anyway, I just wanted to say you're very welcome to hang around if it seems useful.'

'Thanks. You're right: there is trouble. I'm not sure I feel like talking about it just yet. You may not be what you seem to be.'

'Well, I can set your mind at rest on that point at least: I'm definitely not what I seem to be.'

'That's strangely reassuring.'

'I don't want to get metaphysical so early in the day, but it's obvious to me that none of us – I mean literally no one – is what they seem to be. So we should take that as read. The problem then becomes: how can we have intimate relationships if we believe that no one is what they seem?'

'Yes, that's my dilemma in a nutshell. I feel absolutely alone. When I was trying to sleep in the wood last night I was on the point of despair because I felt totally exiled from humanity. And it was my own actions that caused it.'

'Let me stop you there. I don't want to know what you believe you've done. I'm not a guru or father confessor, or a therapist. All I can give you is the right kind of environment to help you gain clarity and perspective.' He poured himself a tall glass of orange-juice and swallowed it straight off. 'Now, if you've had enough to eat, I'd like to show you some more sculptures.'

The room was an entirely different place by daylight. The impoverished, hollow, monotonous dirge of electric bulbs had given way to a rich, multi-channel, ever-shifting harmony of voices from the ascendant sun. Outside, new-fledged birds were just discovering the miracle of space from their dipping ships of twigs in the hushing canopies. It felt as though a new world was bulging into being with each new-minted moment.

'You must have been making these things for years. There are hundreds of them!' I negotiated the creaking floorboards to inspect a low table covered with intricate carvings of all shades and sizes.

'Don't touch any of those yet please. They're not ready.'

I stepped back. 'Ready? You mean they're still being made?'

'Not made, exactly. Tuned would be more accurate.'

'How do you tune them?' It was quite difficult not to touch them; they seemed to sing like sirens as I gazed at them, willing me to pick one up.

'Oh, it's just a question of spending time with them. Charging them with my energy. I don't do any physical work on them generally. It's really a matter of bringing a more and more focussed attention onto them. Some of it is absorbed into the atomic structure. Or even sub-atomic, perhaps. I'm not a physicist. I only know that they change in some way, and other minds can detect that change. A kind of pyschic hologram, if you like.'

I stood awkwardly near the sculptures, trying to absorb the huge implications of what Joe had just told me; particularly what he'd said about not believing what people tell you; but he had a way of speaking that gave the impression that he really didn't care at all whether you believed him or not; that he had absolutely nothing invested in what others thought of his theories – and to my mind that impression carried a lot more weight that the theories themselves.

He had gone up to the far end of the room, where a glass cabinet stood before a wide stone-mullioned window. It must have faced south, for the sun cast soft-edged diamonds of pale amber over the displayed objects. Joe beckoned me over.

'This one,' – he indicated a large obsidian egg balanced on its blunt end in the dead centre of the cabinet – 'isn't one of mine, and I ask you very seriously not to touch it at all. Ever.'

'Is it very fragile?'

'It isn't. We are.'

'How do you mean?'

'I bought this at a market in Wad Medani in Eastern Sudan. It was made by a local artist called Sidike. A few days after I'd got it Sidike himself came to visit me. He said he'd heard I'd bought the egg and he wanted to warn me about it. He told me a demon had accidentally got into it while he was working on it and now it was trapped inside and very angry. He said I should burn it until there was nothing left, and then throw away the ashes into running water. He was very insistent that I followed his instructions to the letter, and made me repeat them. Only that way would I be safe from the demon's anger. Naturally I didn't do anything of the sort. I brought it here.'

'And has anything happened?'

'No. Nothing at all. It just sits there quietly soaking up the sun. If there ever was a demon in it I should think he's chilled out by now. But still I don't touch it. You won't be surprised to hear that I think there could be some truth in his story.'

'Jesus! I'm glad you didn't tell me that last night!'

'Yes. I could see you badly needed sleep. Anyway, you're most welcome to handle any of the other pieces in this room, but please not that one. There are quite enough demons at large in this world already.'

Joe went off to organise fuel for the stove, and I wandered round the room trying to take on board everything he'd told me. There was a childish part of me that wanted to believe everything: wanted to treat him as a reliable, loving father who would straighten me out and see that no harm came to me provided I obeyed him. It was a subtle but strong pull, and I knew I had to resist it. Nobody was going to give me what I wanted, at least not without wanting a lot in return: I knew any deal I did in that department would be perilous. I realized that this place was an opportunity to disempower that particular demon, if no other; it had already wrecked my life in so many respects, and I badly needed to take possession of what remained. For a moment I was tempted to cast all caution to the winds and find out the egg's secret, if it had one: it was, after all, only a bit of polished wood – part of a tree that had grown up from a seed sunk in the earth; everything else I attributed to it was a story that had its origin in ignorance. I stood a few feet away and contemplated its serene burnished surface, its balanced mass, its sense of completeness, and found it impossible to associate with any dark arts, or tales of demonic menace. Yet still I resisted touching it, and after a few moments I deliberately pulled away and let my mind rest on other objects.

Not all of them were carvings by any means; many were stones, minerals and crystals of all hues and shapes. Some were intricate and dense, others simple geometric forms which had apparently resisted more invasive human intervention. I found myself holding a translucent crystal sphere, somewhat like quartz, about four inches across, which felt icy cold to the touch. It was strongly evocative of the sea, and as I peered to see what it was made of I was suddenly back in my childhood, on a sunlit beach digging a hole, deeper and deeper, through layers of ever darker and wetter sand. I was distantly aware of my mother in dry dock a few yards away, sunk in a romantic novel, and my father doing what he always did on seaside holidays: pacing along the water's edge, beachcombing, occasionally bending to inspect a shard of driftwood or a stone with a face on it, or a bit of coloured glass that looked like a star from the crab nebula, sometimes pocketing his loot, sometimes skimming it far out, hoping it might be accepted as a gift by the hungry, snarling waves.

Still I dug deeper, my head eventually disappearing from view below the white shimmering surface. And then an astonishing thing happened: my small red-handled spade hit something hard and stopped dead, like an animal encountering something totally beyond its range of experience. I crouched down as deep as I could, scooping away the grit from the new unyielding surface, and there it was before me: a clear silver wall, slightly convex, reflecting my stunned face and the ragged lake of pale blue framing it. A few years later and I'd have realized that such a thing was impossible: it was my unstable nature, being on my own too much, or reading too much pulp fiction; but at nine I had no such curb: this was clearly an alien artifact, and I was its sole discoverer.

I put my head to the sheer silver surface and listened intently: for a while I heard nothing but the noise of seagulls and the distant crash of waves over shingle. Then something amazing: a high musical tone, or rather two tones, close together in pitch, so that they produced an eery trembling note, which evoked alien civilizations more powerfully that any space music. This, I realized, was the real thing: I'd dug myself an alien spacecraft, and more: a fully functioning one, probably complete with crew, who were in all probability even now desperately trying to communicate with their world to inform them they'd located a virgin planet ripe for colonisation – or, if we were lucky – education. I stood with both sandalled feet on its sheer surface and looked up at the sky, a cry of triumph rising in me from an ancient depth. My mother didn't even raise her eyes from her book at the astonishing sound issuing from a hole in the sand a few feet from where she sat. My dad turned briefly from his vain gazing, but failed to see a boy with bright golden hair and melting wings swoop helplessly into the waves.

The seascape dissolved suddenly and I was again in the memory room: the crystal sphere was back in its place and I was shaking drops of apparently real seawater from my fingers. What had just happened? A hallucination? A clever piece of auto-suggestion? A chemically induced fugue? I'd no idea, but if it was an illusion it was the realest one I'd ever experienced: it seemed like I'd simply stepped through a door into an afternoon of my childhood, with every sense-detail perfect. If it was true that Joe had created most of these objects, he was either a magician in the most literal sense of the word, or else

—

I chose not to complete that thought. I wanted to ask Joe more about his method of making these things, and in particular how conscious he was of planting the visions in them; but my attention was instantly grabbed by another object before me: an oval carving in the form of a platter about eighteen inches long, with rough handles carved at each end. It had an intricate swirling pattern in its surface, formed as far as I could see from the natural grain. It didn't quite make a picture, but its whorls and loops appeared to move towards me as I looked at it, raising themselves above the plane of the surface. I took hold of the handles, which this time felt warm to the touch. Now I could see behind the shapes of the grain, and could make out a desert stretching endlessly away on either hand. There were red rocks before me, and small carvings of figures on the rocks, some holding spears or ritual instruments. The heat was intense, and a searing breeze swept across my body. As I crept nearer, the figures became life-sized, and began to move, and I could hear singing in high nasal voices which pierced the air and seemed to hang in space like a physical object, a harmony made visible.

The figures were alarmingly thin, but undoubtedly human and alive. They danced with minimal movements, clockwise in an expanding circle, throwing their arms high in the air on every alternate beat. Now I'd come closer I saw there was a painting in the sand in the centre of the ring, and one of their number was changing it by degrees as the ritual progressed, adding some details while obliterating others. Then with a frisson of alarm I noticed he'd drawn a small stick figure outside the circle of the mandala, and realized instantly that it represented myself.

Suddenly I didn't want to be present in this scene, but I had no power over my movements: I continued approaching the ring of dancers, and when I was about six feet from them, they parted to create an opening; at the same time the artist on the ground, without looking away from the painting, scrubbed out the figure he'd just drawn, and re-drew it as part of the circle. It was clear that whatever he drew in the sand was at once replicated in the living world: I was in the circle, moving with the rest in the same rhythm, and my individual will counted for nothing.

By now sweat was pouring from my body. Someone thrust a long stake into my hand, and I saw I was naked as the rest of the company. I desperately tried to think of some way of getting out of the ritual, but thinking didn't seem to have any effect in this world: another law, more instinctive and more visceral, had priority; it was like trying to awaken from a nightmare which on one level you know is a dream, but somehow the knowledge has no power to release you.

My apprehension gradually grew to something like horror. I caught a glimpse of what the artist was drawing on the ground, and the dancing and chanting rapidly increased in power. An animal something like a wild boar had just been drawn some way outside the circle; although the dancers could not all have seen this at once, instantly the ring broke up and, still chanting, its members ran off in the same direction, and I found myself running with them, as if some group mentality had embraced me and obliterated any separate will. And then I knew with certainty that there was a wild boar somewhere ahead, and that I would be part of the killing party.

The frenzied caravan of would-be hunters danced on. Up ahead I heard a shriek, followed by a brief silence, a rush of feet in the sand, and a final scream of pain and terror from the quarry. I stopped. Sweat was running down my limns, and people behind me were crowding past to glimpse their prize. I could smell the blood on the breeze. Someone collided with me from behind, and I stabbed my stake into the sand to stay upright. I felt a hand supporting me, and found Joe at my side. In the same moment the desert vanished and the dim room full of motionless sculpture was once more visible. I caught sight of Joe's concerned face.

'Come on. Let's get you downstairs.'

'Mm. I could use a drink.'

'Do you know how long you've been up here?'

'I've no idea. Half an hour?'

'Almost five hours.'

'Holy Jesus.'

He smiled. 'My thought precisely.'

Dusk was already falling as we sat down again at one end of the long kitchen table. Joe lit one of the lamps and brewed tea. The shadows of the trees seemed to lean into the room, as though wanting to leaven our conversation with their quietness. He turned a concerned gaze on me.

'You really looked like you'd been to hell and back when I brought you out of there.'

I told him of my journey – I couldn't think of it in any other way – into the desert. 'I had a growing fear that I'd end up trapped in that world if somebody hadn't rescued me.'

'You could have, very easily.'

'But surely – I mean, it wasn't real. I was in that room all the time. Wasn't I?'

'That depends. If you mean your physical body stayed in the room, yes, it did; but your consciousness certainly didn't, did it?'

'I suppose not.'

'So it comes down to what you identify with, your body or your consciousness. Personally, I'd say I am where my consciousness is.'

'But if you hadn't found me?'

'If I hadn't found you you'd probably still be dancing around naked in the Australian outback.'

'I'm sorry. This is a bit too much to take in. You'll have to give me time.'

'That's no problem here. We've gallons of the stuff.'

'So, let me get this right. There is something embedded in these sculptures or artifacts or whatever, that can directly control your consciousness and take you on actual journeys?'

'Well yes and no. They can't transport you physically like a plane can, but they can work on your imagination, very much like a stage play or a film can. The active element is your mind, not the physical object. I'll give you a simple example of the process. Do you know the Japanese poet Issa?'

'No.'

'Well, he wrote what is undoubtedly one of the greatest poems in the history of literature, which happens to be a haiku: a seventeen-syllable unrhymed poem, part of a very ancient tradition in Japanese culture. It goes like this:

>   A brushwood gate
>   and for a lock
> this snail

'That's all?'

'Yes. Three lines, nine words, ten syllables. Not very sensational at first hearing. But when I first read it it knocked my socks off. I just couldn't forget that image of the snail on the gate; it haunted me every minute of the day. It even appeared in my dreams. Its reality for me was totally overwhelming. Which seems bizarre doesn't it? Considering that it's a very common unspectacular image: a snail on a wooden post. But then I realized what makes it such a stunning poem – in fact what makes it a poem at all – is the huge energy of concentration that Issa brought to it. He saw and felt it so deeply that his feelings are caught in the words and we can sense them four centuries later, and in a totally different culture. If that isn't an act of magic please tell me what is!'

'And you're saying your sculptures work in the same way?'

'Exactly. They are holders of intense concentration.'

'Most people would give their right arm to possess one of those. They have to be worth a fortune!'

'I wouldn't dream of selling them. For one thing I don't need the money. For another I wouldn't want to be responsible for the consequences. They aren't toys; they can be dangerous and unpredictable – as you've already discovered. And not everyone would experience anything at all. In fact I'd guess most people would be too resistant to receive anything from them. So I'd get an awful lot of disgruntled customers. No, I don't need any of that, thank you.'

Joe went off to prepare supper. I needed some air, and went to walk around the grounds, which mostly consisted of unweeded vegetable plots and ragged wildflower patches. Magpies and crows traded insults with each other from the compact shadows of the evergreens. The whole area clearly needed serious attention. There were a few stone sculptures secreted in secluded corners, and I wondered if they too were 'memory sculptures' – though I doubted it because they were nearly all of figures: gods and goddesses, satyrs and nymphs, with a couple of gnomes thrown in to placate the local gods.

I felt profoundly at peace as I wandered slowly around that garden, and realized that if I stayed I might just learn the lesson that had so far eluded me: how to live with other people without the friendship shattering into a thousand pieces around me; yet I had so many shards of unfinished, painful business in my life that I couldn't hope to leave them behind by the expedient of becoming a long-term guest in that fragile wonderland; at some time I would have to go back and mend what relationships I could: Cora, Elaine, Rachel, Magnus, my job; none of it was going to be easy.

When I returned to the kitchen, Joe was surrounded by neat heaps of chopped vegetables, different sized saucepans and little transparent bags of spices and fresh herbs.

'Can I help?'

'You could wash up.'

'Don't you get fed up eating alone all the time?'

'What you must understand, Adam, is that everything – absolutely everything – must be used. By that I mean all our thoughts, feelings, reactions, fears, everything. So that includes what you call 'being fed up.' Of course, being human brings with it all these states of mind all the time: if you look deeply enough into your consciousness at any given moment everything you've ever felt is there, at least in germinal form. So to answer your question, yes, there is a seed of loneliness – not just when I'm eating, but all the time, sleeping and waking; how could it not be there once it's been sown? But no, I try to prevent it growing into the full-blown disease by focusing on it relentlessly and seeing exactly what it is. It's a bit like naming the demons: once you know their true names they cease to have power over you.'

'Right. Well that's me put in my place then.'

'Sorry. I'd no intention of putting you in your place. I'm really happy to answer your questions, and I don't judge you at all for asking them. In fact, judging people is one of the bad habits my mind experiments tend to abolish. However the reality is that the answers often have to demolish the standpoint of the questioner to get anywhere near the truth. Now, if you'd care to give me a hand, I think we can eat.'

Once more the meal was taken in silence: Joe seemed to turn off his awareness of other people while eating. It was an eerie experience sharing a meal at the huge empty runway of the table with someone intent on the primitive act of devouring food, while the small anonymous noises of the house and forest continued around us.

Joe ate slowly, and afterwards sat in silence as though questioning himself about the experience. I realized that this unhurried poise was characteristic of everything he did: it created a harmony and spaciousness around him which was quietly infectious. I was on the point of asking him about staying with him while I clawed back some degree of stability and direction into my life, but he anticipated me.

'You're perfectly welcome to stay as long as you need to,' he said, as though continuing a recent conversation; 'but as I mentioned, there are a few ground rules.'

'Of course.'

'They're very simple and not onerous. We always take breakfast and evening meals together, unless work precludes it. No guests without explicit prior agreement. Quietness at all times. A certain amount of regular work on the house and grounds. Full and open communication to be maintained between us. And if I say it's time to leave you leave. No argument. Is that acceptable?'

'Sounds perfectly reasonable. I appreciate your generosity. What about rent?'

'No money is required. Just your complete and receptive presence.' He sat and thought for a moment. 'I think it might be good for you to have a project. Something physical to counteract all that self-analysis you get up to.' He walked towards one of the windows and stared out at the trees. 'How are you at building things?'

'Pretty rough. But I did a carpentry course once, to try to make me employable.'

'Good. That'll do nicely. What I need is a small workshop away from the house. Just a cabin really, something very simple. There's plenty of material lying around. We might need to buy some fittings. But basically it just needs to be a weatherproof box. How does that sound?'

'Sounds great. How long do I have?'

'As long as necessary. But you'll need to remember that what you're really building is a new mind. The physical aspect is incidental. Still it will be useful for me to have somewhere to retreat to and make my little sculptures in peace. We'll get the site and materials organised this afternoon.'

The next few days were a sustained efflorescence of activity. Joe selected a site for the cabin in a secluded corner of the property, close against the surrounding ring of pines and larches. He found timber, bricks, cement and other necessities, and I began my labours. I quickly settled into a satisfying routine: we breakfasted together, nearly always in silence, then we'd discuss any needful matters concerning the work in hand, then I'd go out to the site and work for three or four hours until lunch. The latter was a somewhat movable feast, and depended on our respective preoccupations. The afternoon I spent walking or reading, or planning the next day's schedule. Supper was another silent meal, but after it we'd talk for an hour or two about whatever seemed needful or claimed our imagination. So the days went by, undisturbed by the outside world.

Gradually however I began to feel that world impinging on my thoughts. There were matters to be dealt with in London, and no doubt a horrendous pile of correspondence was waiting for me. I told Joe I wanted to take a few days off to attend to these things. Oddly, and against my expectations, he was enthusiastic.

'While you're in London you might do a small errand for me. I have a dear friend called Klaus who has a house in Fulham. He's an artist and he made something for me several months ago. I don't want to go to London, and he's fiercely allergic to all public transport. I'd appreciate it if you could nip over there and collect it. I'll phone him and let him know you're coming.'

'How on earth does he manage without public transport?'

'Oh he just doesn't go anywhere. He's an urban hermit. His house is near the river, so he makes occasional raiding parties on the local shops by boat.'

'Lucky man.'

'Possibly. Anyway I think you'll like him. Actually he's a very wise person. An anthropologist, among many other things. Travelled all over the world poking his stick into mud huts. Just be careful not to mention the war.'

'Which war would that be?'

'Oh never mind. Just a bad joke. How long will you be away? No, don't answer that. I was forgetting myself. Just come when you come.'

Chapter Twelve

No. 17 Cowper Road (the address Joe had given me) didn't appear to exist: the odd numbers stopped at 15. Beyond was a white metal fence and a row of unkempt looking fruit trees; I'd got as far as the fence and was on the point of retracing my steps when I saw it: a tiny, squat white-washed facade set back about twenty feet from the rest: '17' was painted in rough orange figures on the wall next to the bell-push. The place seemed ideally positioned to be unfindable unless you had a good reason to find it. I pressed the bell; within seconds the door was opened by a man who didn't look remotely like an artist: well-built, close-cropped black hair, a dark-chocolate coloured Armani shirt, navy blue shorts and black felt sneakers. He offered his hand with a wide smile.

'Adam! You found us ok then?' His tone implied that many didn't.

'Yes. No problem.'

He led the way along a passage to a tiny dining room lit by a window that looked onto an exquisite garden: a mass of yellow crocuses and primroses intermingled with patches of wildflowers as joyful as a Mozart scherzo.

'Joe asked me to collect a packet you had for him. But I don't want to interrupt your work.'

'Oh, you're not interrupting anything. I like to talk to people: it gets me going. I'll get some coffee on. We can have it outside, now the sun's deigned to appear.'

He continued the conversation from the kitchen.

'Where are you from?'

'I live just off the Camden High Street. But right now I'm staying with Joe while I sort myself out.'

'What do you make of Joe?'

'He's clearly an unusual man. We seem to get on ok. But he strikes me as quite lonely. I get the feeling he's wary of getting into another close relationship with a woman.'

'That's very perceptive. I think you're spot on. He can't compromise. He has a powerful vision but is afraid of it becoming dissipated if he shares it. Do you think you'll stay?'

I descended the four stone steps to the even tinier kitchen. 'I don't know yet. It's a wonderful place. But I'm not sure I'm up for the monastic lifestyle. I'm already starting to miss my friends. There's nothing like the countryside to make you miss London is there?'

'I wouldn't know: I never travel anywhere. I've done travelling. And I simply can't bear buses and tubes. Boats I can manage. I often take the boat to Kew or Richmond. And occasionally as a special treat I'll go the other way and have an afternoon at the Tate. But that's about it. I'm a medieval anchorite really. Now why don't we take these outside and enjoy the sun?'

We walked a few yards to a secluded corner of the garden where a small table and three fragile-looking wooden chairs were positioned to catch the sun. Klaus poured the coffee very slowly as though demonstrating a tricky physics experiment. For an artist his meticulous body language struck me as incongruous.

'Do you have a studio here?'

'Yes. You were in it just now.'

'I didn't see any paintings.'

'No. I don't do paintings. Never had much talent for sloshing the coloured stuff around. Mine's all software.'

'Games?'

'No, not really. Persons. You've no doubt heard of SimCity and those land-building programs?'

'Of course.'

'Well, I do the same with minds. More complex of course. Takes much longer to produce. But really far more satisfying.'

'So you're into artificial intelligence?'

'I don't like that term very much. But yes, you could call it that. Actually it's more than intelligence. Nearer to consciousness. I'm trying to explore the point where electronic circuits can simulate self-awareness. Real stand-alone thinking. Lots of people have been working for a long time on that of course. There are people at MIT who've got much more powerful gear than I have. I plough my own furrow.'

'Have you been following those conferences on the Cube technology they've been holding at Manchester?'

'Oh of course. There were some secret ones as well, besides the stuff they broadcast on the net. Did you know that?'

'No. But it doesn't surprise me one bit. Whichever government is the first to crack it will hit the jackpot. Everyone else will be instantly out of the race.'

'Well the Yanks are pretty certain to win: they're pouring billions of dollars into it.'

'Have they got anything conclusive?'

'They're fairly sure there's an alien intelligence of some kind behind it. And that it communicates telepathically with humans: that is, there's a non-physical interaction. But they're still stuck on the nuts and bolts. They suspect it uses quantum non-location as its basic method.'

'Maybe they should be looking at Joe's mind-sculptures.'

'Ah. He's shown you those has he? Yes, you may have something there. Trouble is, conventional science won't touch stuff like that: it's still stuck in twentieth century mindsets. So the real cutting edge work is left to weirdos like Joe and me! Have some more coffee.'

'Have you any theories about how they work?'

'There were some ancient cultures in the Yucatan who had similar things. Actually that's how I first met Joe: we were both researching early Mayan culture. We met at a place called Piste, very near to one of the most important sites, Chichen Itza. It's a tiny place: two small hotels, a few bars, and the never-ending brooding presence of the tropical forest. The place had a truly timeless quality though; it got to you eventually, you ceased to be in the Twentieth Century at all. Anyway, there were a lot of very old artifacts – stone figures and jade winged serpents and jaguars with jewelled eyes: really amazing things. We managed to bring back a few of the smaller objects. They had an uncanny effect on our state of mind.'

'In what way?'

'Well, some would simply induce feelings of intense calm and spaciousness whenever I concentrated on them, like they were dragging me back to their world. One or two I found produced astonishingly vivid images of places I'd certainly never visited in reality.'

'Couldn't it simply have been due to association?'

'No, it was altogether too real. It was like being plucked out of ordinary reality and dropped into a much intenser one.'

'Yes. That's exactly what Joe's sculptures felt like.'

'It's hard not to put it down to some extra-terrestrial source, though of course one has to resist that line of thought. It seems extraordinary that that kind of power would suddenly emerge and then be completely lost again for two thousand years.'

'You're thinking of the Cube?'

'It's a thought. So far I haven't come up with anything better.'

I thought it was time to tell him about Les and Len, and their 'mission' to rid humanity of conflict forever. He sat and chewed on that for several minutes, staring at the brilliant yellow of the forsythia bushes as though hypnotised.

'And how much of this have you told others?'

'Virtually nothing. I've been struggling to believe it myself, to be honest. Anyway, who would believe a story like that? I'd be tabloid fodder for a few weeks, then dropped for something more juicy.'

'Yes, very likely. But it's best kept to yourself in any case. Apart from the press, there's the military. They're more interested in the Cube than they're willing to admit; they realize what a huge impact it could have if they could crack its secret, and anyone with a hot-line to its makers would be a tremendous prize.'

'So you believe me?'

'Yes Adam. I do. I wish I didn't, in a way. But I've been thinking about the Cube ever since it was discovered. The indications are inescapable, when you bother to piece things together.'

'I can't tell you how much of a relief that is. Having to keep a secret like that is an impossible burden.'

'I appreciate that.' He thought for a long moment. 'Tell me, are you still in contact with your friends in the sky? Wait: before you answer, I think this is a two-coffee-pot conversation. I won't be long.'

The sun was emerging from high-banked clouds across the river. I sat admiring the lush garden, imagining what it might be like actually to own such a place; to possess a piece of prime real-estate in the most desirable part of England's capital, and not to have to kill to keep it. Then I thought of the water wars in southern Spain and Africa; the vanishing ice-caps, the incipient south-European deserts, the desperately defended oilfields, and I realized that where I was was a brief anomaly, an enchanted interlude in the tragedy of Mankind's last days. I saw the tides encroaching on more and more of the city each year, fuel becoming a currency more sought after than gold, and parcels of unspoiled virgin land becoming the object of desperate feuds between increasingly avaricious global corporations. Could the Cube save us from this?

Klaus returned with the coffee-pot replenished and a virgin dark-chocolate cake. 'I thought we'd need some sustenance after this conversation. We have a very good local bakery that delivers to my door. I hope you're impressed?'

'Extremely.'

'Now. These... beings – let's call them – that talk to you. Do they still communicate with you?'

'No. I must admit I got fed up with their increasingly ludicrous demands for Russian jokes. I began to wonder if the whole thing wasn't a huge piss-take. But why would anybody bother? They'd need superhuman technology in any case to broadcast directly into my brain. Which leaves hypnotism, or post-hypnotic suggestion or something along those lines. What would they stand to get from it?'

'I don't think it's any of that; it has to be extra-terrestrial in origin, from what you've told me. Quite honestly their silence worries me more than the joke business. You'd think, having established reliable contact with one mind, they'd build on that to get more information.'

'Yes. They could have written me off as an unreliable source of course, and found someone better to work with – which shouldn't be all that difficult.'

'Or the Cube could be giving them all the data they need. That would have the great advantage that it wouldn't arouse suspicions. I think that's the most likely scenario, quite honestly.' He cut some moist wedges of chocolate cake and tipped them onto side plates. A mass of blue tits instantly descended from nowhere and perched on the nearby branches of a silver birch in readiness. 'You know Adam: I do think the time has come to take a more active stance. If those who know what's going on don't act, sooner or later the big guns – literal and metaphorical – will be rolled out, and the whole show will be unstoppable.'

'Yes. Obviously I've thought of that a lot. But nobody's going to believe a couple of lone individuals with a story about aliens trying to save us: it's classic B-movie sci-fi material isn't it?'

'Of course you're right; that's why we have to re-establish direct communication with the Cube and its makers, and let them know we're willing to do whatever it takes to render their work effective.'

'And when the media bandits find out?'

'They mustn't. That has to be rule number one: secrecy is our main strength. And the fact that there are few of us.'

I was a little bit worried about that "us". I'd never felt part of an 'us' before, and it didn't feel comfortable, considering I'd never met the man before that morning. I reckoned if we were going to be an us, he'd better know a few things about me.

'There's something else I need to tell you: I may be a murderer.'

The ghost of a grin played over his face. 'You aren't sure?'

'Well, it sort of depends on which reality I'm in.'

'Ah yes. I get the picture. How about we address ourselves to this wonderful cake and then you can tell me about it?'

Chapter Thirteen

While I was in town I decided to bite the bullet and pay Cora a visit. I hadn't seen her for nine months, and there was a mountain of unfinished business growling between us. Since she'd been taken on by Wallace & Steele – her so-called publisher – she could afford to rent an elegant top-floor apartment behind the cemetery in Hammersmith, only a couple of stops up the tube line from Klaus's minimalist bunker. But Cora's tastes betrayed far more concern with lubricating the essential social gears than did Klaus's.

'Sorry about the chaos. You're lucky to find me home actually. I've been having a loft extension put in. They only finished it this morning.'

'That's ok. I'm used to it. It's good to see you after all this time, Cora. You're looking well.'

In fact I'd never seen her so flushed with vigour. If she'd put on some weight it only served to point up her newly blooming lifestyle. She bore all the signs of a successful, taste-setting young executive. And the flat mirrored it with its downbeat decor suggestive of scrupulously avoided kitch. I guessed that Martin, her opportunistic editor, had moved in with her; the place had that feel of desperate domesticity, evidenced by an unneccesary number of scrubbed-pine chests of drawers and Laura Ashley floral curtains hung on fat varnished beechwood runners. The niche-carving mindset.

I didn't mind all this: it was clearly what she'd always been after; I only regretted I hadn't seen it a lot sooner. No wonder she'd silently resented my obstructive waywardness. Although I was sure she wasn't remotely aware of it, I could see she was already planning to be, in her fecund middle-age, a sought-after arbiter of educated, honey-scented Englishness. And what was wrong with that, you ask? Oh, only that there probably wasn't going to be any Englishness left, or any England to practice it in, for very much longer: it will be a luxury item that fewer and fewer people outside Russian oil billionaires will be able to afford.

'Thank you. Hard work seems to suit me. I must say you look a bit peaky. I bet you're not eating properly.'

'Oh I'm fine, really. It's just been a crazy few weeks.'

'Still chasing aliens?' She set about clearing a space on the nearest scrubbed pine table by the window.

'I never did really chase them, Cora, if you remember. It was more the other way round. But anyway they seem to have turned off the heat recently. Possibly because now they've got the Cube working properly they don't need to use me.'

'Oh yes. Your wonderful Cube! It's creating quite a stir these days isn't it?'

I suddenly realized she was only making polite conversation: her mind was already away somewhere planning her next media coup. I felt an intruder in her scrubbed elegance, and her polite interest in me seemed a kind of abuse.

'Is it? I haven't heard any news at all for quite a while.'

'Which planet have you been on Adam? It's been on TV fifty times each week. Conferences, documentaries, politicians claiming to have found out where it's from, crackpot alien experts, the lot. I'm surprised they haven't got hold of you. They've interviewed just about everyone else who's had anything at all to do with it.'

'I've been in a very strange place these past few months – pretty well incommunicado.'

'Probably wise. Now, what will you have to drink?'

'Anything that's not coffee.'

'I've got Nescafé.'

'Well—.'

'Or grapefruit juice?'

'Perfect. Do you live alone here?'

'That depends. You remember Martin?'

'How could I not? He tried to get me killed.'

'That's dramatizing Adam. He thought you were a spy, as I recall. With some bizarre story about an alien invasion. Can you blame him?' She filled a large jug with iced water and sat down. 'Anyway, he sometimes stays here, on the few days he's in the country.'

I'll bet he does, I thought. 'So you are having a relationship?'

She froze halfway through opening the juice carton. 'Adam, why on earth shouldn't I have a relationship? I'm not married to anyone else am I? Do remind me if I am!'

'No reason at all why not. I was just asking.'

'If all you've come for is to lecture me about faithfulness then I think you'd better go. I've done my stint at taking lectures thank you.'

'No. That's not what I've come for Cora. I genuinely wanted to see how you were. If you're happy. And I can see you are. But I must confess now I'm here it's painful. We have a lot of past between us.'

'Yes.' She supported herself on the table. 'But as you say, it's past.' She seemed suddenly regretful. 'I'm sorry I snapped. Your turning up caught me on the hop.' She handed me a tall glass of ice-cold fruit juice. 'I am glad to see you. Really. And you're right: I'm not rubbishing our time together. There were some great moments. Some very loving moments. But I don't think we could have reconciled our differences. We were in such very different places.'

'Love is not love which alters——.'

'Don't throw Shakespeare at me Adam. We all alter all the time. A relationship isn't a legal contract, you know. And I did try very hard to give you what you needed, though you may not believe that.'

'I know you did. I was just going slowly crazy. Nobody could have supplied my needs then. I was on the edge of an awful abyss, and barely managed to avoid crashing into it, if the truth be known. I stopped being able to tell what was real and what was purely in my imagination. That's a terrible place to be. I came very close to real despair.'

'Well you seem to be on dry land again now.'

'I think I have a perspective on it, which is a start. Trouble is, the things I started out believing to be aspects of my madness seem to be taking up residence in my life.'

'What things?' She was surreptitiously glancing at the clock, which was a sure sign I hadn't entirely captivated her.

'Well the voices for a start. And people dissolving into nothing while I'm looking at them.'

She gave me a dark look, meaning: I bet you haven't even considered getting professional treatment for this. But much too correct to say it. Instead she asked:

'Have you got a job at the moment?'

'Not what you'd call a job: I'm building someone a cabin to make sculpture in.'

'And he's not paying you, right?'

'He's paying me in board and lodging. And experience.'

'I think, if I could give you a tiny bit of advice, what you need's an ordinary job. You know, one of those boring things where you work for normal people and they give you money? It would provide an anchor.'

'It would drive me to drink, more like. You know me better than that Cora. If my imagination is fenced in I start going loopy. Like the voices.'

'So you admit they were your creations?'

'No. Of course not! They were – are – real beings! For a long time I tried not to believe they were real but they gave me incontrovertible evidence. Like the Cube.'

'Oh please don't let's go there again! This is why we had to separate: you weren't dealing with your real problem. You were giving in to the fantasies.'

Perched on my stool with my finger-chilling tumbler I suddenly saw why Cora needed to keep these monsters safely in their cages marked 'dangerous fantasies': if they once got out into rational territory her hopes of a comfortable, settled, middle-class social life would be shattered forever. Now for the first time I could feel real compassion for her: she was trapped, just like millions of others, in her world of desperate social mechanisms, where what really mattered was having the right people at your next dinner party: people who could lubricate your ascent to the next echelon, who had villas in the parts of the Algarve and Croatia where the movers and shakers wintered. I felt genuinely sorry for her, because she would never escape from the pursuit of these ends, and neither would they satisfy her once attained. But she hadn't always been like that. I remembered when she'd lived the bohemian life in Paris in the seventies as an art student; I think that was when I really fell in love with her. I was doing the hippy thing, living in a squat in Vincennes, thinking up desperate strategies to meet her at lunchtime, walking along the river together eating just-baked warm baguettes bulging with runny Camembert. She'd rented a tiny flat and taught languages at a local primary school (yes, languages plural), but eventually gave that up to become a 'philosophe minimaliste' – a concept for which there is no English equivalent. She explained it to me as something like an experimental existential artist – one who makes her life her artform, where the actual 'work' of art is not an object but a state of mind. As far as I could tell, the main thing it involved was lying in bed most of the day and having endless rambling discussions about art and revolution with one's friends all night long, and at all costs avoiding anything that might be construed as productive work. Her redeeming feature in all this was her complete sincerity. She wasn't trying to take anyone for a ride: she believed totally in her lifestyle as an end in itself, and she had a genuinely enquiring spirit: she wanted to know everything without bullshit, let or hindrance. When I once went to visit her she'd organised an installation which consisted of a dozen artists clad in white vinyl jump-suits sitting in white plastic chairs in a featureless white gallery. Their only action was to make and maintain eye-contact with anyone who wandered into the gallery for as long as the person allowed it. Needless to say, the event (or non-event) was minimally successful. I don't think she could ever understand the indifference and cynicism of observers and critics towards her art: for her not to make art, or to make art which was bland and unchallenging, was spiritual death; In any case, for her the whole thing was an experiment, with no preconceived outcome: whatever happened, happened: the outcome was an integral part of the work. But she was viciously attacked in the various media that bothered with the arts, which hurt her a lot: everyone assumed that, because she was young, female and pretty, she was as cynical and thick-skinned as the rest of the art establishment: but she wasn't at all. She found it very hard to take all the flak and personal abuse that came her way, especially from those she'd long regarded as her friends and fellow artists. About a year after that she wrote to tell me that she'd burned herself out as an artist-philosopher.

Yes, bliss was it to be alive. But what happened to that radicalism? Radicalism without roots. Of course, really it wasn't radical at all: just the same adolescent naughtiness wanting to make ripples in the adult world. To affirm the anarchism of the life-force, start everything afresh, show the cynical world of money how shallow it was. But money got most people in the end – even if most people hadn't got any: they were still in its thrall. Money was the one remaining key to fulfilment, after first philosophy, then religion, and finally beauty had been kicked off their pedestals. The fact that in the end it just didn't provide satisfaction was never mentioned except by the Hyde Park nutters and doorstep God-botherers.

'I'm sorry you see them that way,' I said, staring at the sun-patterns playing among the ice-cubes. 'But yes, I realize now that our interests were fatally diverging. At least, I see that with my head. The trouble is that my head and my heart tend to live in different worlds. And that meant asking you to live in both. A classic prescription for conflict. Anyway, I think I have changed. Though I still like Floyd and Grateful Dead.'

She smiled. 'I still have an embarrassing number of their LPs. Mostly yours, I suspect.'

'Well, if they're embarrassing you I'll take them off your hands. Which reminds me why I came. We have the matter of the flat to sort out.'

'What do you want to do?'

'Ideally I'd like to sell up. Get out of London for good. Maybe travel round the world.'

'Well it's your choice. I don't need it. And you could probably use the money. I'll bet you haven't bought a suit since I last saw you.'

'True. I haven't really been into suits for a while. They seem rather—'.

I felt another diatribe against materialism coming on, and decided it would serve no purpose. I wasn't going to change the world by railing against fashion.

'Rather what?'

'Never mind. There is one thing I would like to ask you, if I may.'

'Of course. Anything.' She smiled like one who has nothing to fear in the whole wide universe.

'Were you in love with Martin last year?'

I thought I detected a momentary paralysis of her features before she answered.

'I couldn't say. I certainly liked him a lot.'

'What I mean is, were you seeing him while I was slowly losing my mind in Scotland?'

'Well of course I was seeing him Adam: he was my editor. It isn't a secret.'

I noticed the smile had gone into deep cover.

'So you deny you were sleeping with him?'

'Adam, I really don't feel like being interrogated about my sex life.'

'I'll take that as a no then.'

I put both hands flat on the table and pushed down with all my strength, as if it was about to ascend to the ceiling like the instrument of some outraged poltergeist. There was a particularly interesting knot-hole in the part I was looking at, which reminded me of the unsleeping eye of

Sauron, the Dark Lord. Which was not good news at all. 'Look. I'm just trying to get a straight answer to one simple question. We're you and Martin fucking on our kitchen floor? Or any floor come to that. Did he get into your knickers? Did he dip his wick? Did you open your front door to him? Or your back door for that matter. Whatever expression you care to use. A simple yes or no will do fine.'

'I'd like you to leave now, Adam. You're clearly still as full of bile as you were a year ago, despite all that therapy. I really would suggest you get some proper help.'

'Ok. I thought I was asking a reasonable question. After all we were still having a relationship at the time. But apparently I was mistaken. I'm sorry to upset you. I'll see myself out.'

'Don't nurture resentments Adam. It does no good. Not to you nor anyone else.'

'Oh, right. Thanks so much. I'll try to remember that.'

In my fury I almost ran the hundred yards back to the tube station, as I realized bitterly that it had happened again: the same old dreary circle had re-drawn itself. I'd been taken for a long ride, and then made to feel guilty for alluding to the fact. But the real pain was suddenly seeing I was still in love with Cora. Her elegance, her clear-headedness, her energy, her confidence, her talent for making people like her – I could go on – they were a heady mix for someone who'd come up from being a complete nobody to a total nonentity without any help from anyone. I realized I was beginning to recite another catalogue of woes and disappointments, and stopped myself in time to buy a ticket and get myself onto the escalator. Today was not a good day for going to pieces: I had too many tasks to address myself to. So I held off until I was on the train to Kings Cross. I tried to read the ads above the windows and found I couldn't: my eyes were streaming with tears. Here again was the great mystery nosing right up to me: Cora was happy, I was on a path of discovery, I had found stimulating new friends, the world was an ever-changing cornucopia of miracles, and I was spinning out of control at the loss of an adolescent romance. Could any of this be reconciled with my long-sustained idea of myself as a sophisticated, civilized member of homo sapiens?

A voice was speaking forcefully into my left ear.

'You ok man? You look like you could use a drink or something.' The accent was vaguely Glasgow with a splash of Millwall.

'No. I'm ok really, thanks.'

The face looked as though it had been formed a long time ago by a process of reverse metamorphosis from one of the Cairngorms. It reminded me of a famous description of Auden's features: a wedding cake left out in the rain. I glanced at the book he was holding: 'The World as Will and Idea.'

'Good story?'

'Oh aye. A bit light on the sex though, for my taste. Listen, you sure you wouldn't like that drink? I know a place.'

'Thanks. But I just need some space. I've just been to see my ex-partner, and she's not, well, quite as ex as I'd thought.'

'Oh yes. I've been there pal. It takes time. Well see here. If you need to talk, here's my phone number.' He scribbled a number on a piece of yellow card. 'You know what the Buddha said about that? "Hatred isn't stopped by hatred. Only by love."'

'Sounds cool.'

'Yeh. It is. So it's a start anyway.' He threw me a wide, timeless Cairngorm grin.

'Thanks. I have to get off here.'

The encounter had calmed me. As I climbed into the early evening sun I regretted not taking up his offer. I glanced at the number he'd scrawled for me: it was written on his ticket.

The train journey back to Joe's was blissfully uneventful. No dissembling actresses, no mysterious envelopes with explanations that didn't explain a thing. Just soundlessly sliding landscapes and indecipherable announcements every few miles: exactly what I needed. I wanted to think about Cora, and Joe, and Klaus, and most of all about why my past never seemed content to lie down and simply be past. And for once the world allowed me to do it.

Klaus was a conundrum; after our chat in his garden he'd taken me inside to see some of his 'pieces': unlike Joe's, these were entirely insubstantial, being computer programs. He slipped a knife-thin disc into the machine and the screen came alive with tiny mugshots of attractive young men and women.

'You're sure this isn't a porn site?'

'Absolutely. Choose one.'

I chose a man with a short beard, oriental looking, with black eyes and an intense gaze. Nothing happened.

'Oh sorry. That must be a dodgy link. Try this one. I only finished her yesterday.'

He clicked a picture of a short-haired female in her thirties, olive-skinned, with greenish-blue eyes. Her face immediately bloomed at me in delicious colour and live action.

'My God!'

'You may ask her questions.'

'Do you guarantee I'm not going to end up on a sex-offenders' register if I do this?'

'Absolutely. This is as clean as Father Christmas.'

'That's meant to reassure me?'

'Ask her something.'

I shuffled nearer to the image. It smiled alarmingly.

'You sure that's not a real person in there?'

'Of course it's a real person. Do you really think I'd waste months of my life creating someone who wasn't real? Now for God's sake ask her something before she gets bored.'

'Ok. What's your name?'

'Anna. And may I ask yours?'

'Adam.'

'Very nice to meet you Adam.' So far so unspectacular. I could have done the code for that dialogue on a single pot of Columbian. Then she added:

'You don't sound happy.'

I was stunned. 'She can analyse my voice?'

'Of course. Why wouldn't she?'

'That must have required a colossal amount of code.'

'Well, yes. But she does have continuous access to the net and thousands of audio files, so she isn't exactly deprived. And she doesn't need to sleep.'

'Sorry, I didn't mean to insult her.'

'I daresay she'll forgive you. Why don't you ask her about her interests?'

'Hello Anna. I'd like to know what you're particularly interested in.'

'Hello Adam, I have a large number of interests. History perhaps is my chief interest. And anthropology of course. And biology, particularly primates. Also palaeontology, geology, minerology, deep ecology, astronomy, particularly stellar evolution and the physics of the very early universe. And linguistics and the structure of proto-languages.'

'Er, what do you do in your spare time?' I glanced at Klaus, who was looking as smug as a new father.

'I read the classics of literature.'

'Is there anything she doesn't know?' I said to Klaus, sotto-voce.

'Oh, she hasn't got around to music or politics yet. Possibly because they're not my strong points either. Although ultimately that shouldn't affect her learning.'

'I'm glad she can't have children. If she could the human race might soon be surplus to requirements.'

'Yes. Well. I'm sure she's thought of that. Maybe in a decade or two...'

'But why are you doing all this? Do you sell the programs?'

'Oh God no. I've no interest at all in going commercial. I suppose I do it for companionship. I don't get out very much.'

The image on the screen said: 'See you around Adam,' and with another heart stopping smile her face faded.

'But don't you get frustrated with having relationships with a lot of binary code? I mean, you can't really discover anything you haven't already written in, can you?'

'That isn't remotely true actually. Let me demonstrate.'

He called up Anna's image again. This time I thought she revealed an especially charming smile, but that might have been simple envy.

'Hi Anna. Good to see you looking so well.'

'Thank you Klaus. I enjoyed talking to your friend just now.'

'I'd like to discuss the Mayan artifacts with you.'

'I guess you're referring to the jade serpents, right?'

'Yes. What have you discovered about them recently?'

'Well Klaus, you remember last time we talked I thought they dated from the sixth century?'

'Right.'

'Well, they appear to be much older, about 300 AD. They were found in the Temple of the Magicians. They seem to have been dug up and reburied at least once.'

'That's interesting. I wonder who dug them up?'

'That isn't known. But I have discovered an interesting paper on them by a Professor at Merida. Would you like me to print it for you?'

'Not just right now Anna. But thanks. Could you summarize it for us briefly?'

'Of course. He says tests have been done on the crystal structure, to see if that could account for the effects, but they showed nothing conclusive. He thinks one would have to go down another order of scale – at least to atomic level, perhaps sub-atomic – to find any structures that might be affected by psychic forces, and be able to hold images. The human brain doesn't have enough energy to directly affect crystal structures in the way that lasers can.'

'Thanks for that Anna.'

'You're welcome.' The smile she gave Klaus sent a shiver through my entire body; surely, I thought, it was not possible to programme that?

'You're impressed, eh?' He dimmed the monitor.

'It's... mind-boggling. The rendering is flawless.'

'Thanks. But the point is, she learns stuff that I know absolutely nothing about. Having unrestricted access to the net is like opening up the world to her. It's what computers always lacked before: a world of experience to learn from. And she learns twenty-four hours a day, three hundred and sixty-five days a year.'

Before I left, he administered his *coup de theatre*. He took me upstairs to a tiny attic room. Inside it was quite empty, except for a young woman sitting at a bare table in front of a white wall. In front of her was a video camera.

"Adam, meet my little sister Anna. Anna, this is Adam.'

She smiled a stunning smile: exactly like the one I'd just seen on the monitor. I felt slightly sick.

There had been so many practical jokes in my life recently I thought one more ought to run off me like duckwater. But it hadn't: it shocked me more than Rachel's or Cora's, or Jane's, or Martin's – or Les's for that matter; that someone who didn't know me at all, who stood to gain absolutely zilch from me, who had everything he could possibly need, should spend so much thought and ingenuity on a practical joke with no other conceivable outcome than my discomfiture worried me in a part of my being that didn't often get worried; sure, I was often paranoid about the conspiracy there undoubtedly was to destabilize my sense of reality; but I knew all about that; I'd co-habited with it for years; it was just part of the universe's unfathomable sense of humour. But the universe didn't often make such elaborate and detailed plans to achieve its diversion; this one had required the organisation of serious hardware, as well as Klaus and his delicious sister to give up several days of their time to play their parts. No, something about this one simply didn't hang together. Maybe I'd find the invoice already waiting for me back at Joe's.

And then Cora. In hindsight it had been a bad mistake to visit her: it had probably set back our friendship by several lifetimes. The flat could have been dealt with by solicitors and email. What was it, I wondered, that made me do it? I'd not merely upset the apple cart, but systematically stamped on every one of the apples. Why hadn't that slinky bitch of a therapist picked up on that? Obviously to keep me hurting enough so I'd go back for more lucrative humiliation. Clearly it was mugs like me who kept the whole shrink industry going.

No, the truth was I couldn't let go of Cora: she held too much of my life-energy. She was successful, I was a failure. She had close friendships, I made enemies everywhere. She admired and trusted the world, I abhorred it, I wanted to beat it until it confessed its falseness. She aspired to an oil-fired Aga, I aspired to a Tesco's microwave that didn't fuse all the lights. I'd been so attracted to her because I believed a sexual liason would by slow osmosis replenish my precious resources of life-juice. It hadn't: it had simply deepened the sinuous canyon of incomprehension that wriggled between us. So ok, write it off to experience: wipe the slate. Reboot the system. Pick yourself up, shake yourself down, start all over again.

But wait. I'd done exactly the same with Rachel: a lovely, uncomplicated good woman who'd just wanted to help me. Perhaps that was what I evoked in most women: pity, a desire to stop me hurting. And I lapped it up like a starving kitten, eyes tight shut in ecstasy. So perhaps I should go on a fast? Stop rushing after people who got their kicks from rescuing me?

The train slowed. We were coming into Taunton; wheels squealing to a stop between huge, tasteless hoardings for hypermarkets and internet companies. As I walked up the High Street I suddenly realized I was thinking of Joe's house as home; I didn't think he'd have been too overjoyed to know that.

Chapter Fourteen

Once back at the house I fell into the daily routine as easily as if I'd never left: we breakfasted together, talked briefly, usually about practical matters which needed to be addressed, then I went out to my 'building site' and continued the work on Joe's 'studio'. He didn't interfere with how I went about the work, merely giving me the information I needed to find the materials and implement his specification. Our evenings continued, as before, with a generally silent meal followed by discussion of anything that happened to capture our imagination.

My work on the cabin's foundations was going well, even though I had practically no real-world experience of laying concrete and levelling brick courses. After all, he wasn't going to live in the place, and he'd made it clear I shouldn't be over-concerned about 'finessing' its appearance.

On the fifth morning after my return, Joe made an unwonted visit to the site.

'How's it going?'

"Pretty good.' I wiped my forehead with the back of my hand to show him I was learning the builder's language. 'I'll need to get some more cement soon.'

He paced around the perimeter and then called from the far corner: 'It's not big enough.'

I thought I'd misheard him.

'Too small. It needs to be three feet longer. Sixteen feet. Those were your instructions.'

'I'm sorry Joe. But it's exactly the size you asked for: ten by thirteen.'

I stepped carefully around the stacks of bricks to reach him.

'It's too late to change it: the foundation's finished.'

'Ten by sixteen was what I asked for. You must have written it down wrongly. Change it please.' And without further explanation he strode off back to the house.

I was dumbstruck. There was no question in my mind that I'd laid it out exactly to his specifications: I had written evidence of it. To change it now would set me back weeks. I tramped around the site in a state of high dudgeon, trying to guess what had triggered this change of mind; I was quite certain it was more than a simple mistake: there was an agenda behind it.

When I went inside for lunch there was a note waiting for me. It said simply:

'Adam: I'll be away for a couple of days. Please ensure you have the dimensions right this time: 10 x 16. No more mistakes! — Joe.'

I was furious almost to the point of physically shaking; as if some huge armoured engine had shuddered into life inside me, ready to lay waste everything within reach. But there was practically nothing to hand (apart from the massive wrought iron cooking pots) to lay waste, so I paced between the table and the stove and reasoned it out like Oedipus must have done the night after slaying his Dad at the crossroads.

Not only was Joe causing me enormous extra work by his fickleness but he was blaming me for getting it wrong originally, and then absenting himself so I couldn't resolve the problem with him. It was simply inexcusable. I couldn't say it was uncharacteristic of him, because I hadn't known him long enough; but he didn't strike me as the kind of person to make a mistake and then blame it on someone else without at least listening to their side of the argument. Maybe something had gone seriously wrong with a project and he'd temporarily lost the plot; or maybe he'd received bad news. Or maybe he was subject to uncontrollable emotional instability at irregular intervals: this would certainly explain the failure of his last attempt to sustain a close community of friends.

That afternoon I took a long walk in the woods in a state of high indignation alternating with abject self-recrimination. The trouble was I could not completely rule out the possibility that I'd written down the wrong measurements in the first place; but how could I possibly check them when Joe had only given me verbal instructions? Maybe his story about his experiences in Australia was nothing more than bullshit. Maybe he was mentally ill, and had come here to get away from the trouble caused to others by the inevitable breakdown of his faculties? It was impossible to know the truth, and yet I couldn't carry on without at least having some stable hypothesis to start from. I considered writing Joe a long letter explaining my conflicts and anguish, but then realised in all probability he wouldn't bother to read it.

Which left me with the one remaining option: change the foundations to accord with his new requirements, as though he had simply made an error which it was my job to put right.

I struggled with this possibility for the rest of that day; it felt like giving in to gross injustice; accepting blame for no reason other than a quiet life. Yet by the end of the evening I'd accepted that it was the only reasonable path to take: any other approach would simply ignite more conflict, and in the end it was Joe's project and Joe's property, and I had no rights at all as to his methods or the direction he chose to take it. Looking back on that decision, it strikes me as bizarre that the one thing I should have done – leave without doing any more work on the cabin – didn't even occur to me; it was as if I'd totally accepted that I was in the wrong and had to atone for my mistakes.

The next morning I set to work on the task of altering the foundations; every step of the way I felt irritated by the knowledge that it was all completely unnecessary, and this irritability made me work sloppily, without checking measurements or levels, so I frequently had to change things I'd already done. By mid-morning I was exhausted and had made little headway. I began to question my motivation for doing all this work for no payment, and for a man I hardly knew; but time and again I returned to the realization that it was as good as anything else I might do, and after all I had come here to sort out my life and learn what I wanted to do with it.

By lunchtime I'd dug out most of the earth needed to make room for the enlarged foundations, and although still far behind schedule I decided to stop for the day: the weather was warming up, and I wasn't used to such sustained physical work. After lunch I decided to change my usual pattern and go upstairs for a short game of snooker: I thought I'd take the opportunity while Joe was away to improve my technique; however to get to the games room it was necessary to pass the sculpture room, and on an impulse I drew the curtain aside and went in. Sunlight flooded the room and lent its contents a timeless, surreal beauty; it reminded me of the story of the magic toy cupboard: I felt as if I were walking into a room full of people who had been moving about and living their lives normally only a moment before.

I looked down the length of the room and saw the carved egg bathed in the soft lights of the stained-glass window; I slowly walked towards it and stood admiring its lustrous surface, as I had done when I'd first seen it. Joe's injunction against touching it seemed ridiculous in the calm, confident spring sunlight; maybe, I thought, it was just another of his tests, to see how far I'd acquiesce in his fantasies; maybe he really wanted to see if I was man enough to do something he had expressly forbidden, and his tale of a trapped demon merely served as a ruse to appeal to the quixotic hero within; maybe it was one of the tests he gave everyone before deciding if they were mature enough to share their lives with him – and if they failed he would simply find some excuse to expel them.

With these thoughts thronging in my head I found myself stretching out to caress the egg. It's surface felt unexpectedly soft and yielding, as though some kind of benign energy field enclosed it; there was nothing remotely demonic about it. Just for an instant though, as my fingers rode lightly over its warm curve, my mind went totally blank, as though someone had gone over it with an extremely powerful magnet and pulled out every thought: I had no idea where, or who, or even what I was, I'd become less than unconscious: I'd become something without being of any kind; without even the capacity to be endowed with being. But this is merely my attempt to render a tiny fragment of a remembered moment into entirely inadequate language; before I could react or register the anomaly I was back in the room, my hand hovering over the egg, as though still deciding whether it was safe to touch or not; and the sun's warmth was already working on my skin to make my recent fears seem ridiculous.

Joe didn't return for another two days, by which time I'd completed the alteration to the foundation and begun to lay the first course of bricks that would form the lower walls. I desperately wanted his praise for the work I'd done, but all he said when he saw it was: 'Did you remember the damp course?' It hadn't occurred to me to include a damp-course on what was essentially a day-cabin; but Joe insisted, and again I revised the plans to include one. I thought it was a waste of effort considering its use, but again there was no point in protesting, and I lurched off to find suitable material.

The second night after Joe's return I had the first of the nightmares. I was on holiday, in a large hotel somewhere abroad. I found myself in a long shadowy corridor searching for my luggage. On the walls were paintings of previous owners of the building. As I went along they became more like wild beasts, and more and more realistic. The corridor seemed to stretch forever and the air became hotter and hotter. I came to the room where I'd left my luggage several days ago. I felt guilty because I'd abandoned it and not given it any thought for a long while, but I was afraid to go into the room: there was something very dangerous in there that had to be kept locked up. So far so typical. But I needed my luggage because it had my return tickets and all my money in it, so I screwed up my courage and went in. The room was empty, apart from a brick in the furthest corner that had been detached from its place in the wall. Suddenly I knew with that horrible certainty one has in dreams that my precious luggage was in that hole left by the detached brick, and there was simply no way I was going to get near it, let alone go inside to retrieve it. But neither could I go back the way I'd come because of the wild animals that were guarding the corridor. I woke up sweating my skin off.

After breakfast the next morning I told the dream to Joe. He listened with total attention while I spoke, and then appeared to lose interest.

'Good, Adam. Things are happening. So how's the work going?'

'Fine. It's slow, but no real problems. What do you think about the dream?'

'Nothing. I have no opinion of it. It's purely your business. Tell me about the cabin. Did the damp course work out?'

I was devastated by his calculated indifference; it was as if he were trying to humiliate me and deny any previous intimacy. I thought of tackling him about it, but he was already on his feet and looking restless, as though he'd just heard of an urgent matter that had to be dealt with immediately somewhere else. I asked:

'Do you want me to leave?'

'No. No, of course not. I want you to get on with the work you've started. You're a long way behind with it.'

'I thought we didn't have a schedule?'

'Oh, but we do. I need to be using it by the end of the month.'

'That's the first I've heard of it. Why didn't you tell me before? You've always said there was no hurry.'

'I have told you before, Adam. You weren't listening. You were away with the little people. Now please get on with it.' And with that he was out of the room.

I found it extremely difficult to work in this suddenly changed atmosphere. Again I considered leaving, but I'd already left so much unfinished in my life I felt I had to stay and see this through, no matter how painful.

Over the next two days the fine weather broke: there were sharp rainstorms and winds which made it impossible to work outside. I defied Joe's rule and took my meals in my room so as to avoid the strained atmosphere between us. I spent a lot of time reading the Russian masters in the library: I browsed through Tolstoy, Dostoyevsky and Chekhov, and when the weather allowed, took long walks in the surrounding woods and uplands. These walks calmed me, and made me realize there was a world beyond the confines of Joe's domain that was uplifting and nurturing, and didn't undermine my shallow confidence with overt or implied criticism.

It was a fortnight following Joe's return that the second nightmare came. Again the same dark corridor and at its end the grim uninhabited room; except that this time the room was not entirely uninhabited: a small naked figure about a foot high crouched in it, and stared directly at me with merciless coal-black eyes. It was, I knew without doubt, the demon of the egg.

It didn't speak, but in its malign stare was one plain and dreadful message: I had to kill myself. Without hesitating I strode over to the tall window and threw it open; only then did I realize we were at the top of a very tall building: spread out far below was a city I didn't recognise. With a mixture of terror and relief that finally I knew what my duty in life was, I stepped across the sill.

The sudden swoop of vertigo immediately woke me; I found I had already got out of bed and was starting to walk towards the door. In my disorientated state for a few moments I couldn't remember what house I was in, or where it was; all I thought of was the horror of the final few seconds of the dream, and the sickening sensation in my belly and legs when I realized what I had been about to do.

I very much wanted to tell Joe about this second dream, because I felt sure it had some connection with our relationship; but his studied indifference inhibited me from talking to him at all about my inner life. I knew exactly what he would say if I tried to untangle some emotional snarl-up: 'Why aren't you working on the cabin?' Or rather he wouldn't say it like that; he'd merely stonewall me with some practical question about roofing felt.

When the weather at last cleared I went back to work outside; but I'd made a pact with myself: I'd ignore all nit-picking criticism, all whimsical changes of brief, and simply carry on at my own pace with the original proposal. It was the only way, I decided, that I had any chance of staying sane. I took the brickwork two feet up from the ground, then started on the wooden frame that would hold the door, windows and roof. I began to feel pride in my work: I slowed right down, took my time rooting out the best timber, bought new brass fittings instead of using rust-eaten iron ones, sharpened my tools, planed edges until they fitted as snug as bugs in rugs. Through all this Joe left me alone, and if he didn't say anything that could have remotely been construed as encouragement, he at least backed off on the cruder manifestations of criticism. But I knew he was watching me; occasionally I'd catch sight of him intently carrying tools and complicated objects on circuitous routes around the garden, like a delivery man suddenly bereft of instructions, or someone forlornly searching for a drain to clear.

I was sitting on a packing case one morning contemplating the final stage – lifting the roof frame into place – when Joe strode up and gave the cabin a long, intense scrutiny. In spite of recent experience I felt confident he would approve the work I'd done, and said cheerily:

'What do you think?'

Without a moment's hesitation he replied:

'You'll have to move the windows. You've put them facing north.'

'And west. North and west.'

'But I told you I'll be working in the mornings, which clearly requires south and east light.'

'No Joe, you didn't tell me that.' I felt myself inwardly seething with anger. 'You didn't once mention that.'

'They'll have to be moved, Adam. How do you expect me to use the place like that? The whole thing's useless.' And once more he performed his vanishing act without a syllable of apology, leaving me to stew in my fury. If there had been any doubt about it before, it was clear now he was deliberately choosing to undermine me; but what was his motive? What had I done to provoke such treatment? Instead of slinking away to breed further resentment, I decided this was my High Noon moment: I stomped up to his private study on the top floor and marched inside without knocking.

The room was lit by a bare but generously proportioned window: Joe was standing before it gazing out at the forest, for all the world like a general on the point of deciding to send in the army to put down a native rising. I felt my rage well up uncontrollably.

'I've had enough of this, Joe. If you don't explain your attitude to me I'm leaving immediately. You can build your own fucking house.'

Without deigning to turn round he said calmly:

'Adam, you are entirely free to leave anytime you please. I shan't be in the least offended.'

'Do you want me to leave?'

'What I want isn't the point.'

'So what in hell is the bloody point?'

'The point is to do something well. To do something without your ego running the show.'

'Oh, I see. And I suppose your ego doesn't come into it?'

'That's right. It doesn't.'

'Well that's just ridiculous! One law for you and another for everyone else? How very convenient for you! No wonder your previous attempts to live with people fell apart.'

He sat down on the sofa facing the window and stretched with an unnervingly feline motion, as though I'd just been complimenting him on some recent artistic achievement. His words were slow and measured.

'It doesn't, not because I don't have an ego, but because what we're concerned with here at this moment is your stuff, and to get it mixed up with my stuff would fatally confuse the issue. This is an opportunity for you to overcome something that's dogged you all your life, right here and now. You can clear it up and be free of it. What's happening now is material for you to use, if you can only see it.'

'What absolute bullshit! I've never heard such a justification for an ego-trip at someone else's expense in my life! You should be ashamed of treating someone like you have done. Anyway, I'm leaving. I've realized I can't work with you if you carry on denying your own weaknesses.'

'I'm sorry you've chosen that route, Adam. Genuinely sorry. I thought you had more guts.'

'Fuck you, Joe! You simply don't care a shit about me, do you? All you've ever been concerned about is preserving your precious pathetic little empire where you control everything. You can't bear anyone to be free to do things differently to you. Well all I can say is I feel very sorry for you: because as long as you're in control of everything you'll never learn to respect others.'

I didn't bother waiting to hear his reply; I hit the corridor, leaving the door behind me wide open. As I was taking the steps three at a time I heard his door click shut, very softly. In my mind I could see him smiling to himself as he turned back towards the window to plan the rest of his war.

I have no memory at all of the rest of that day; I probably walked until my legs blindly rebelled against further demands. I knew I'd reached another major point of decision, but I was too embroiled in the plot to think clearly about it; I felt humiliated, sidelined, used, deceived, ripped off – but this time it wasn't a woman who had abused me, but a man I'd opened myself to more fully than any other person in my life. This was actually a significant step forward, because this time even I couldn't blame that duplicitous man-hating half of humanity for my present ills: it was one of my own tribe doing the abusing.

Yet the much worse thought that maybe it was I who was somehow bringing this doom down upon myself looped back again and again like an obsessed wasp. No doubt this idea had been skilfully planted by successive tranches of svelte psychiatrists: how else, after all, would I be even distantly entertaining such a bizarre notion?

That same night the third nightmare came. Exhausted as I was, I lay awake for hours, unmoving, captive to the sounds of constant rain pounding on the roof, almost as if I knew what lay ahead the moment sleep's fingers found me. Once more there was the same interminable corridor with its gilt-framed prints which morphed into gateways for wild animals; once more the huge empty room with its pall of concentrated evil. And once more the crouched demon with its all-seeing, unavoidable stare. This time however I tried to avert my fate by speaking to the creature, on the premise that introducing discourse might somehow humanize the situation. 'I can change,' I earnestly told it, at the same time vaguely realizing that I was here precisely because I hadn't changed. But this was a non-speaking demon; its expression remained utterly implacable. Then I realized that I simply had to go through with the ordeal: the demon wasn't a judge to whom I could appeal by laying before it the grounds for mitigation: it was a simple embodiment of the law of action and consequence.

I walked with acute consciousness of my last living moments towards the waiting window, slid it open, stepped across the sill onto the outside ledge. In a last gesture of hope I looked back to see any possible rescuer, but the room was now an inferno of flame and smoke, the floor a gaping cavity through which I could glimpse streets of the city sickeningly far below. I leaned out into the void, and felt my feet lose contact with the ledge. The last thought I remember was that I'd been given a priceless gift and wasted it in lifelong shame and self-hatred.

Chapter Fifteen

Two things I knew: I was alive and mostly functioning, and someone was looking after me. For now, that was more than enough.

Someone – perhaps the same person – had thoughtfully arranged a tall tumbler of wildflowers in the sun on the window sill, where it braided and unbraided the light into a million dancing colours. By my bed was a tray containing a jug of cold water with leaves of lemon, a plate of thin sliced bread and butter already halved, and a rolled napkin. Some colourful knitted blankets were neatly stacked on top of a pine chest of drawers nearby. The only snakes in the sand-pit were that I couldn't move my right leg, my shoulder ached like hell, and there was something oddly absent about my mind.

With considerable effort I worked backwards from the present, trying to piece together the raw fragments of images that presented themselves. A doctor. A needle in my hip. A hospital ward. Daffodils. The Agnus Dei from Bach's B-minor Mass. Then an ambulance, a lot of noise and crashing about, tremendous pain. I couldn't get back earlier than that.

But of course there was something before that, and my mongrel of a brain knew it, and gnawed away at the memory's raw edges until it found a scent. Inch by inch I dragged it into the open: the dream, the egg-demon, the fall from the window – which turned out to be a real window, and real ground. But there was still nothing before the dream.

The door opened a little, and Joe peered in. At least I knew him, even if his grin was unfamiliar.

'The dreamer awakes'. He came into the room carrying another tray laden with tea and biscuits.

'Joe! Thank goodness. Did I really jump from a window?'

'You did. Second floor. It's a miracle you survived. Here.'

The tea was quite wonderful.

'I've never tasted anything so good. How long have I been sleeping?'

'Three days. On and off.'

'Jesus! I'm sorry.'

'Don't apologise. I should be apologising to you: I was probably to blame, for making your life such hell.'

'What do you mean?'

'Don't you remember building the cabin?'

'I built a cabin?'

'Most of a cabin, yes. I'm afraid I didn't make it easy for you though.'

He told me about the 'work' as he called it, and how I'd predictably revolted against his criticism. I remembered nothing.

'It'll come back. As soon as you're ready to walk I'll show you what you made: it's pretty impressive.'

'Did I break a leg?'

'Yes. And dislocated a shoulder. And got concussion. But they'll all mend. What's really worrying me is that demon.'

Then I remembered the egg, and Joe's strict injunction against touching it.

'You knew I touched it?'

'Of course: your fingermarks were all over the bloody thing. Don't worry: I realized all along you would have to touch it; that was never in doubt. It took me all my strength of mind to avoid doing the same myself.'

'But I thought you didn't believe in that demon story?'

He helped himself to some of the slices of bread from my tray before answering.

'Adam, I didn't want to go into this now, but I think I have to tell you: it's happened before. That story I told you about the two guys who lived with me was only partly true: they did fall out over the privacy issue, but one of them tried to do the same as you, though by sheer luck I caught him before he jumped. He'd had a nightmare about a demon in an empty room that told him to kill himself.'

'Jesus Christ.'

'Quite. I take it you had a similar dream?'

'Three. Within a few days of each other.'

'So you see, I really had no choice but to believe it.'

'What will you do with the egg?'

'Already burnt it and buried the ash. That fellow won't be coming back. But of course it had huge implications.'

'For your sculpture?'

'Of course. If one's demonic mental states can get embodied in matter –.'

'But you didn't make the egg did you? Your own works haven't caused any trouble I presume?'

'So far, no.'

'So no problem.'

'The thing is, I don't really know how they work. Whether it's some quality of the material, or some outside agent –.'

'You're thinking of the Cube?'

'Possibly. If the Cube can change the laws of physics there's no limit to what might happen.'

'But it's supposed to be benign. According to Les its purpose is to heal humanity, not destroy it.'

'And you believed him.'

And I suddenly realized I had believed him. In spite of everything that had happened, once I was convinced he was not himself a hoax, I never thought to doubt what he'd told me: he was a super-intelligent hyper-being after all; how could he possibly sink to the essentially human failing of telling lies?

'What could he conceivably gain from lying?'

'Er – a planetful of suckers?'

'Well, yes, apart from that,' I grinned.

I had plenty of time for thinking about all this in the days that followed. As my leg healed I began to feel restless, but Joe expressly forbade any recreational movement, and I was totally content to acquiesce. Since I awoke he'd looked after me with unstinted solicitude; he even broke his own rule and brought me news magazines and papers from Kingston, which brought home to me the fact that, despite our personal differences, we were a bulwark of some sort against a chaotic and beleaguered world. Despite endless summits and other high-level meetings, the Middle East was seething with resentments and incipient conflicts. The issues were generally about control of land and perceptions of historic injustices. The Gulf states could never resolve their ambiguous relationship with the powerful west, and were forever making alliances that soon disintegrated because of the fear of American hegemony, driven by its endemic insecurity and insatiable need for oil. The UN played its perpetual firefighting role, but was seen by the Arabs as being in the pockets of the Americans, and therefore deeply distrusted; consequently there was no supra-national body with enough clout to quell the conflicts and at the same time not be seen as partisan. Added to this there were the smouldering remnants of the Iraq war which threatened to re-ignite because one or the other of the factions perceived itself to be ignored or unfairly treated. At the moment Tehran was thumping its chest and asserting its right to be an economic power that couldn't be ordered around by America; further west Damascus was feeling itself economically and culturally squeezed between Jerusalem and Ankara. For the moment the oil pot was big enough for all, but there were abundant signs that this wouldn't last forever, and the nuclear option was becoming more and more attractive to those excluded from the feast.

Into this witch's cauldron came the Cube.

By now of course the entire world was familiar with its image: the vast obsidian monolith frequently lit from within by brilliant, flitting rainbow lights; and also with the stories about it: the lights were aliens spying on us; it's an American plot to enslave the rest of the world; a Martian reality-TV show; a mass hallucination created by scientists experimenting with a new generation of superdrugs. And of course inevitably: it's the Beast predicted in Revelation waiting its moment to consume the world in terror and flame. Strangely, as time went on the only explanation that came near the truth began to be discredited by most people on the grounds that if it were an alien spacecraft, having got here they wouldn't just sit around in their ship playing four-dimensional chess: they'd have laid waste the whole planet within hours of landing; it occurred to no-one of course that the invasion had indeed been underway for almost two years. But what effect, if any, was it having? Conflict was every bit as rife in every direction you cared to look; injustice bloomed like a cancer wherever there was wealth and power; but who's to say it wouldn't have been just the same, or far worse, without the Cube? It's like the London advert for elephant repellant: obviously it works because there are very few elephants in London. And coming nearer home, my own relationships could hardly be said to be repairing themselves; I even managed to fuck up my brief visit to Cora, and doubtless convinced her I was a complete no-hoper: no healing evident there. But it was early days still: Les had said it would take decades to have its full effect – by which time either nuclear holocaust or irreversible climate change would have made it redundant.

Two days later I was judged recovered enough to hobble out to the site of the cabin I'd allegedly built. I still had absolutely no recollection whatever of having done so, and would have found the idea ludicrous if Joe hadn't insisted on it.

'You've probably repressed the memory because I made it so unpleasant for you,' he said as we stood gazing at the half-finished structure.

'I've never made anything like this before in my entire life.' I inspected the level brickwork and the meticulously chamfered four-by-fours. 'I don't have the skills to do this sort of work. Honestly.'

'Well you obviously do have the skills. Se monumentum requiris circumspice...'

'Pardon?'

'Look around: all your own work. Anyway, in a way I'm glad you don't remember: I said some pretty stupid things which in hindsight would have been better unsaid.' He scrambled between the heaps of timber and broken bricks, and stood looking up at the sky. 'I suppose you'll be wanting to get this finished as soon as your leg's healed?'

The moment he said that I had a flashback which felt like recalling a previous life: there was a sudden familiarity about the whole thing, as though I was a ghost dragged back to haunt the site of former intensities. For a moment I glimpsed myself setting plumblines and levels, hefting support beams into place. I pushed against a door jamb to see if it would survive the impact.

'Well, I suppose if as you say I started this, maybe I ought to finish it.'

'Good. Take your time. And if there are any problems don't hesitate to talk to me about them.'

We strolled back to the house across the rapidly burgeoning garden.

'By the way, there'll be someone joining us shortly.'

'Oh. Who?'

'Someone who wrote to me. Chap from Paris called Philippe.'

'A bloke?'

'Yep. He's been studying philosophy with some teacher. But it all seems to have blown apart. He wants to meet me because of some old articles I wrote in *Philosophy Today*. Says they impressed him with their "acute insight into the human condition."'

'Sounds a bit of a wanker to me.'

'We're not rushing to judgement there just a tiny soupçon, are we?' He grinned for the second time as we stooped to enter the cool kitchen. 'Anyway, are we not all when it comes down to it, em, wankers, in our own way?'

Chapter Sixteen

'So what's he like to work with?' I asked Philippe when we'd assuaged our initial hunger.

'Passionate! Everything is passion. Feeling. Ideas are a commitment, not a pastime.'

'That's not at all his popular image, is it?' Joe replaced the iron pot on the stove and shuffled back to the table in an odd evocation of an ancient curmudgeonly waiter.

'Oh, but I don't care about his image! What has that to do with the man himself? No philosopher should care about such things.'

Philippe was tall and slim and had an assured air about him, which immediately caused my hackles to edge a few centimetres higher. He also affected the raised eyebrow when he didn't have an immediate answer for something, as though the questioner were being faintly ridiculed. There was an air of the dandy about him, which, coming from Paris, he may have felt obliged to play out for our benefit.

I found myself wondering why he was here: surely not because he wanted to meet the author of some obscure philosophical essays in an English academic journal. Maybe the CIA had installed him to find out what was going on; I recalled the bizarre incident of the government agent sent to the Quantocks to spy on Wordsworth and Coleridge in their innocent forays around Alfoxden, and laughed out loud.

The raised eyebrow was turned on me, but I couldn't explain.

'Were you at the Sorbonne?'

'Oh no. Before Paris I was studying music at Salzburg, with a wonderful piano teacher called Daniel. Music was my whole life: I was going to be the Brendel of the next century. Anything less was inconceivable.

'So what made you change to literature?'

'I was climbing and broke my wrist. It didn't heal well: I had two fingers unusable. About the same time my mother was killed in a chairlift accident. Suddenly everything was reversed: music was useless; it couldn't stop tragedies and pain, so what was the point of it? It was just another toy which I was using to distract myself from suffering. Then I came across the philosopher George Seton who was writing books that said everything I was feeling. So I left Salzburg for Paris, and went to find him. He became my dear friend and teacher.'

'You got on well with him?'

'Not particularly well. But that wasn't the point. He was extremely honest. If he thought I was deceiving myself he would tell me at once. Self-honesty was his number one tenet; it was what everything else was built on. But when he put it in his books people didn't like it: they thought it was just world-hatred and envy of others' happiness. There was a lot of bad blood around. But George just said, 'it's inevitable, if you try to be honest, you stir up strong demons.'

'Well it's true,' said Joe. 'We have our share of demons here. The trick is to use them, not let them use you. And to that end, we have some rules which I would ask you to follow while you're here—.'

Philippe's whole body seemed to quiver like a provoked squirrel.

'I'm sorry, I can't accept rules. If you insist on rules, I will leave tomorrow.'

'What's wrong with rules?' I asked.

'They are antithetical to philosophy. Someone has to make the rules and then impose them – usually the one who has money and property and is in a position to impose his will – we've been through that stage of humanity, and paid a huge price for it. Now we must move on to real freedom. What is the point of just repeating failed social models forever?'

Joe leant back in his seat and steepled his hands over his mouth, a characteristic pose when he was about to proclaim something he thought radical. I assumed he was about to issue some sort of anti-Marxian rhetoric, but instead he said:

'I think you have a valid point. Rules are against freedom, and freedom is the highest good; therefore we will have no rules while you are here. You are henceforth free.' He smiled at Philippe.

'Thank you. I appreciate it. I will stay.'

Joe's response deeply shocked me: I thought it was a complete sell-out, but I said nothing.

After the meal, Joe took his guest on the mandatory tour of the house, while I strolled outside to consider my unfinished cabin.

It was that part of the year when summer hands over its prizes to autumn to work into something more conducive to contemplation. Trees, birds and other wild creatures basked in the glow of their supreme achievement: survival, before the change to a darker key which heralds an even greater mystery. I sat on the edge of the concrete base and allowed the evening's music to seep into me. A question hovered before me, as though an angel who chanced to be passing had noticed my looming depression and for once decided to intervene: 'why is the world so beautiful?' And immediately this was followed by a second question, as though another angel, following on behind the first, had not wanted to be outdone in inventiveness by his colleague: 'and why don't I realize it more often?' Even further questions followed this, as though—

But I won't try your patience by proliferating comparisons. What it all came down to was, why do I allow my lollock of a brain to dictate the story so much – when there is so obviously a much bigger story going on all the time right under my nose? And why, despite the ample evidence, do I constantly deny the existence of this bigger story?

I had no answers, but then this Rousseau-esque moment wasn't about answers; answers never answered anything. Maybe that was the lesson Joe was trying to bang into me when he refused to ask me about my Hammer Horror past?

A late bird was singing his heart out somewhere in the honeymoon suite of a nearby oak tree. It seemed an apt metaphor: that something so small and self-contained should be the source of a cry so gigantic, far-reaching and heart-piercing. I was certain that Les, with his parsecs of computing power, could never, with all the time in the universe, have comprehended that song, not even with all his vast mad schemes for the correlation and unification of everything. And the fantastic thing was, we didn't have just the one bird, but millions, a seemingly infinite supply in fact, all embedded in those reticent fairy curls of DNA, which never reveal themselves, yet express themselves so eloquently.

Slowly the late summer evening darkened, and those vaster mysteries, the stars, appeared, "like something almost being said," as Philip Larkin so succinctly put it, though he was talking about trees, not stars. Would they ever say it, I wondered, that thing they were perpetually on the brink of saying?

Or was mankind destined to blossom, peak and fade without ever hearing the momentous annunciation?

I would stay and complete the cabin, I decided, since it seemed I'd started it; a kind of rite of passage: the first time I'd finished something and got it right; and also by way of saying thanks to Joe for his unusual hospitality.

We seemed to be having an Indian summer, and I spent more and more time outside: when not working I passed hours each day reading and writing. When the sun was above the treetops the three of us took our meals in the garden, pretending we were living the high life in the Italian Alps, or in the anarchic hinterlands of New South Wales. Slowly I began to notice a dynamic emerging between us, where Joe would play the slightly patrician master, watching over his proteges, but always keeping one or two steps ahead of them, never lost for a sly riposte. Philippe, ever the precocious and admiring student, was full of questions positioned to show off his wide reading of twentieth century philosophy and aesthetics, which Joe generally dismissed with a zen flourish, or answered obliquely in a way that made me suspect he'd never even heard of the author in question, yet still managed to give the impression he was addressing the implicit question that Philippe would have asked had he been slightly more *au fait*. I for my part, instinctively took the role of the maladroit novice, taking refuge in a smouldering silence in preference to the risk of appearing to compete for the master's approval.

Joe himself continued to confound all my many attempts to confine him into a fixed character whose behaviour I could attribute to simple psychological causes. He always seemed to see this coming long before I was aware of doing it, and so was able to become instantly invisible to my crude reductionist armoury.

One particularly balmy afternoon after lunch we got onto the subject of women's aptitude for philosophy – a topic on which Philippe had strong views (one might, if permitted, say prejudices).

'Why do you even consider bringing women into a philosophical community? They have no reason to be remotely concerned with it. It's merely selling out to conventional expectations.'

I allowed my outrage to slink red-eyed into the arena.

'Women are people, Philippe, just in case you hadn't noticed yet. They have as much right to an intellectual life as you or I have. The fact that they have to bring up children and generally provide a nurturing environment should qualify them more for philosophical enquiry, not less, because their ideas are more grounded in reality than men's.'

'This is quite wrong thinking,' Philippe went on. 'Very typical of current liberal egalitarian misconceptions. You try to placate women's anger by allowing them mental equality. But the way of nature is not equality: it is adaptation. Men are adapted to philosophy precisely because their lives are free from the need to make homes and feed infants, so their minds have been selected to become more expansive and suitable for asking the big questions, such as how we should live, and to what purpose. Women have no need to ask these things.'

'And how many women have you bothered to ask about their concerns?'

'Oh it's irrelevant how many! That's statistics, which is the science of lies. I deduce from primary facts.'

'But can't you see? Even if your adaptive theory is true, it's based on a massive injustice! And guess who perpetrated the injustice?'

'People doing what they're best at can't be injustice Adam. If women had been naturally suited to a philosophical life they would have been following it for thousands of years! Why not follow Nature's way? Women raise families as they instinctively know how to, and men think about what it's all for and the best way to live. It's really so simple, when you let go of these politically correct excuses for thoughts!'

'Oh you're really too kind.'

'No, I'm not kind at all. Just right.'

The arrogance of this continental humbug sponge stunned me; his ideas seemed proofed against all self-doubt – little tracts custom-made to justify the depredations of the dominant male of the species. I didn't see how we were going to inhabit the same house for two days together without terminally irritating each other. But the ways of Joe were mysterious: maybe Philippe had been invited for a specific purpose, I thought; maybe this beacon of European enlightenment in the Anglo-Saxon darkness was about to have his wick trimmed.

I looked hopefully at Joe, who was rocking serenely back and forth in his creaking wicker chair, no doubt hugely enjoying the miasmic undercurrents. I guessed he wasn't going to be teased into taking sides.

'What do you think?'

'What do I think?' His features sharpened into a Holmesian smile balanced on the verge of pouncing. 'I think... nothing.'

So far so predictable. The creaking was beginning to irritate me. Such positionings of non-combatance were usually the prelude to an engagement of shattering finality. The formerly loquacious birds had subsided into their afternoon siesta. The fir trees bordering the lawn leant furtively down to savour the rare scent of our hiatus. Everything waited for Joe's meditation to bear its reclusive fruit.

He caught our expectancy and played with it like a well-fed cat with a mouse.

'What should I think? What *could* I think? I suppose I could think that one of you must be wrong and the other right. And if I express an opinion on that I'll probably upset one of you and inflate the ego of the other. Or I could think that each of you had a point, although neither was entirely correct. Which might get me off the hook nicely, if I was bothered about that. Or I could be a little bit zen-like and say rightness and wrongness are empty concepts, entirely without value. Or I could be even more zen-like and just walk away and make some more tea – which might very possibly be the most creative thing to do. But right now I really don't know which of those I'm actually *going* to do. And the more I wonder, the less inclined I am to do any of them.' The smile relented, relaxing into the guileless grin of a child who's just mastered a delicate balancing trick. A light breeze from the south rustled the smaller branches of the inclining trees.

'I suppose the really useful thing would be whichever brings about the greatest self-knowledge in the participants. But one would need to be wise indeed to foresee that.'

'Aren't you wise?' Philippe fished for an approving glance.

'Ah! You think I'm going to fall into that old elephant trap? I think you should make the tea for expecting me to make a claim like that.'

'I assure you I didn't expect anything at all,' said Philippe, gratifyingly embarrassed. Joe stared intently at the teapot, and gave no sign of moving.

Chapter Seventeen

It became more and more difficult to talk with Joe without Philippe being present. Conversations tended to degenerate into a point-scoring match, with the two acolytes vying for the master's approval. I hated it, but felt powerless to change it: I imagined I was being marginalized, under-valued, and generally regarded as a nuisance, a trouble-stirrer. Philippe spent hours each day reading, or talking with Joe. I lavished more and more attention on finishing the cabin. There were many small details to consider: plumbing, electrics, weather-proofing, window and door fittings, furniture; in the absence of any discussion Joe had taken to leaving his version of post-it notes for me each day, as his thoughts about his needs for the building developed. Sometimes the notes were contradictory – deliberately so, I sometimes thought: it was Joe's way of giving me "material" for my personal edification. A point came when we ran out of electrical fittings, and I took a bus into Bridgwater to hunt down supplies.

I was very happy to have a reason to get away from the incestuous atmosphere of the house. By ten o'clock the day was already warm and fragrant with autumnal scents. Nature was showing off her little genetic experiments in every direction: the fact that she'd demonstrated their viability several million times already didn't seem to reduce her delight in them one jot. It was like Mozart in an opera playing with a tiny four-note motif: it could produce joy, mystery, exuberance, caprice, mischievousness, rage, banality, despair, horror, triumph; the fact that he'd already tried it out in a thousand different contexts and it had produced interesting responses each time only served to enhance its essential mystery: the simpler it was the more it could contain. Think of the four ciphers of the human genetic code, and how many unique expressions they were capable of: the fecundity of its permutations was mind-numbing to contemplate.

I went rapidly through my list in the electrical superstore, grabbing 3-core cable, 2-gang sockets, switches, lamp-holders, cable clamps, junction boxes, fuse units, a circuit-breaker; all the time feeling impatient, snappish, frustrated and resentful, but I didn't know about what. I paid for everything with my Visa, being careful to key my PIN without reading the total amount; then trailed to the newsagent to get a paper and a few goodies to keep my brain sweet about continuing to work with me; something told me I was going to need its cooperation in the months to come.

When my backpack was bulging with signifiers to remind Joe what an industrious and thoughtful worker I was, I decided to visit the cafe by the river and catch up on the world's stampede to oblivion. The early sun had vanished and been quietly replaced by convincingly black stormclouds. I was lucky: despite being past midday the place was almost empty. I installed myself in a corner with a good view of the terrain, in case the world ended and I had to get to a cash machine very quickly. Which wasn't all that far off the mark as it happened, because when I opened the paper the first article my eyes fastened on was tantalisingly if confusingly headed:

CUBE 'ANGELS' NOT A THREAT TO MANKIND SAY EXPERTS

"Space experts from Manchester University have completed the first comprehensive study of the artifact popularly known as the 'Cube', which was first discovered on a North Yorkshire farm almost two years ago. They are confident it does not constitute a threat to our civilisation, although they have established that the intense comet-like lights frequently seen inside it are probably images of alien intelligences.

"Powerful iridium-ruby lasers fired into the object for long periods failed to alter the atomic structure or even the temperature of the material of which it is composed, leading scientists to conclude it is enclosed by a 'force-field' protecting it from any human-originated energy. This has led some physicists from the high- energy lab at the University to believe the Cube relies on a phenomenon known as 'quantum non-location', which states that two objects separated by a vast distance may behave as a single object in all respects once they have been 'entangled' before separation. Which has in turn led scientists to question our conventional view of the attributes of spacetime, ie, that faster than light travel or even time travel is essentially impossible because it would contravene the energy equations of Einstein's relativity theory."

None of this was particularly news to me of course. But what did worry me was the final paragraph of the article, which was added by the writer almost as an afterthought – a kind of 'would you believe it?' space-filler you used to find in the 'Readers Digest':

"An Iranian sect known as the Brothers United in Global Harmony, which has been growing in strength since the Cube's existence became known world-wide, yesterday issued a statement on their website that the Cube was an agent of ultimate evil and would eventually destroy Mankind to prepare the planet for colonisation. The group pledged themselves to destroying the artifact with nuclear bombs. They are understood to have the tacit support of many other terrorist groups around the globe, including the Students of the Heavenly Vision (a previously little-known Islamic pressure group), the Swords of Liberation, the Guardians of Sacred Truth, and the United People's Front of Turkestan. They are being taken seriously by the Combined European States Intelligence Services, (COMSIS) and the UK has been put on an Orange state of alert – only one level down from the maximum Red Alert signifying Imminent Attack Status."

'Mind if I sit here?'

I looked up: a thin shaven-headed man in his thirties with thin lips and an intense chin full of black stubble was eyeing me. He had very dark serious eyes and a gaze that seemed to say 'nothing in this world can shock me any more'. His seriousness made me warm to him at once.

'Please do.'

'I'm Mark. You're reading about our friends in the Cube.'

He dropped his pack heavily onto the table and sat down. He seemed so thin that half the chair remained vacant.

'You think they are our friends then?'

'I know they are. If we let them.'

I instantly began to listen a lot harder.

'You know? How?'

'Because they talk to me.'

At that point my brain began to record every thought and feeling in extreme slow motion, as follows:

0 - 100ms: Fear

200ms: Beginnings of the thought *Oh no, another bloody nutter!*

300ms: Corresponding strong desire to remove myself from the situation.

450ms: Recognition of the irony of meeting another Cubehead by chance in a provincial town cafe.

600ms: The thought that I'd been deceived by Les into believing I was the sole human communicant. (This was accompanied by some emotion akin to jealousy mixed with fury, plus a small percentage of relief that I could now share some of my feelings with another human being.)

800ms: Slightly unpleasant body odour in vicinity of Mark.

1200ms: Recognition of the need to devise a strategy for informing myself of the exact degree of Mark's interaction with the Cube, and how much I could trust what he told me.

1500ms: Awareness of reluctance to doing this.

Beneath all this, and running concurrently, was a persisting sadness that had to do with relying on weirdos – human and otherwise – for one's friendships.

I nudged my chair twenty centimetres further from his, so I could take in his almost quivering figure.

'They talk to you? How?'

He tapped the side of his skull.

'Here. Inside. Very quiet.' He made a listening-hard gesture with his finger and thumb. I was getting a lurching feeling somewhere in the dark of my stomach that said: *here be dragons*.

'Do they talk English?'

'Yes. Very good English. Considering they're from the Frog Nebula.'

'Pardon?'

'Yes. Most people say that. I don't mind explaining. The vast majority of people smile for a bit and then make an excuse and leave. I expect you'll do the same. But it doesn't matter.'

'Did you say frog?'

'That's right: the Frog Nebula.'

I couldn't take my eyes off him for a moment. 'Please go on. What do they say?'

'That they're a massively intelligent and ancient life-form located 40,000 light years from earth. They occupy almost a thousand light-years of space. They're not planet-based you see: more like a very tenuous intelligent cloud stretching between the stars. And they've just discovered that we humans are a threat to their existence, so they want to upgrade us. Still here?'

He blinked to check that I was still there. As you may imagine, I was.

I thought it was time to ask a high-risk question.

'Have they mentioned anything about needing Russian Jokes?'

He didn't flinch, not for one millisecond.

'They've contacted you too, haven't they?'

So now there were two of us.

Frankly I didn't know how to respond to this new poke from the universe. I was no longer alone, assuming my new found Cubehead was real, and wouldn't break up into a heap of clattering pixels at any second. And of course it flagged up the other question: were there others? Hundreds? Millions? And was Les purveying a different story to each person he contacted?

'Thank God', Mark muttered, 'I was beginning to feel like the bloody elephant man.'

'Me too. But did they ask you to find jokes?'

'Yes. But only Irish.'

Something clicked into place.

'It's clear what they're doing: yes, of course! They're building up a psychological picture of all the world's peoples through their jokes. We'll probably find they're made contact with someone in every country. Then they'll integrate all their data and decide what's wrong with us. Are you Irish, by any chance?'

'My grandmother was from Galway.'

'There you are then. There are probably thousands of us around the globe. Each with our own allocated joke-field.'

'But I don't want this,' Mark said. 'It's scared off all my friends. I was a good musician before all this happened. Well, fairish, leastways. I had a good woman. She got off with the drummer. I didn't mind 'cos he was rubbish. I even had a job: not brilliant, but it paid the bills. That went down the tubes. Even me dog's gone. And when a man's dog leaves things are bad. My mates were just breaking onto the scene. We'd have been big, no question. Those voices took me brain over. Day and night. Month after month. No one was interested. Nobody wanted to know did they? They all thought it was drugs. Well, I mean why would you believe a no-hoper who thinks he's been chosen by aliens to reform humanity? You wouldn't want to go there, would you?'

'Are they still talking to you?'

'If you can call it talking. They fire Irish jokes at me and I have to analyse them: tell them what they're about, why they're funny.'

'And do you?'

His voice became conspiratorial. 'I make up stuff. I can't see it matters much anyway. Most of them even I don't understand. It keeps them happy. And when they've done all their number crunching on them I reckon they'll get the picture of the human mind that they want.'

'So you believe they're genuine?'

His eyes narrowed. 'How would I know? But you've got to wonder. I mean, who could come up with a scam like that on a student budget?'

He slurped his tea noisily and fell silent.

My brain was still trying to absorb the fact that there was someone else like me, in contact with the aliens, who'd been turned into some kind of freak by their messages. Maybe we should all get together and plot our strategy to turn events to our advantage. Together we'd be enormously powerful: if we could get the aliens to talk only to us, we'd have unprecedented influence: governments would hang on our every word and whim. The new technology would be ours for the asking. State of the art condos in Dubai and Havana would be placed at our disposal; no one would dare offend us, in case we put it about that certain individuals were opposing the aliens' plans.

But could I handle the responsibility? Did I want my life tangled up in high-level politics? Did I even want the dubious advantages that vast wealth would bring? Dammit, I didn't even have a serious bank account.

'I can't help feeling,' I said, 'that everything we do – I mean, all those who've been contacted – is being comprehensively watched and analysed.

They're throwing tests at us like we'd give tasks to white mice: to work out how their minds operate. Then when they've got all the data they need, they'll program the Cube to remake us into rational beings, just like them. Then they won't feel threatened, right?'

'Right. With you.'

'The problem is of course, humans won't want to be rationalized. They want to be free to wreak havoc throughout the galaxy, and beyond, if necessary. I can't imagine any human saying, ok, yeah, we're a bit loony, and these aliens seem fairly sussed, so why not let them reprogram our brains so we don't threaten them? Can you imagine that?'

'Not with all the fog in Galway. We wouldn't be human if we said that, would we?'

'Quite. So once the story's out, we've got a serious problem on our hands, as go-betweens I mean. We'd get hit by both sides, wouldn't we?'

'I see where you're going. Could be nasty.'

'So basically we've got to keep our heads down. Work invisibly. And we can't play games. The aliens'd know instantly if we started mucking about. And I do mean instantly. We have to be absolutely straight: give them the data, plus our knowledge of how humans work.'

'But what if they're right about us? What if we are a hopeless case? We'd be colluding in our own extermination.'

'I don't think they want that. They want us to get over our obsession with power and destruction. I think they see us as prototypes for something more like them. A higher plane.'

'And our job's to sell that to our own side, right?'

'A hard call, I'd say. It'd be like selling chocolate to the Venusians.'

'Except that the chocolate man is here, and he wants to talk. We have to respond somehow. I mean, look at the pig's ear we're making of our planet. We have to do something.'

Suddenly I had an idea.

'I'd like you to meet Joe.'

'Who's Joe?'

'A mate of mine who I live with while I'm getting my life sorted. Bit of a magician on the quiet. You'd get on.'

Mark stared at the table as though it might give him guidance.

'Ok, I'm up for it. Just so long as he doesn't try to sell me anything. I can't stand opportunists that think I'm an easy touch.' His face suddenly darkened. 'He's not queer, is he?'

'No, not remotely. He's just a bloke with very interesting ideas. And he really does know some magic. The genuine article.'

'Ok, you've got me. How do I find him?'

On the way home I tried to sort out my feelings about Mark. He struck me as passionate and naive, and therefore potentially dangerous; he was like someone whose world had collapsed and in the nick of time had found a cause, and was hanging onto it by his fingernails. What if the aliens turned out after all to be another bunch of crop-circle comedians with a powerful microwave transmitter in a white van? What would he have left? Al-Qaida?

Despite that, I found myself wanting to trust him – maybe because like me he had little to lose. And his eyes had a dark intensity that didn't waver when they met mine. And we'd both been weighed in the balance by our women and found wanting. And above all perhaps I needed someone I could talk to about the aliens without being laughed at or lectured or told to pull myself together and get a life.

But then a more unsettling thought floated quietly by me: suppose he too was nothing more than a character playing his assigned role in the giant computer game that the Cube had made of the green and pleasant land we called Earth? The next thought didn't get a chance to form, because a thirty-ton fuel tanker chose that moment to roar by me, drenching me with an icy mix of mud and rainwater.

Chapter Eighteen

It was after sunset by the time I got back to Joe's. There was something different: a change in the psychic environment. Nothing visible; everything apparently just as I'd left it. But – it was not the same place I'd walked out of that same morning. I felt like an intruder.

I slouched to the cabin, unloaded my hoard of pristine power cable, steel sockets and gleaming brass escutcheons, and wondered how I was going to put it all together into something that wouldn't instantly go into meltdown on being connected to the mains.

Joe didn't appear until late evening. He seemed in a good mood.

'Good raiding party?' He positioned a small battered saucepan of milk on the hob and adjusted the flame.

I was instantly on my guard: had he sent Philippe to trail me all round B&Q and Wickes? Was he one of the over-dressed people pretending to read papers at the bus-stop opposite the cafe? I couldn't rule it out, because logically it was possible; therefore he must have done, therefore he knew I'd met someone who might possibly—.

I went for non-committal. 'Pretty good. I got everything except the halo.'

'Oh, there was a man here earlier with a halo. Must have been yours. I sent him away; he looked like a Christian.' All this without the ghost of a smile.

'Oh good. You did the right thing. We can't have Christians snooping around in our dustbins.'

'Speaking of dustbins, have you eaten?'

'Yes.'

'So how's the human race getting on?'

'It's losing.' I stacked my little hard-won luxuries in the freezer, trying to distract Joe's attention with my news. 'There's a worrying article about the Cube in the Guardian though. There are a whole lot of hotheads wanting to nuke it. I think they're serious. We could be set for another 911. Iran and Pakistan have nuclear capability. Syria's manouvering for time. Anything could set it off: a small diplomatic incident: a kidnapping, a spy being caught, an oil pipe-line exploded.'

'I've a feeling the Cube will look after itself. Meanwhile there are plenty of little wars nearer home that maybe we could influence the outcome of.'

'What have you got in mind?'

'Oh, I don't know. There are so many. How about, for a start, the war between openness and the desire to secrete little personal treats in the freezer?'

'I can't imagine what you're referring to,' I deadpanned as I fumbled plastic bags into the waste-bin.

No matter how hard I distracted myself with problems of cable-ducting and junction box positioning, the image of Elaine refused to leave me. On my knees, on the concrete, sorting masonry and roofing nails, she would be there in front of me with her wistful, intimate, sanguine gaze. While I was fixing socket housings and trying to interpret circuit-breaker instructions, she was beside me with her soothing indolent river voice and her fine jasmine-scented hair. But falling in love was strictly off the agenda. This wasn't love: it wasn't even the beginnings of it; it was loneliness, pure and simple; my very own bete-noir that I should have suffocated to death many years ago. Loneliness and failure and the despair of ever escaping it had led me here, to Joe, and now to Philippe. I'd thought this building idea would carve me a place in Joe's affections, but it manifestly hadn't: I was still stuck in the same circle of hell I'd been in ever since the Rachael affair; only now I felt even more desperate, if that were possible.

It still depressed me enormously that I still needed affection and approbation so much, whether from attractive younger women or clever older men. I told myself over and over again I shouldn't need it; I was fine just as I was; I was capable of constructing a building from scratch that actually worked (ie, didn't immediately collapse when the door was slammed). I'd helped people to be happier and achieve their goals; I'd written articles that had been praised for their insight and originality; I'd even developed a few decent games that had been state of the art for a few moments at the end of the twentieth century. I'd prevented numerous old people crossing the road at moments when crossing the road wasn't in their best interests. I'd once saved a child from drowning in a water tank (he'd later been convicted for massive fraud while working for an international aid organisation, but one can't know everything). And (what might someday be regarded as my crowning achievement) I'd had direct mind-to-mind contact with the creators of the Cube and possible saviours of mankind. Yet all this didn't seem to weigh significantly against the things I hadn't done, or hadn't done well, or had done positively ill; and as a consequence I needed to be forever buoyed up, shaken out and set running again by people who saw their mission in life as saving people like me (setting aside for the moment the more or less infinite possible interpretations of exactly what constitutes being 'saved'.) This, in essence, was the task I was up against and frankly I viewed it with no great relish. But as has been observed, if you want to make an omelette you're going to have to have some full and frank discussions with the eggs. And what eggs are going to relish their own enforced non-existence?

A day came in late July when Joe announced he was ready to move into his summer palace. The electrics worked, the roof kept the rain out, and the rudimentary plumbing somehow avoided flooding the place. I didn't plan on getting any lavish praise, but I did expect some kind of acknowledgement that I'd done a competent job. But the silence was deafening. There was not a syllable of recognition from Joe that I'd ever had anything to do with the cabin's mysterious appearance at the edge of the garden. The three of us spent a hot and windless day moving Joe's essential furniture and working materials across to the new structure, and installing it according to his precise instructions. Philippe, I noticed, moved lethargically and with frequent gaps for contemplation and drinking many litres of bottled water. When he saw this, Joe merely smiled indulgently like a proud father who sees his offspring as the epitomy of pre-lapsarian purity. In spite of myself, my already well-exercised hackles rose, as my brain fussed about inventing imminent catastrophes like a panicked sheep.

And then it came to me that I no longer had a visible role in our fragile living experiment. We were having dinner under the trees one sultry August evening when I mentioned this to Joe. The comment launched him into a typical invective against conventional society.

'Are you complaining?'

'I suppose I am, yes.'

'You see the way your mind works? You spend years doing a job you despise, participating in a social structure you see as pointless and self-serving; you finally find a way out of it, you end up here, where you immediately create another role for yourself, another structure for getting approval and security, and when that fails to achieve that, you bellyache like hell. This is why we have the societies we have. Now you're free of all roles and structures, and still you're not happy.'

I found it impossible to answer him. Instead I looked at Philippe, who'd been listening in silence to Joe.

'What do you think about roles?'

'I agree absolutely with Joe. We must abandon all roles: they are prisons. You made yourself a prison in building the cabin: now it is finished you can be free. So what's to complain about?'

'Well I'm not really complaining. I'm merely confessing my discomfort.'

'Good,' said Joe, draining a bottle of Merlot over his glass. 'We should never complain, because everything that comes to us is a gift. Everything. When we have a role, it's very difficult to see how trapped we can be, especially if it's a pleasant role, or a role where we have power. So we're generally not strongly motivated to abandon it.'

'This is how France has been turned into a terminal invalid after three hundred years of mastery.' Philippe took up Joe's lead and spoke as though to a table crammed with acolytes straining to receive his insights. 'We began with the role of the philosopher-king spreading culture through darkness. Then wisdom was usurped through greed. Then the revolution forced equality on everyone. At last we had what we thought was the holy grail of civilization: for a few moments we had equality in our grasp, but we immediately reverted to our old comfortable role of master and servant – we couldn't live without that sacred model. As the great Sartre knew well, we couldn't endure the freedom to be just ourselves. So we blew it. Now we're all slaves of mediocrity.' He smiled at his own articulacy. 'We're all nobodies going nowhere.'

Suddenly I felt an overwhelming need to get away from this revisionist hot air. I needed to think about Elaine, and that needed space uninfected by testosterone-fuelled sociology (of course my testosterone had nothing to do with it). But there was something else I needed to get straight: why did I have such a visceral antipathy toward Philippe? He was merely a young, inexperienced, foreign music student who was somewhat over-idealistic in his revolutionary zeal. He was harmless, and would probably leave soon after he'd exhausted the novelty of being a small but perfectly formed fish in a very small pond. Could it be I was jealous of him? After all, I'd been the ascendent star of this gripping drama until now; suddenly I had to get used to being in the wings rather than the limelight. Maybe I was simply resenting having to share parental attention (all those expensive therapy sessions had paid off after all: I could now precisely identify every one of my irremediable neuroses).

But why couldn't I tell him? Or Joe for that matter? What about our brave new world of total honesty? Surely all that hard graft couldn't have melted into gnat's piss so soon? Could I be so terrified of rejection that I was deprived of the power of argument by a few subliminal but skilfully aimed glances? Was this the grim end result of my lifetime of obsessive mooching and yearning?

Dusk was draining the warmth out of the tree shadows. The birds had long since fallen silent. A sinuous indigo scarf of vapour twisted along the sky in the west. I glanced up: a couple of stars were shining high in the south, like the first glyphs in a yet to be understood alphabet. The world emanated tranquillity, yet I was anything but tranquil. Somewhere up there behind the deep blue gauze was something so far beyond my comprehension that it made the whole of humanity's evolution seem an irrelevance, a sideshow that had somehow got started by mistake, and would now have to run its course regardless of the havoc it caused its participants. The main action was happening somewhere else, a colossal distance away, beyond our present technology's ability to probe. And yet while all this was true, at the same time what I did from moment to moment seemed crucial, not just to myself, but to the total picture: somehow the tiniest, most transient detail of a life was also critical to that main action, but in a way it was entirely beyond me to fathom. In the idiom of the most turgid and sentimental love lyrics, the gods were looking down and blessing every one of us, without exception, everywhere.

The windless, characterless days succeeded each other with very little change. Joe was seriously into his new sculpture project, and hardly ever left his studio, as we were now required to call it. Philippe had moved into Joe's attic study, and the house suddenly seemed like a silent mausoleum. During the middle part of the day I took to aimlessly haunting its corridors and neglected rooms like a twenty-first century Des Esseintes, lethargic and disconsolate, unable to take the step I knew in my heart I had to take. As the summer imperceptibly shifted into its maturity the interior of the house seemed to respond with more and more darkness, to become more and more its own kingdom – a place with its own laws and time. The hours of the afternoon in particular seemed to sussurrate with voices I hadn't heard before: voices verging on music, yet pulling back just short of it; voices singing the songs of dying things through drying rafters, shrinking garden pools, yellowing window lights, dust suspended in long-unswept passageways.

I felt abandoned by Joe: now he had his new admirer he made no effort to put his precept of openness into practice; yet at the same time I wondered how much of his attitude was deliberate shock tactics to jolt me out of my emotional dependence. I found my brain going round in ever decreasing circles in its hopeless attempt to square this circle: one moment I'd be in despair over my rejection by someone I'd looked up to as being above all emotional ego-games: the next I'd persuaded myself it was all a piece of theatre deliberately designed to induce an existential leap into a new orbit. And then one morning at the very end of August the world decided my days of self-indulgent brow-beating were over.

In the absence of any imposed role, I'd adopted that of gardener; it suited me very well because it didn't make any intellectual demands, and it kept me connected with the earth and with growing things. I loved the feel of soil: its texture, coolness and moist depths made me feel part of something that seemed to know why it was there, what its relationship was with everything else – and I relished the sense of wholeness that came from that contact, even as, in another part of my brain, I was pouring scorn on the whole paraphernalia of mystical mumbo-jumbo that fed so many people's sad lives. So on this particular late August morning I'd given myself the task of thinning out the brambles and bindweed that had been having a ball, as only convolvulus can, in the once meticulously ordered borders that ran inside the southern boundary fence.

I looked up to give my eyes a respite from staring at bramble vines, and saw a young woman gazing towards the house. For several seconds I saw nothing strange in this: she could have been anyone – a misplaced traveller, a seller of home insurance or fitted kitchens, someone in search of a lost relative – but then she turned and waved: it was Elaine.

'Hello Adam!'

It was a whole week since I'd thought of her, and I'd convinced myself she was safely consigned to that part of my memory carefully labelled 'nostalgia'. (In retrospect I should have had another folder in there with it, labelled in red capitals: 'LIVE NOSTALGIA'. But it would be bulging to destruction).

She edged tentatively up to the fence as though about to ask for directions. She looked entirely different from how I remembered her: she was dressed in a white tiered cotton skirt with a close-fitting sleeveless top, her hair cut short with a fringe that artfully contrived to lend her a carefree, gypsy-ish air. I stared at her, willing her not to fade.

'The gate's along that way. Unless you want to chance the fence.' I felt an unfamiliar feeling distantly related to elation tug at the edges of my mind. She'd come back. I wasn't a complete un-person: I still had an existence in her mind.

I'd barely finished the sentence before she'd stepped neatly over the wire where it sagged between the rotted posts.

'I hope you don't mind my turning up unannounced. I could come back later if it's not convenient?'

Something in my eyes must have betrayed horror at the prospect of losing her so suddenly, because she smiled the kind of smile that had stopped olympic athletes in their tracks and got them thinking of loft-extensions.

'Absolutely no problem. To be quite honest I didn't expect ever to see you again. After my awful behaviour, I mean.'

'Don't worry about that. I understand how you must have felt. It took me some time to adjust, that's all.'

I led the way towards the house, deliberately taking an indirect route around the burgeoning rosebeds, reluctant to break the spell and allow time to continue.

'So you got my post-card? I wasn't sure if the post was still functioning with all the disruption.'

'Yes, I did. But I've moved. I've bought a cottage in the Blackdown Hills. A fantastic location on the edge of a village called South Brockley.'

'And Jack?'

"Still in the old place. He realized I needed to be away from him. I was amazed how he accepted it all in the end. He realized his job was his world, and other people were marginal. I think it was harder for me than for him.'

'It's good of you to come.'

'I wanted to. I hated the way all those violent feelings were left in the air.'

I took her into the 'morning' room, where we were less likely to be disturbed. She stood with her sun hat and her white Gucci bag on one shoulder and admired the view like a prospective purchaser.

'You're very lucky to live here. It's so peaceful.'

'Yes, it is, if you ignore the inhabitants.'

'And you? Are you... sorting your life out?'

She looked at me with a touch of her old disarming softness.

'I think so. Joe's a relentless teacher. Though sometimes it feels like persecution.'

'Tell me about Joe.'

So I told her Joe's story, of his years of experimenting, his wandering in search of 'authentic' experience, his vision of an experimental community, a brotherhood dedicated to living out their knowledge, and how that vision had drawn him to this place.

'He sounds like a lonely man to me,' was all she said at the end of it.

'Perhaps. But he's also driven by this need for truth. I think it's stronger than any other need in him.'

'He doesn't sound altogether human to me. Is there anything beautiful in his life?'

'I could show you something beautiful if you like. Or perhaps beautiful is the wrong word. Would you like to see?'

'Absolutely. Yes.'

I took her up to the sculpture room. All the way up she was goggle-eyed at the unexpected spaces and vistas that unfolded at every turn. 'This place is like the Tardis!' she exclaimed when we finally entered the room.

'I know. I think it's to do with its being continually added to every few years. And the people who lived here, of course.'

'Doesn't it feel weird living with all this stuff around you? I mean, it must be like having a zoo full of wild animals under your feet.'

'It's interesting you chose that image.'

She moved towards one of the long shelves. 'Can I hold one?'

'Better just look, I think. As I said, they're unpredictable.'

She walked slowly towards the figure of a horse half-way along the central aisle. It looked inoccuous enough: about ten inches high, carved in a light, fine-grained material like walnut. Its head was caught in the moment of rearing as though it had been suddenly startled.

She moved to inspect the carving, and instinctively her fingers darted to caress its head. Instantly she let out a cry as though she'd been electrocuted, and staggered back, almost toppling the figure.

'My God! What was that?' She looked scared, her wide eyes glancing to the window.

'What happened?'

'I don't know. I need to sit down.'

I led her to a seat by the middle window, shocked by her reaction.

'There was a real horse charging at me: I only just managed to get out of its way. Jesus! It was so real!'

'That's because you touched the figure.'

'It was as if it was willing me to; I had no power to resist. Adam, what are those things?'

I sat by her on the window bench. 'I don't know.' Her features were still riven with the shock of her encounter, but curiosity hovered about them, softening the fault-lines. 'It has something to do with concentration: the state of mind of the artist while he's making it. But of course there must be more to it than that, or we'd have these things all over the world. Think of Michelangelo for starters. Or Leonardo.'

'It almost makes you think magic.'

'It makes me think the Cube actually.'

'Really? How come?'

'Have you noticed how the world has gradually changed over the past few years? I mean, things seem to be happening that go against physical laws. I don't just mean climate change and the ice-caps melting. I mean human interactions. Changes of culture. Barriers between people softening.'

'I must say I hadn't noticed. People still hate each other as much as ever. There are still terrorist attacks every day in some parts of the world.'

'True, but there's a will to resolve things. As if people have looked over the edge of the precipice and seen what lies ahead. They've been invaded by a sense of perspective.'

'Well I can only hope you're right. But the Cube? Surely it's just a stunt isn't it? That's what everyone believes now: a desperate gambit by governments to distract us from their appalling cockups and malpractice. Don't you think?'

'No. Actually I don't. I think the Cube has real power to change things. And is doing, despite our collective paranoia.'

'And you really believe it can affect inanimate objects like these?'

'Well, what's inanimate? Joe believes there's only the mind, and it has no limits. What we call 'inanimate' is an artificial construct to make us feel in control.'

'Frankly that sounds to me like new-age claptrap. It's far more likely it's a clever bit of technology dreamed up by one of the new mega-chains to promote their brands. I'll bet if you look closely all those lights will have logos attached. You have to hand it to them: it's a brilliant concept.'

I heard the downstairs door slam, and voices in the hall.

'Let's go down and meet Joe, shall we?' I was apprehensive about the meeting, so soon after our row, but in the event he was the embodiment of charm; though by now I'd discovered how quickly he could assess a situation and turn on whatever charm was needed to achieve his desired outcome. Philippe smiled stiffly before vanishing into the kitchen.

After mutual appraisals Joe fetched her a tumbler of ice-cold orange juice and said: 'Tell me about your life Elaine.'

'My life? Where should I start?'

With the most important part, of course.'

'Well, I'm still finding that out. I went to art school, realized I had no talent whatsoever, changed to business school, got bored out of my mind, met my partner, fell hopelessly in love, began to live with him—.'

'Do you know why you're alive?'

'Of course not. Do you?'

'No. But it's the question I wake up with every morning and the one I grapple with every day. What else is there to do?'

'Well, there's doing something to reduce suffering, for starters. Changing the world just a little.'

Joe sat down, as if preparing for a long instruction.

'Would you lift your left arm for me please?'

Elaine hesitated, meeting his eyes, then slowly lifted it and held it level.

'Do you understand how you did that?'

She held his gaze. 'Only very vaguely. I made a decision to lift it, and then... well it just lifted. It all goes on behind the scenes, doesn't it?'

'Well, maybe there aren't any scenes. The point is, you made a decision. You had a thought which led to an action. Every single thing begins like that. An electron thinks before it changes its energy state.'

'No. I can't go along with that. Surely thoughts are the preserve of conscious beings?'

'And considering we've not the first idea what consciousness is, who's to say an electron isn't conscious? Anyway a thought is whatever precedes change. It doesn't have to be conscious, in the human sense. However simple thoughts are, they create the world we live in. And if we see what conditions our thought processes, we've as good as cracked the conflict problem. Who would kill another person once he's clearly seen the chain of thoughts that led up to the impulse to do it?'

'Isn't that a bit simplistic? We're not generally motivated by thoughts, are we? We get angry, or fearful, or outraged.'

'All those states begin with thoughts. You just have to catch them early enough. What I'm doing is writing some pauses for reflection into the program. And reflection introduces freedom. Choice. "Oh, maybe I won't do that thing after all...". If we get enough pauses wired in we might stand a chance of really changing things.'

'And 'we' are?'

He smiled, acknowledging the irony. 'Well, yes, as you rightly noticed, we are still few. But all great changes start in invisible ways.' He got to his feet and then astonished me by asking her: 'Will you stay to lunch?'

She gave him her most radiant smile. 'I'd be delighted.'

The midday sun was scorching, and Joe put up the shades over the table. Within five minutes he'd conjured up cheese, olives, bread, avocados, tomatos and a bowl of herb salad, plus two chilled bottles of Reisling – presumably to demonstrate that philosophers in the twenty-first century don't need to be hopelessly unhinged hair-shirt hermits. For some reason Joe seemed uncharacteristically responsive to her questioning, giving her answers that explained more than she asked for, or seemed to. I suddenly found myself wishing he would get up and leave, because with every sentence I felt he was in some obscure way digging a trap for himself.

'Morals have no place in a truly open society,' he was saying, 'because when there is complete trust there is no need for a code of conduct. Confucius said: "Morality is born when vision dies." Morality is always outdated. You have to be authentic. Then all your actions will be based in desire for the welfare of others.'

'I don't see how that follows. It sounds like the sort of thing they used to say at Sixties love-ins. For instance what do you do when there's a genuine conflict of wills? Or when someone is set on getting his own way regardless of others' needs? You can't resolve that by being 'authentic'.

"Well, you have to listen. Often what's really being asked for or demanded isn't what's being said. To take the Palestinian example, what you have there is two groups of passionate people expressing their past and present pain to each other. Each group believes itself to be the abused party. Each believes it has a divine right to the disputed land; and each believes it is justified in retrieving its rightful territory by force. Neither is prepared to listen to the other's pain, or accept responsibility for causing it. So how to get out of this prison? What do you think?'

'Make both sides listen?' Elaine looked like a cornered schoolgirl faced with a trick question.

'But how do you 'make' anyone listen? That's using force, isn't it?'

'I suppose. What's your answer?'

Joe assumed his inscrutable smile. 'I don't have an answer. Answers are part of the problem. People always have 'answers'. You go into any cafe in Jerusalem or Basra or Ramallah and you'll hear any number of people who have 'answers'. No. Something else is needed.' He allowed the silence to gather around us like a conjuror teasing out his yards of amazing silk.

Elaine sipped her glass hesitantly, then dragged her gaze back from the trees to Joe.

'Something else?'

'We don't have an adequate term for it. "Receptivity" is too weak. It's more like empathy. An active, incandescent touching of hearts. A complete abatement of the will to dominate, or the fear of being dominated. That's what I meant by authenticity. "A lifetime burning in every moment", to use Eliot's wonderful phrase. It's the only thing that has a hope of working. And hardly anyone knows it's even possible.'

Joe was weaving his magic, and Elaine, despite herself, was captured. She drank her wine and tried to put Joe's voice back into its box – reduce it to one man's opinions among a world of conflicting theories – but found she couldn't, and this angered her. Her hands fidgeted self-consciously with the empty glass, while she considered a different tack.

'Have you had children Joe?'

For a fraction of a second Joe hesitated. 'Not the biological kind.'

Elaine sensed her advantage. 'Oh, you really should try it. Looking after totally helpless humans is an essential learning experience. For once in your life someone else calls all the tunes. You're a servant in the very best sense. You have absolutely no freedom to indulge your ego.'

'And you think I'm indulging my ego here?' The cat poised to pounce.

'Oh no, of course not. How could I possibly judge that? I was thinking of our great leaders and their advisors – those who cite national security as an excuse to bomb half a million families. They simply couldn't do that if they were able to see the consequences in human terms.'

'The trouble with that is that bringing up children doesn't automatically endow one with imagination. That's something that has to be worked for. And it can take a lifetime. Young leaders are usually too full of testosterone to have the inclination to reflect on consequences. And old leaders have seen too many failures and are therefore too cynical.'

'And leaders of just the right age are too ambitious.' I offered.

Elaine took off her hat and laid it on the table as though accepting a challenge. 'I'd like to ask you about your sculptures.'

'What about them?'

'Well, Adam took me to see them, and I happened to touch one—.'

Something icy came into Joe's voice. 'Why did you do that, Adam?'

'Because she's an artist, and wanted to see them at first hand.' I suddenly felt defensive, realizing that the real reason for inviting her had nothing to do with art.

Joe said: 'You're not an artist are you, Elaine? No more than you're an innocent satisfier of curiosity.'

I watched her face as she gathered her resolve. She almost looked a different person as the high summer afternoon light rebounded from the white flagstones and remodelled her face into something irresolute and ill at ease among this dangerous intensity. She and Joe were not just on opposite sides of a deep-bedded boundary, but were the issue of opposing histories.

The struggle in her features relaxed into a smile. 'Well it's true I'm not here because of art: I'm writing an article on communities for the local paper. At least I'm hoping they'll take it.'

'You're here to destroy us.' Joe's tone made it clear it was not a question.

Elaine was stunned. 'No, of course not! For a start, why would I want to do that? What would I gain?'

'It's not important,' said Joe quietly. 'Whatever I say, or refrain from saying, you'll spin your story. And whether you consciously intend it or not, you will destroy us.'

'I assure you I've no desire at all to destroy you! I'm shocked you think that's why I'm here. And ok, I'm not a very good artist, but I am interested in how the mind makes sense of the world. I'm proposing to write a book about it. So this is personal research. Nobody has commissioned me to get a story out of you. That's the truth.'

Joe smiled and appeared to soften. 'I'm glad to hear it. Anyway, as they say in the films, I don't want to waste any more of your valuable time.'

'I rather think it should be me saying that.'

Elaine stood up and arranged her hair, claiming back some of her lost dignity.

'I'm very grateful for your time, really. And the great lunch. And I wish your project well.'

I walked with her to the gate.

'I'm really sorry it went so pear-shaped. Perhaps it was naive of me to expect you'd hit it off.'

'Oh that doesn't matter. I'm not upset by Joe. I think he's just a lonely man in need of care and friendship.'

'I've never thought of Joe like that.'

'No. He disguises it well. But he needs love very much. You can see it in his eyes: a hunger that's always hoping. And always denied.' She looked at me candidly. 'But he'll never admit what he really wants, so he'll go on drawing people to him and then reject them as soon as they find a fault. Which they inevitably will of course, unless they are brainwashed clones.'

'My God, how come you saw all that so quickly?'

'My turn to be silent, I think!'

With a coy smile, she swung her bag onto her shoulder and turned for the gate.

Regretfully I watched her trim figure dwindle down the drive and merge with the islands of brilliance beneath the trees. Then I walked slowly back to the house, and as my hand touched the cool metal of the kitchen door I felt a stab of loneliness and loss – not this time the loss of a potential lover, but of the very dream of love itself.

Chapter Nineteen

My decision to leave Joe's house came quite suddenly early one morning, as though a new chapter of my life had just been opened. Yet despite the feeling of freedom it brought, some sense of work unfinished tied me to the place, and to Joe, and of course he knew it. And I made the fatal mistake of arguing with him.

'I need one more thing doing Adam, if you wouldn't mind.'

Night hadn't quite left the bare and frigid corners of the kitchen. It was a part of the house that never got around to negotiating with sunlight, and the greeny daylight from the windows constantly unsettled it. Joe concentrated on cooking toast in the recalcitrant oven, staring into its black interior as though some alchemical transformation were underway.

'I need more space in the cabin. I thought you could extend the south wall out about four feet and glass it over, so I can have more light in the working area. As it is there's no room for us both to work together.'

'Is Philippe going to be here through the winter?'

'Yes. He's learning ceramics. I think he's got huge talent. I'd rather like to take him to Spain next year, to see the great art collections at Granada and Seville.'

'I don't think there's any place for me here.'

'I don't agree at all. I think this is exactly where you need to be. What would you do if you left? Probably waste your time with some entirely unsuitable woman.'

'Well, to be frank, I find living here with you almost impossible.'

He gave the oven door a stab with the rake, as though warning it of the consequences of disloyalty.

'But not absolutely impossible?'

'Near enough. You seem to go out of your way to be difficult and unpleasant. You were so rude to Elaine, I couldn't believe what I was hearing.'

'What you call rudeness is a value-judgement Adam. I don't make judgements. I try to act appropriately to the needs of each unique circumstance. But really none of that matters; you must learn to focus on what matters, and ignore everything else. Only one thing matters: self-knowledge. Being awake at all times. I take it as read that you're here to attain that state. If you're not you're wasting your time and everyone else's.'

All this time his eyes were fastened on the toast as though a moment's loss of vigilance might allow it to escape. Now he snapped off the gas and swung open the transparent door. A wave of heat assaulted the air.

'So are you up for it, this work?'

At some moments great and small forces compete for dominance in the mind, and the tangible world crowds in to witness them, unable to help itself, as though the unending millennia of stasis had been too much for it. And from where we stand inside these moments, there is simply no way to tell apart the momentous and historic from the merely familiar and contingent. Indeed from where we stand all moments look identical; there is seldom an opportunity to stretch on tiptoe and peer ahead to see what kind of world might flow from our tentative, feather-like choices, though I longed, in that ramshackle cubby-hole of history, to do just that.

'If you want it I'll do it,' I said at last.

I've still no idea what impelled me to make such a reckless statement, but as soon as the decision was made, of course, I realized what a ludicrously self-thwarting choice it was, and began to regret it bitterly. I wanted more than anything to get away from the place, to begin to live a normal human life again: receiving letters, meeting friends, buying trousers and towel rails, browsing in markets for that unsuspected bargain I'd never find a use for in a hundred years. Of course it was the freedom to do it that was crucial. I could still leave, clearly; I wasn't going to be hunted down and dragged back in chains, at least not by Joe. All the power Joe had was what I'd given him, in some desperate deal to win love and approval – and it wasn't working. So why not leave? I could escape all that instantly and go back to my vagabond existence, without ties, obligations, fear of rejection. It would be the easiest thing in the world. But it would be another failure, another avoidance in my quest of myself.

And now Elaine had come and insinuated her potent seed of doubt. Strange, I thought, that it hadn't occurred to me in all my months in Joe's company that he was simply lonely, and needed admiring and interesting people around him to give his life purpose. Could someone acquire such a persona of power and charisma, and yet be just as much a victim of his needs and fears as I was? Could someone who placed a state of total honesty at the very heart of his philosophy behave towards others with such evasiveness and duplicity? I couldn't accept this: it dropped too many doubts about the bedrock of human nature into my mind. People were weak, inconstant, subject to confusion, greed or overwhelming desire; they forgot their principles, or applied them partially or injudiciously; but they didn't cynically and consistently profess one thing, and in the same moment behave in complete contradiction to it, unless they were clinically schizoid. Therefore I was forced to conclude that Joe had been unaware of his callous behaviour and the effect it had had; that he'd been acting under some misperception of what motives were in play, and what their outcomes would eventually be.

After long hours of walking and thinking I watched the weary circle complete itself once again. I would stay; I'd do the work Joe wanted done, but this time in my own way, to my own standards, and without expecting any approval, help or praise. In this way I could stay sane and keep my self-respect, my pride in the work. But through the declining days of the autumn I couldn't keep my mind from trying to square this fiery circle, and my gut-criticism of Joe kept me separate and ill-tempered, unable to relax under the thoughtless beneficence of the sun. Despite my building work, from which I derived a unique satisfaction, (and increasingly so as my confidence in my skill grew) something inside me remained ignored, and was slowly starving to death.

Again Joe left me largely to my own devices as I worked on the alterations. Generally it went well, the early autumn weather was calm and fine, and I took frequent breaks to explore the surrounding countryside. I even asked Philippe to come with me on one of my walks. He and I had largely avoided each other after the first week or so of his stay; but I began to realize that such strategy only aggravated resentments and pre-existing clashes of temperament. So I was surprised when I discovered we actually had much in common: not least a chronic loneliness and distrust of women. As I didn't exactly celebrate these qualities in myself it wasn't at all surprising that I found them irritating in him. But being of simple European stock he didn't benefit from the good old Anglo-Saxon tradition of equivocation. He was hurt, and the pain ran directly to his belief centre, and took up permanent residence.

We turned north and headed for a hill I'd skirted on my way down from the Quantocks. Climbing briskly through the sparse scrub I felt my optimism returning. Philippe stumbled along behind, stopping frequently to get his breath, and complaining at the pace I was setting.

'It'll do you good', I shouted back. 'Get good English oxygen into your brain! Stimulate ze little grey cells!'

The summit of the hill was free of trees, and the view was stunning: the Brendon Hills in the west shimmered in yellow heat haze; there was no wind, and the spell of calm weather seemed to hold the landscape beyond time's grasp. I unpacked our philosopher's picnic and made myself comfortable in a shallow bowl of dry grass. Philippe crouched beside the paper plates and eyed them from different angles like a crow who can't quite believe his luck. Looking at him I had to recognise an uneasy empathy.

'You know Philippe, I don't think we're all that different after all. Allowing for our different backgrounds. We're both non-joiners.'

'What do you mean?'

'We both hover at the edges of things, waiting to see if they'll bite.'

'I don't understand. How should they "bite"?'

'What I mean is, you don't trust things to be what they seem. So you keep your distance, until they've proved themselves.'

'I suppose so.' He immediately looked deflated.

'I'm not criticising you. It's a good habit. But it makes for a lonely life. It means you don't grasp opportunities. And the people who do get the worms.'

'Worms?'

'You know the saying, "the early bird gets the worm"?'

'Oh, yes. I see. I'm not early enough?'

'Not aggressive enough.'

'I'd rather not have worms than betray my principles. The world's in such a terrible state because of aggression. If my highest aim is to be authentic in all situations what justification is there for aggression?'

'No, you're right of course. There isn't.' I addressed myself to our crow's lunch. 'Tell me about your teacher. What were his methods of teaching?'

Philippe's eyes brightened. 'He had many methods. He lectured and gave seminars the way most teachers do. But he also had his special circle that met at his house. They were the students who he'd invited to study with him after they'd been to his philosophy courses. You didn't apply to join the circle: you were chosen. And you were told never to talk about it outside the circle to anyone.'

'Oh. Why the secrecy?'

'He had a big thing about not becoming popular: he believed to be popular was philosophical death. The fewer people who knew about you the more effective your teaching could be. So he actively discouraged students from coming to his classes. For instance he'd also switch classrooms at the last moment to confuse people. And later on he took to turning up disguised as a student himself, and just sit down at the back and ask where the hell the fool of a lecturer was. Things like that. Sometimes he'd come in wearing a dirty brown cleaner's coat and carrying a metal bucket and mop, so he wouldn't be accosted by students on the way to his class. But in the end those things only made people more curious and determined to seek him out. So he had to resort to more serious methods.'

'Such as?'

'Oh, he announced he was resigning from the faculty. He disappeared for a whole term. He even somehow managed to get the authorities in on it. They appointed another professor of philosophy to run his official course, while his own course was going on at the same time up in an unheated store room hundreds of metres away from the main block. He still ended up with more students than the official course, because word quickly got round that it was another of his ploys to put people off the scent.'

'It sounds like he was a very clever self-publicist.'

'No. That wasn't his purpose at all. He was actually immensely shy. If he could have stopped teaching altogether he would have. But he also had a deep love of teaching real people: those who had the genuine philosophical spirit of ego-free inquiry. There were very few of those. At one point he dismissed a student from the course because he left half an hour early to go shopping for his girlfriend's birthday. And yet it wasn't unkindness: he didn't care a hoot about punctuality or conforming to the rules; it was just that he demanded total commitment to the spirit of acquiring true knowledge. He sometimes said there were thousands of good teachers prepared to teach ordinary people, but very few able to teach gods.'

'So what happened to him? I mean, if he was so exacting why wasn't he better known? You'd think some of his devotees would have promoted him a lot more.'

'He instilled in everyone his own passion for privacy. It was a bit like the masonic tradition: no one would admit to being in his circle, even to others they knew were also in it. They'd go so far as to ignore each other completely if they happened to meet socially.'

'One wonders how he actually managed to teach anything at all.'

'Yes, well few would have recognised that he ever did teach anything. He always insisted he never taught anything to anyone. But then so did Socrates. It was a kind of tradition wasn't it? But people still learnt something. That was his secret: by just being authentic he was giving his real teaching. It wasn't anything you could see. On the surface he was just a bit of an unworldly professor teaching the usual academic stuff that people expected so they could get diplomas and so forth. But to his few true students he would disown all that as worthless dross.'

'And do you think those methods worked in the end? I mean, did they have a lasting effect?'

'It's hard to tell, because nobody talked about the teaching, and few met each other socially, even long after they left. It's like none of it existed except in the moment it was communicated. Something strange happened for an instant and then it all just disappeared like smoke. But I think it did have an effect: people don't completely forget, do they? An almost invisible change can have incalculable consequences way down the line. So maybe it changed their lives in subtle ways.'

'And what about you? Did it change you?'

'I think so... well it must have done.' He weighed a small green apple in his hand, but hesitated to bite into it. 'You can't meet someone like that without being changed, can you?' He contemplated the apple before replacing it uneaten, and instead took a handful of walnuts, suddenly cramming them into his mouth like a starving man. Then a sadness clouded his eyes. 'The only thing is, he was impossible to get close to, in any way. He would always avoid talking about his feelings, or showing tenderness. I never once saw him be close in that way. So I think he was very lonely himself, and attracted lonely people to him. He didn't really know how to handle that side of people, their emotions and neediness. I think that's why in the end those students who wanted a more personal friendship left. Many of them got married I think.'

'But you didn't?'

'No. I came here instead.'

'And do you find Joe different? I mean, easier to be close to?'

'Oh yes, much easier. There's no comparison. I could never imagine ever being George's lover, not in a million years. He was definitely against physical intimacy.'

'His lover? Are you saying—?' I ground to a halt, unable to get the words to form.

'Of course, yes. We've been lovers for several weeks. I assumed you knew.'

'No. I'd no idea. You're sleeping with him?'

'Yes. It surprises you?'

'Yes. Frankly it does. I'm really shocked.'

'But why? It's completely normal. I mean, he's normal, and I'm normal. Why shouldn't two normal people be lovers?'

'But he's not just a normal man: he's a teacher. How can you possibly learn anything from him if you're having a sexual relationship?'

'I think he would say: how can you possibly learn anything if you're not having a sexual relationship?'

'But, the point is, it's not a relationship of equality. You're his student. He's in a position of power. It skews the whole thing to introduce sex.'

'This is just your bad English conditioning. You keep philosophy and life all in airtight little boxes so they can't smell each other: here is religion, here is philosophy, here is love, here is friendship, and here is sex. And they're all kept in ignorance of each other's existence. So how can you possibly learn from any of them? This is what Georges couldn't understand. He tried to believe the feelings could be kept away from the philosophy without reducing both to travesties of themselves.'

'But it's all so dangerous! Can't you see that? Sexual feelings run so deep! It's like tossing a match into a dry forest. Once it's started there's almost no way of limiting it.'

'But that's exactly the point! Why limit it? This is your fundamental English fear: letting the fire out of the box! Why be afraid of it?'

'Because it destroys people! It creates emotions that can ruin people's lives. Surely that's obvious?'

'You're mistaking free-energy with imprisoned energy. It's only imprisoned energy that's destructive. Energy that's not allowed to flow. As your beautiful William Blake said, energy is eternal delight. Why be afraid of eternal delight?'

His question and his revelation reverberated in my brain as we retraced our steps down the hill. It was a good question: why indeed be afraid of delight? Surely it was the fundamental force that nurtured us and made us able to love one another? Without it we are merely machines for surviving. Yet there had been so little of it in my life, and the need for it had possibly driven me to kill someone I loved dearly (But still not proven, my lords).

I wasn't a worthy vessel, I concluded. That was it. No delight would ever settle in me until I'd purified myself. I could suffer all the humiliations at the hands of women (and now men) I liked; build all the perfect cabins I liked; even throw myself from second-floor windows – it would make no difference to the fundamental fact: I was a house built of guilt, an edifice of age-old impurity. I had to be burned up, so I could start again with a clean slate. Then I might stand a chance.

I was following behind Philippe trying to keep my balance on the steep ground when I chanced to look up: far in the distance across the valley to the west there was a pale grey haze. When I looked more carefully I could make out an irregular red smear stretching along the hillside: fire. Philippe looked up and saw it too.

'Will it spread here to us?'

'Oh no, not a chance. There's no wind. It'll burn itself out in an hour or two. In any case the woods are too broken up. Lots of nice damp pasture in between.'

'That's a relief. In France we've had huge fires that burned for weeks. Nobody could stop them.'

'Ah yes. But our English fires know their place. You wouldn't find an English fire joining forces to overthrow the medieval oaks!'

We arrived back just as the sun was grazing the hilltops. A rich golden light suffused the western flank of the house, so that it seemed like a scene from Samuel Palmer's mystical period. Reluctant to go inside whilst any remnant of its benediction remained, I stood and tried to take in the majesty of the colours while Philippe went ahead into the house.

When I finally entered the kitchen, Philippe and Joe were hunched over an open newspaper spread out across the table. There was a black silence that made me want to retreat immediately to the sun's golden magnanimity. Philippe turned to me with his jewel-sharp eyes.

'This is bad news Adam.'

Not understanding his glance, I joked:

'Have the aliens come?'

'Yes,' said Joe, 'and with your invitation.'

I read the headline:

POWERS OF DARKNESS THRIVE IN SOMERSET CULT

'Is this about us?'

'Read it,' said Joe from the window. I sat down, hoping the world hadn't ended while we'd been playing philosophers.

"English teacher Adam Stone is the most recent addition to the dark world behind the decayed and forbidding gothic edifice of Moreton Rectory, just a stone's throw from the peace-loving village of Kingston St Mary. In an exclusive interview he told me: 'We're trying to destroy our social conditioning. [The sect's founder and resident guru] Joe Baker believes it's possible to de-condition anyone by a series of mental exercises, so that they act without fear or desire. We're ultimately trying to create a new human who will far outstrip all present humans just as ordinary men outstrip monkeys.'"

'Is that what you said?' Joe asked quietly.

'Of course it isn't! Not remotely. Who on earth wrote this garbage?'

'Your beautiful friend Elaine.'

'I don't believe it. I can't believe she'd do this!'

'She's a journalist Adam. It's her job to provide stories. And boy has she provided a story!'

It got worse. Apparently I'd said we were using mind-altering drugs to achieve states of sexual abandon and euphoria; that we had regular orgies in the house; that we invoked devil-worship and conjured demons; that Joe ruled the whole place by playing on fear and threats of terrible retribution if we ever thought of leaving; and that he used his powerful physical charisma to draw impressionable young men to him and then made use of their bodies for his gratification before growing bored with them, when they would be summarily dropped from the inner circle on some pretext of having failed the initiation. The article used just about every innuendo in the book to paint the grim picture of a dangerous cult led by a man bent on using guilt, shame and fear to satisfy his perverted desires. When I'd read it to the end I felt nauseous, and there was cold sweat standing on my brow.

'You must realize this is a bagful of bat-shit from start to finish. I didn't give her the slightest basis for these stories.'

'Adam, journalists don't need a basis; all they need is half a word – and more or less any word will do. You shouldn't have even thought of inviting her here: if you'd asked me I would have categorically forbidden it. You broke a fundamental rule.'

'Well maybe it'll just be seen for what it is. After all, people know that ninety percent of what's printed in these things is garbage.'

'They might know that but they still want to believe it's true. This culture starves our imaginations so much that we thirst to distraction for this kind of poison. That's why the populist press thrives like a rat in a sewer.'

'God, Joe, I didn't for one second imagine this would happen.'

'Well it has.' Joe sat down and fixed his stare onto me. 'Now you listen to me. We can't afford to have any dealings at all with these people! They have no interest in finding the truth: they want sensation – whatever transgresses our insane system of taboos. And anything slightly different from tedious suburban normality is fair game. So we need to be prepared for what will inevitably follow: have no doubt they'll root us out. There'll be apparently innocuous requests for interviews. There'll be photographers trying to capture compromising images. They'll fly kites and hope we respond. We'll be waylaid whenever we leave the house. We must be on our guard every single minute of every day. Niether of you must say anything to strangers, no matter how plausible they might seem. If we stay under cover they'll eventually lose interest and go after some easier quarry. Is that completely clear?'

I had no choice but to assent, even though I believed Joe was overreacting. I didn't think the media would consider us interesting enough to pursue beyond a day or two. I was wrong. It was barely beginning.

The first sign that things were not as they should be was the increase in 'passers by' outside the house. Prior to the appearance of the article we'd had about one person a week go past the gate; now there were two or three each day, and most of them stopped to gaze or take photographs before moving on. This in itself wasn't a problem: they generally kept at a distance and seldom stopped for more than a few seconds. But after them came the hate mail: letters typed in capitals or scrawled on grubby scraps of paper that made it clear the writers believed everything printed in the article, and thought we were scum and dangerous lunatics who should be either thrown into a deep pit and set light to, or deported to Siberia – or ideally both. And of course there were the threats, the violence of which made me wonder if we hadn't unwittingly slipped collectively back into the Dark Ages. One such letter said if we didn't immediately release the dozens of helpless children they knew for a fact we were holding locked in hidden windowless rooms (and they knew because they had happened to come past in the night and heard their terrible heart-rending screams) they would set fire to the whole house and us in it and make the world a safer place to bring up innocent children (and if the police refused to take action they personally knew of a dozen local stalwarts who were just itching for the chance to take things into their own very capable hands). And so on and so on. Every day there was some new intrusion. The photographers became bolder, while a local campaign was raised to harry us into abandoning the house.

We adopted a siege mentality, subsisting on our own produce and what we'd been able to store before the article had appeared. Joe remained amazingly upbeat throughout the ordeal, always relying on his principles of using whatever happened as a valuable resource for self-knowledge.

'These events are gifts, if we can only recognise them,' he told us gravely. 'When this happened in Australia I survived because I was able to be completely free from any desire to avoid the situation, or punish the perpetrators, or even justify myself. They had nothing to grab hold of. If I'd given way to reacting against them I'd have been finished. We have to remember at all times that it's their own fears they're attacking, not any reality. The world brings us these situations in order that we can grow beyond them.'

While the outer conflict gorged on its own fantasies, I was locked in my own inner battle. Joe couldn't be argued with on his principles; he had worked everything out meticulously into his own self-consistent philosophy. But I couldn't so easily dismiss what Elaine had said as she was leaving on that fateful day: Joe was a man dependent on those around him for the satisfaction of his emotional needs. Without the sustaining energy of our admiration he might well have sunk into indifference and self-destruction. I tried to convince myself this was a forgivable human frailty and of no consequence; but still it was a flaw, and my unforgiving mind could admit no flaws in those I'd appointed as my mentor, and especially in one who'd been so viciously contemptuous of my own weaknesses. And the outcome of this inner battle was that I couldn't give him my unqualified support at just the time when he most needed it. Added to which, Philippe's revelation that they were having an affair seriously darkened the issue. The fact was I was secretly furious about this and had not the slightest idea what to do about it. I desperately needed to talk to someone, but as I couldn't leave the house this was clearly impossible. The pain of being incarcerated in my self-generated hell gradually became unbearable, yet neither could I leave without branding myself a traitor – a rat slinking away from a burning ship.

Then one evening when I was feeling particularly oppressed by loneliness I remembered Klaus. He was someone who knew Joe well and would know how to deal with him without falling into a destructive role. I went into the games room and slid the bolt shut. The phone rang for ages, and I was on the point of giving up when at last I heard Klaus's voice.

'Adam. How good to hear you! How are things?'

'Not good Klaus. We have a full-scale siege brewing up here. Did you read the article about us?'

'Fraid not. Newspapers bring me out in a rash.'

'Well it let mayhem loose among the locals. I think we're in danger of becoming a scapegoat for all the changes going on around here. I wish you could come down.'

'If necessary I will. But I'm sure Joe will have a strategy for dealing with the problem. He may not be the best communicator, but he's usually ahead of everyone else in an emergency. And he knows what he's up against. Give him space.'

'I may go to see a friend for a couple of days. I don't seem to be much use to Joe now he's got his new student.'

'Just remember his mind doesn't work in the same way as most people's. With Joe things are rarely what they seem. So be slow to judge him.'

'I'll try to remember that.'

'Oh and Adam: there is one very important thing he may have overlooked. One of the sculptures in that room is extremely dangerous. It's not one of Joe's making: it's one we brought back from Mexico: a black bull with gold hooves and horns. We didn't realize what we'd got until I inadvertently held it. You mustn't handle it, or let anyone else do so. It's lethal.'

'Joe's got the room locked up now. It's safe for the time being.'

'That's good. Best not go in there. When this craziness has blown over I'll come down and destroy a few of those carvings in the proper way. They shouldn't have been allowed to survive once we knew their nature.'

'We've had letters from people threatening to burn the house down. I don't feel Joe's safe here. I think he underestimates how angry some people are. And needless to say he won't tell the police.'

'I think I'd probably best come over anyway. Can you let him know I'll be there just as soon as I can arrange it?'

'Will do. Thank you. I'm really grateful.'

In view of the threats, one might have expected Joe to temper his behaviour with respect to Philippe, but far from it: he made no attempt at all to conceal his habits or his beliefs – even after we'd discovered a press photographer with a portable ladder and a thermos flask skulking in the garden at six in the morning. His strategy for dealing with outsiders (if he had to deal with them) was 'never apologise, never explain'. But increasingly I felt relegated to the status of outsider myself: maybe I simply wasn't good looking enough, or didn't praise him enough, or wasn't compliant enough, or asked too many questions (I didn't). Whatever the truth, I woke up very early one morning in October and instantly decided the only sane thing to do was to try to find Elaine. I had no illusions about having an affair with her: that seemed firmly off her agenda; but I very badly needed to find out why she wrote that article, and why she'd been so evasive with me. I suppose I simply couldn't believe that someone would behave like that without having a very good reason; especially someone with such beautiful, generous and guileless deep brown eyes.

Before six I was safely in the lane to Kingston, my green backpack loaded with bread, dried fruit and cheese, a huge vermilion sun floating free of the golden chestnut trees, and my heart lighter than it had been for more weeks than I could remember, not knowing if I would see Joe or Philippe or the room of lethal sculpture ever again.

Chapter Twenty

I phoned the number Elaine had given me from a kiosk in the centre of the village. It rang for a long time before a young girl's voice answered.

'Mum's asleep. Can you call back?'

'About an hour?'

The child seemed doubtful. 'I'm not sure. Who are you?'

'My name's Adam. I'm a friend of your Mum's.'

'She has to go out to be tested.'

'Oh. Sounds like it's not a good day to see her then.'

Elaine's voice came on the line.

'Hello. Who is this?'

'It's Adam.'

'Oh yes, Adam. Hello. Sorry about that. It's a bit early.'

'I'm sorry to get you up. It's just that I'd really like to talk to you.'

'Oh dear. The article I suppose.' I could hear her daughter trying to get her attention, and beyond that, a dog barking.

'Well, not really. It's more advice I need. I really would appreciate it if you could spare an hour.'

'Well – it's not the best time, but—'

'I'll buy you lunch.'

'Later would be better. Let me think... could you make it about five o'clock? I'll do supper. How does that sound?'

'Sounds absolutely wonderful. Thank you.'

I scrawled her address, my spirits already lifting. The prospect of talking to someone who was neither Joe nor Philippe made me quite euphoric.

I had the whole day free before my appointment with Elaine. The address she'd given me was in a village in the Blackdown Hills, and I reckoned I could easily walk there by five o'clock – almost ten hours for uninterrupted thinking and enjoying the maturing colours of early autumn. But as I made my way along the footpaths south of Taunton I saw there was something disturbingly different about the landscape. It was as if there wasn't enough space for the material that had to be fitted into it, and two gigantic slabs of rock had jammed up against each other so that they'd broken through the earth, carrying up everything that had been above them: trees, fences, telegraph poles, even roads. If we'd been in Turkey or Indonesia I wouldn't have been too surprised, but earthquakes of this severity were unheard of in Britain in modern times. Luckily the faults were discontiguous so I was able to negotiate them fairly easily. I crossed a few fields in which there were cattle huddled into one corner, hard against the boundary fences. I came to a small village in which an entire church with its steeple was leaning at least ten degrees from the vertical, and yet it seemed not one stone of the structure had been displaced. A small group of people had gathered in the churchyard to gaze up at it. One was taking photographs continuously as though at any moment the entire edifice might collapse into rubble. I snuck open the latch of the gate and walked past the nearly horizontal gravestones to the cluster of onlookers.

'What happened?'

The photographer turned to me. He had a short grey beard and intense fearful grey eyes.

'That's just what we're all wondering. Best guess so far is it's some kind of subsidence. On account of the drought.'

'Subsidence my arse!' said a younger man behind him. 'It's our messing with the climate that's done this. It was on the news as it's all across the country. How can that be subsidence, I ask you?'

When I came to the village square there were more people huddled in twos and threes in sullen debate, while children chased each other around the fountain near one end. It seemed the disruption was very recent, and not confined to one part of the village. I found a cafe that was just opening, and went inside for some coffee and toast.

'Does anyone know what's causing these changes to the land?' I asked the woman at the counter as she was preparing the coffee machine.

'There's no shortage of theories. Everyone's got their favourite. But as usual the government's caught on the hop. Useless bloody shower if you want my opinion. Beats me how they got in in the first place.'

'Have there been any earth-tremors?'

'Not as I've heard. Do you want milk?'

'No thanks.'

She placed the tray noisily on the counter. 'Saturday everything was normal. I remember because there was a wedding in the afternoon. Then yesterday morning I got a phonecall from my sister to go and look. I couldn't believe what I saw. I had to go back twice before it sunk in. And now they're saying it's the same everywhere. Things all tipped over. Roads stuck in mid-air. The world's gone totally mad. I've been saying that for years but now it really has. There's plenty of butter there if you want it. Have it while you can, eh? You don't know what tomorrow's going to bring.'

I took my breakfast to a small wooden table by the window. There were no newspapers, so I sat and watched the people outside as they tried to make sense of events. For a moment there was an almost tangible rumour in the air, and I felt as though I were in a Prague café on the eve of the communist revolution, waiting for the tanks to grind down the undefended streets. I looked at the group of people nearest to me: two young women and a middle-aged one; there was real fear in their eyes, and the older one repeatedly glanced down at the flagstones around her as though expecting them to erupt and reveal some kind of monster from the deep forcing its way into daylight. Even the dogs were standing around looking nervous and growling at nothing. I could almost hear them muttering to each other (the dogs, I mean) 'there's something not right here, something's going badly wrong with the world – let's run away while we still can.' And then I realized I had heard a voice. But it wasn't a dog's; more to the point, it wasn't human.

'Hello Adam. I'd like your help with a little problem.'

It had been a long time since I'd heard that disembodied voice, and I couldn't decide if I was relieved or horrified to hear it. I now knew it was coming from a source a thousand light years away, in the Great Bear constellation; and its owner was a telepathic sentient super-computer called Les. Les had sent the Cube to earth as a little gift in recognition of services rendered, to wit, providing him with thousands of human jokes to analyse: actually, to be quite accurate, they were Russian jokes. Why did he think these were so important? Because he'd decided they held the key to the irrational – and it was this irrational that threatened the entire galaxy, and beyond, with chaos and destruction.

The really irritating thing about Les and his cronies (yes, there were a few of them) was he had an absolutely appalling sense of timing. He'd break into my mind without warning at any time of the day or night, regardless of who I happened to be with, or what intimate activity I might be occupied with – and ask the most idiotic questions you could possibly imagine about the precise meaning and cultural significance of some ridiculous joke, and expect an instant and detailed answer, which he would feed into his colossal data bank spread out among the stars. A fraction of a second later he'd be back to say my information had significantly deepened his 'people's' entire understanding of the nature of sentient life-forms throughout the sector. Not bad for explaining a single crummy joke, eh? But I'd become mindful of the saying, 'beware of aliens bearing gifts': apparently this had been a problem throughout human history, and this particular alien was proving no less troublesome. Unsurprisingly, no-one actually believed the Cube had been sent entirely for our benefit, and a few singularly ungrateful individuals were plotting to blow it up with nuclear warheads, which for some reason they imagined would be effective in rendering it unusable. The trouble was, I was the only person on earth who knew – because I had it from the horse's mouth, so to speak – where it had come from. Les had told me himself (and of course I believed him unconditionally) that he had made and sent it to help us overcome our little local difficulty. And now here he was again, with his usual immaculate timing, wanting my help. He knew how much I enjoyed crunchy hot buttered toast, but did he care a hoot about interrupting my rare solitary pleasure?

'Hello Les,' I said out loud, out of pure habit. 'How's tricks?'

Les had long since given up the futile effort of analysing human colloquialisms, although I still enjoyed throwing a few at him from time to time, to see if he'd take a swipe at the bait.

'You've probably noticed our little present is beginning to be more active in your world.'

'Oh, you mean stuff like making people fade out while I'm talking to them? And churches acting like they've been out on the tiles all night? Yes, it had come to my attention. In fact it's come to the attention of quite a few people it seems.'

'This is merely an anomaly, Adam. It's an inevitable part of the process of transforming the way you behave towards one another. It's altering the electron-spin equations just a little, just enough to normalize consciousness to a level where it can't threaten other races.'

'Normalize? I'm not sure I like the sound of that. Do you by any chance mean restrict?'

'Adam, what we're changing is the strength of the nuclear interactions within atoms. A very small weakening of one of these forces will have the required effect. Sadly it will also have a number of other effects which we can't completely predict. But we think on the whole it's worth doing.'

'A pity you didn't think to consult us first.'

'But you would not have agreed. And then we would have alerted you to the nature of the operation, and you would have opposed it. As it is—.'

'As it is there are desperate groups of fanatics aiming nuclear weapons at a certain population centre in Northern England, even as we speak.'

'We are aware of that. And this is your part in the mission, Adam: you will communicate with the terrorists. Persuade them by any means that the Cube is benign – in fact it is their only chance of survival. Tell them you are the channel of communication between the Cube's creators and humanity, and that we have your welfare and continuation as a species as our sole motive for intruding into your affairs. Also tell them—.'

The other extremely irritating thing about Les was his naive and unshakeable belief that all intelligent races spoke the truth and nothing but the truth at all times. Heaven knows why he persisted in this belief when his communication with so many other races over zillions of years must have shown him that the exact opposite was the norm. I'd tried many times to demonstrate that the jokes he valued so highly and found so richly laden with insight were themselves founded on the fact that the human race had, at best, an interesting relationship with truth. But it all fell on deaf uplink processors.

'Les, I do appreciate your faith in me, I really do. But I simply can't do what you ask. It's not in my power. To begin with, these 'terrorists' don't operate from any one point, and probably none of them are even in this country. It would be extremely difficult to find them. Secondly, I have absolutely no authority or status in anybody's eyes. I'm totally unknown: they would simply ignore me. And if I made it impossible for them to ignore me, they'd just have me quietly disappeared. No one would worry about it. This happens all the time to anyone who tries to prevent terrorism or injustice. It's not even considered worth reporting on in many countries. Who needs troublemakers? And thirdly, many people who are not terrorists greatly fear your machine: they believe it's part of an invasion force quietly waiting for the rest to arrive. So I'd be very unpopular indeed if I got up on my soapbox to try to explain that, while it is in fact alien, it's also a friendly alien. We've had too many evil-alien films in our culture for people to imagine there are any good ones.'

'But Adam—.'

'And fourthly, I'm on my way to a dinner engagement with a beautiful young woman, and I'll be late if I stay gassing with you any longer. Oh yes, and I almost forgot to tell you: I'm unemployed, almost penniless and probably also by now homeless. Not a strong position for an intergalactic ambassador to be in.'

I'd been sitting in the same position so long my left leg had gone catatonic with boredom. I dragged it over to the counter to pay my bill. But of course Les, not having the slightest concept of physical bodies and their innate limitations, went on talking to me as though he was simply tagging along behind.

'You must try to overcome these human limitations. The stakes are very high: if the Cube fails in its mission we shall have no other recourse than to render your world harmless by more direct means. But I'm sure you will find a way. Our detailed study of your history has shown us that your entire evolution has been mediated by lone individuals acting out of conviction, unsupported by the belief of their contemporaries. They succeeded in saving their world by force of will alone. Why are you different from these?'

'I am completely different from them!' I shouted as I was negotiating the vertiginous flagstones of the square. An elderly man with a pipe turned to stare at me, as well he might; I gave thanks that most people just assumed I was talking on my mobile, and didn't give me a second glance.

Still, his question brought me to an abrupt halt, causing a small child to crash into me and let his bleeping and flashing plastic strato-cruiser dive in imagined flames to the ground. It was a stunningly apt question, and I'd no ready answer to it. I wasn't Homer, Aristotle, or Seneca, or Wat Tyler, or Cromwell or Fox: sure, I had a functioning brain, two eyes, arms, legs, feet and all the basic apparatus required for survival; but there was still something rather fundamental missing: the gene, maybe, responsible for turning a run of the mill Caucasian layabout with a propensity for philosophising into a great reforming leader or revolutionary hero.

'Les?'

'Yes, Adam.' I still couldn't believe the crystal clarity and immediacy of this voice coming from a thousand light years distant, but I'd somehow 'adapted' so that my disbelief didn't interfere with the reality.

'Les, you need to go back to you database and look up "human genetic disposition." It should answer your question quicker than I can.'

'Our reading of your literature implies that genetic disposition is modifiable. Otherwise evolution would not be possible.'

Match point.

I was beginning to find the old tedium returning to my conversations with Les, because there were some things you shouldn't ever need to explain: they were blindingly obvious to anyone over five with the normal complement of chairs in his kitchen. But I suppose alien hypercomputers were different.

'Evolution takes thousands of years for even the smallest imaginable change to happen. For someone's genetic makeup to change significantly enough to turn him into an Alexander or a Caesar within one lifetime would require literally a miracle. It just can't happen without the intervention of the gods, and since they don't exist—.'

'Oh but they do exist now, Adam. We've created them. You have one with you at this moment. Would you care for a demonstration?'

It sounded like one of those offers one should *always* refuse. But reckless curiosity beat me to it.

'Ok, why not?'

'Do you really want me to answer that question, Adam?'

'No, thank you Les.'

'Watch the fountain.'

The fountain just across the square was an old black millstone grit affair doing what old fountains were pretty good at doing: throwing narrow jets of water up into the air and letting them curve gracefully to earth again, showing us in a poetic way how the water of life endlessly issues from the depths for our spiritual nourishment, and the great cycle of creation completes itself in returning to its source, and so everything goes on harmoniously in accordance with the Word. Well, as I watched the water streams were in an instant transformed into four blindingly bright arcs of fire, shooting upwards into the morning sky to a height of over twelve feet, but of course not falling back to earth as the water had done. Everyone in the square instantly froze in their positions and stared at the fountain as though their heads had been suddenly magnetized and locked to its irresistible pole. One or two people with more presence of mind than most whipped out their mobile phones and managed to capture the moment in all its B-movie improbability. For maybe ten seconds the spectacle persisted, before just as suddenly reverting to normality again, and the familiar plashing of water cascading coolly into the pool resumed. But for many more seconds the involuntary spectators continued locked in their poses, so that the scene resembled nothing so much as a still photograph capturing the instant following a famous disaster such as the crash of an airship or the sudden cacophonous arrival of tanks. Then one by one the figures began to move and turn to one another, as each one tried to convince himself he'd experienced a momentary failure of sanity – an effort which became easier as the seconds flicked by and the fountain continued to throw perfectly normal water into the air with gestures of immemorial blandness. I didn't dare meet anyone's eyes, in case they suspected, from my unshocked appearance, that I was the instigator of such a singular transgression of the natural order.

'Ok Les,' I muttered, turning to face away from the statuesque crowd. 'You've made your point. You've created a topic of conversation that won't be exhausted for decades. But I still don't see how being able to turn water into fire is going to help me appease the men with a grudge against the Cube. We're in the twenty-first century now, not the tenth. Small-time itinerant miracle-workers don't cut much ice these days. Everyone's seen far better tricks on TV. The point is, if I start defending it I'll be immediately identified as one of the Enemies of Mankind. And you may just possibly have noticed that I personally don't possess any nuclear warheads. I don't even have a catapult. So really what I'm saying is, I'm not the man for this job. Sorry.'

As I'd been talking I'd left the square and taken a narrow road winding westwards towards the Blackdown Hills. I felt very relieved to be away from the crowds in the village, where I'd felt increasingly like the Martian at the wedding party. I couldn't help thinking that Les was losing the plot slightly: to put on that sort of spectacle in the town square couldn't but make people suspect the Cube and its minions were the modern equivalent of witches and were responsible for the present global troubles – which to some extent they were.

The road climbed and dipped and zig-zagged around the lower slopes of the hills. There was almost no traffic, which puzzled me, until I came to a bridge over a small river and saw that the entire structure had sheared half way across, so that each half projected out over the water; there was nothing to prevent traffic from overshooting and ending up a wreck on the riverbed. I was surprised that the police hadn't installed warning notices, until I realized this must have happened very recently. So why hadn't I felt any ground-shocks of any kind? If it was some kind of geological fault causing it, why had no one detected it earlier?

Then I had the idea of calling in the experts.

'Les, are you there?'

'I'm here, Adam. How can I help?'

'Well, you can call your dogs off, for a start.'

'Dogs?'

'The land around here resembles the aftermath of a battle. It's impossible to carry on with normal life in many places.'

'An effect of the minor adjustments we've made to the lower level nuclear binding force, which will mostly affect the lighter atomic weights. We went to great lengths to ensure there would be no instability effects in the elements you use for nuclear fission.'

'I suppose we should be grateful for that.'

'By all means, if it makes you feel better.'

'What would make me feel better right now is if I could get across this bridge. I'm a hopeless swimmer. Any suggestions?'

'Have you tried jumping?'

'What I'm afraid of is that it's changing all the time. It's as though the metal is boiling.'

'We have no power over low level individual effects. We program the Cube, but from there on it implements the transformations at the atomic level. But you could probably jump the gap safely if you hurry.'

'You mean it's still moving?'

'The territory is unstable, probably because the altered orbital energy ratios are modifying the valencies and creating new chemical reactions, which in turn are altering—.'

'Yes, ok Les. I can do without the figures.'

I ran onto the bridge, but as I reached the middle I could see the shear area was indeed still changing: its edges were rippling and curling back as though the metal was a fluid under the influence of extreme tidal forces. I began to experience a degree of vertigo at the thought that my feet were standing on something insubstantial rather than steel and tarmac. Gathering my courage I leapt over the gap, and was hugely relieved to meet stable ground on the other side. When I glanced back I saw there was now a four foot gap between the sections, and the edges were melting back all the time. Les's 'minor adjustments' were having effects far beyond the changes he'd planned. A bit embarrassing for a god, I thought. I wondered if he'd get demoted to a lower-profile domestic project after this.

Beyond the bridge the countryside seemed normal enough; at least the landscape stayed still long enough for me to walk through it; I made good progress, and by mid-afternoon I was only a couple of kilometres from Elaine's house in the hamlet of South Brockley. I was looking forward to seeing her and sorting out the muddle of the article: I was certain she hadn't written what was printed; it just wasn't in her to be so vindictive. And yet no-one else had access to the stuff about the sculptures, or about my role there: she must have been at least complicit in its writing.

It had turned into a perfect autumn afternoon: a sharpness in the air, mitigated by a caressing warmth from the intimate apricot sun. There was no wind, and I sensed a peace and beneficence in everything I passed. I realized I wanted to share this with someone – but everyone I'd tried to share it with had seemed to get entirely the wrong message. Maybe falling in love was not the best way to embark on this process. Still, I hadn't fallen in love with Joe or Philippe, and I nevertheless ended up adrift and alone – albeit with a sexless, disembodied, joke-obsessed alien supercomputer to talk to whenever I felt the need.

Elaine's cottage was halfway up a steep lane running between tall ivy-clotted hedges. Indeed the hedges had grown so luxuriant that I passed her entrance twice without realizing that the small square of rusted green scrollwork I'd noticed was a gate. A leaf-strewn earth path wound between larches and sycamores to a whitewashed mock-Tudor facade. A water-butt covered in wire mesh stood by the front door, together with a few recently used garden tools propped against the wall. Everything seemed well tended but not over-tidy; the owner had not wished to banish the wilderness, but merely present it with boundaries against which it could only pine and dwindle.

There was no bell, so I optimistically knocked on the door and waited, trying to hold on to the atmosphere of calm I'd felt encircling me as long as possible. This was almost a ritual with me when visiting people: meeting someone was to lay oneself open to their state of mind, which might threaten a state of mind of my own I'd been enjoying (or, of course, not). I was generally loth to let go of my own thoughts in such circumstances, and allow some foreign influence to disrupt them; I suppose this is why for millennia we've had threshold rituals for entering someone's dwelling place. The truth was I couldn't see any way to be immediately open to the new environment while the sensations created by the previous one were so strongly present.

After a minute or so I pushed the door, causing it to yield a few inches, revealing a dark passage stretching straight ahead, and a scent that seemed to be a mixture of mildew, disinfectant and lavender. I stood wondering what to do, reluctant to trespass on someone else's space. Something moved in the shadows: then a grey, long-haired cat stood mewing up at me. I took it as an invitation to go in.

The cottage appeared to be deserted. Although the light outside was bright, the interior was hard to make out, and I almost went flying into the rear kitchen when I failed to see the two steps leading down to it. I was surprised to see modern appliances surrounding me like a ruminating half-circle of well-fed cows. I'd somehow assumed Elaine to be a wood-burning stove kind of person, but everything here was uncompromisingly twenty-first century: even the mandatory white pine welsh-dresser had been replaced with sleek glass-fronted cabinets. I crossed to the wide window and saw a large unkempt garden with a circular fishpond at its centre. Beyond, a wheelbarrow piled with bramble cuttings gave the only sign of present habitation.

I finally discovered Elaine, secateurs in hand and clad in ancient threadbare jeans and a ravelled green jersey behind some clumps of wilting rose and blackcurrent bushes.

'I meant to leave a note on the door, but got distracted. How was your journey?'

'Fine. Just a few, em, minor anomalies to negotiate, such as fountains spontaneously turning into flame throwers, you know the sort of thing.'

'Well, I'm glad you've come. I did want to talk to you. I'll get some tea going in a sec, when I've cleared up this mess.'

'Is Nicola here?'

'She's out playing with a friend. She's at the age when she's beginning to demand her independence.'

'How old is she?'

'Six and a half.'

'Don't you worry about her going out alone?'

'Yes. But you can't imprison them, can you? You have to believe they'll be ok somehow, else you'd go mad very quickly. At least she's safer here than in London.'

I watched her pick up the long prickly stalks with great concentration and drag then over to the barrow. She moved with a slight hesitancy, as though contending with some great sadness or setback.

'Fantastic place you've got. Is it yours?'

'I wish! There's no way I could raise the cash for this. No, the owner spends most of his time in Spain, making disgustingly lucrative business deals. The arrangement is I look after the place in exchange for a cheap rent. Safe pair of hands.'

I wondered about that last point as we went inside. The place felt cool and spacious; I imagined the deeply upholstered beds that undoubtedly lay fragrant and inviting in shaded rooms somewhere above my head.

Elaine was asking me something that seemed pertinent to my reason for being here.

'I'm sorry?'

'Was Joe very annoyed at the article?'

'It's hard to know when Joe's annoyed. I suppose it's fair to say he wasn't exactly over the moon.'

She reached for a large yellow teapot and slopped boiling water into it.

'The thing is, as you probably realize, it was taken out of my hands. If the sub decides it's going to have a certain angle, he just rewrites it. It's all about readership. Scandals sell papers. Truth doesn't. So guess which goes to the wall.'

'You should have vetoed it. He falsified your work after all.'

'I'd have been out of a job.'

She sat down to stir the pot. Somewhere in the house a clock chimed resonantly.

'There was terrible fall-out from that article. We're still getting hate-mail. Someone even threatened to burn the house down. They said we were torturing children.'

'I'm sorry if it sounds naive, but I didn't remotely imagine that would happen. What I wrote was entirely unsensational. I admit I didn't like Joe much, and it was probably mutual. But I didn't in any way sex it up for the paper. They didn't even tell me they were going to change it. It just appeared like that. I was absolutely horrified.' She poured milk into the mugs and produced a tin of biscuits. She seemed genuinely remorseful, but I thought the sadness that surrounded her was connected with something else, something that weighed heavily on her spirit.

'Joe certainly isn't an easy person to know. And he's been pretty outrageous in his behaviour. But he's also a genius.'

'Do you think that excuses him?'

'Not at all. But it seems genius comes at a price. He thinks more deeply than anyone I've ever met before. If we want that depth we probably have to accept the inconveniences.'

'I'm not sure I go along with that kind of pragmatism. The bottom line should be respecting other people, don't you think?'

'But what does it mean, respecting people? Does it mean pandering to their fears or compromises? Or does it mean encouraging the best in them? Joe, whatever his faults, always has his sights on what someone's capable of; he wants to stretch people to live their full potential.'

Elaine pulled a disapproving face. 'Oh I don't like the sound of that. Stretching people? Come on! You can teach by example and stretch yourself if you like, but stretching others sounds sadistic. Actually that's what I felt about Joe as soon as I met him: there's a strong streak of sadism in him.'

'Are you sure that didn't influence your article?'

'Yes, pretty sure. If anything I deliberately went the opposite way because I didn't like him. It was the sub who put all that rubbish about black magic in.'

I wasn't convinced. 'The thing about Joe is, he pushes himself to the edge because he genuinely wants to understand himself, and he believes that only *in extremis* can we see ourselves naked, so to speak; but this makes for a very lonely life, and he needs close friends around him. It's not a comfortable equation. And it's not one I'm sure I can handle myself.'

'You're going to leave?'

'I'm considering it. I wanted to talk to you about it. Joe's a wonderful person – unique in my experience. He's taught me a huge amount I wouldn't have learned from anyone else. But he's absolutely remorseless: he pushes everyone else to the edge as well as himself, and he doesn't seem to realize that others may have less clarity and resilience than him. His uncompromising philosophy strains any human intimacy to breaking point.'

'So what attracted you in the first place?'

'I needed something I thought Joe could give me. He has a charming side to him, which he uses to draw people in to his circle. It's not exactly a deception, because he really does have people's interests at heart; but there's something else as well, that's hard to pin down: it's this tendency to exploit people's naivety and need for a strong father-figure. He can play into that; exploit people's innocence. It took me a while to realize I was being manipulated like that.'

'Yes, there are many people like that around, and they're very destructive, because few can stand up to them. They turn into little tin-pot gods with their own fragile coterie around them.'

'As you yourself put it so well in your article.'

'Correction: as the sub-editor put it.'

'I wish to God that piece had never been printed. I don't think Joe deserved it.'

'But maybe he needed it.'

'What do you mean?'

'Well, as I said, people like that don't get challenged: they rule by default. That's how child abuse in the Church managed to survive so long. We prefer not to think about it.'

'I think you're misrepresenting him. If you'd got to know him before unleashing your journalistic dogs I think you'd have written a very different piece.'

'Maybe. I don't know. I don't think it was a hundred per cent unjustified. There is a sadist lurking inside him. As well as all the good things, of course.'

'That's true of all of us, to my mind.'

'It sounds like you're defending him.'

'Well why not? He's an amazing man. His sculptures are unique.'

'Hitler was an artist too, don't forget. And no, before you jump on me, I'm not comparing them.'

'I suppose this whole thing turns on whether or not you think the price of genius is worth paying.'

'Yes. And I don't. It's too easy to justify cruelty and megalomania by saying they turned out some great works of art. I mean, if the price of Wagner's operas is his wife being abused for fifteen years, I don't want to buy it. You can't do that kind of art-ethics equation: art should reduce suffering, not contribute to it. Anyway, rant over. Some more tea?'

'Thanks.'

'You think I'm wrong about Joe.'

'I think judgement is always premature. How can anyone know another well enough to condemn them?'

'I'm not condemning him: I'm condemning his actions.'

'So all his insights and teachings are worthless because he had a few personal faults?'

'No, of course not. Just not worth the price.'

'If we costed all of humanity's insights we'd still be in the stone age. Knowledge always has a high price.'

'But if the price is abuse and exploitation?'

'You see, I don't think there is exploitation. I think we exploit ourselves.'

'That's semantics. People are allowed to be exploited because it serves his purpose.'

'I'm afraid there's no learning without pain. If I have a need for an all-wise father figure, and he has a need for an admiring compliant student, you're going to get some kind of dependent relationship arising. But if there's genuine love and respect both sides will grow through it.'

'I think that's too idealistic. Far more likely the teacher will abuse his position of power. It's happened so many times through history. When humans find themselves in positions of power they always end up abusing it and doing great damage. It's a law as old as gravity.'

The phone rang, and she hurried away to answer it. I began to think it had been a mistake to come; we were already taking sides around Joe, and I didn't feel happy being maneuvered into defending him. And yet I knew that Elaine was not playing fair: Joe had stirred something in her that she didn't want to look at, and her article inevitably reflected that. The more I thought about it the more pointless the whole argument seemed. I made a decision to leave as soon as she returned: I could easily tell her I'd left some things behind and needed to get back before dark to retrieve them. But when I looked deeper I saw there was fear on my side too: fear of invoking Joe's anger at being deserted – even though of course I realized if anyone had been deserted, it was me. Which in turn bred resentment against Joe for his unintentional manipulation of my indebtedness. Another double-bind, and another compelling reason not to get closely involved with anyone on any level, for any reason, ever again.

Elaine seemed to be gone a long time, and when she finally returned she was transformed. The jeans had been replaced with a silver embroidered muslin dress, and the green jersey with a pale-blue tight-fitting blouse. I couldn't avoid the impression that a message of some sort was being sent.

'That was a friend of mine in the village. She just heard on the news that half of Ireland has sunk without trace.'

Chapter Twenty One

Nicola came in while we were discussing the strange case of the vanishing island. She grabbed a chocolate bar and knelt close to the screen to watch the evening news with us.

'How can an island sink, Mummy?'

'That's just what everyone would like to know darling.'

'If it's connected to the ground it can't sink can it?'

'Probably not.'

'Because if it did it would squash the world wouldn't it?'

'Listen to what the man's telling us, then you'll know.'

The news of course was dominated by the event, displacing even a sex scandal involving a millionaire world-class footballer. Top scientists were invited to give their explanation, and as the programme went on more and more bizarre elements of the story were revealed. It seemed that Ireland hadn't actually sunk or disappeared, but had shrunk dramatically. Entire towns had been downsized to the diameter of a football. It wasn't possible to say at this stage whether deaths had occurred, or if people had continued to go about their business on the scale of bacteria. Despite the evidence of the shrinking, the most-offered theory was a Syrian cruise missile strike, possibly one that had gone off course; the government issued an immediate Red Alert status to the military, and advised a total ban on travel to the affected region – not that anyone could find much of the affected region to travel to. Strangely nobody mentioned either the Cube or aliens.

Somehow in all the excitement my resolution to leave had evaporated; no doubt Elaine's sudden metamorphosis had something to do with it. I didn't even make a gesture of demurral when she invited me to stay the night.

'There's tons of space here,' – she swept her arms around to indicate the celestial regions of the house – 'you can stay in the fish room, if that's alright.'

'So long as I don't have to sleep with the fish.'

'Oh no. The fish has his own bed.' She laughed, and for an instant the shadow of sadness floated off her, and she seemed a pretty, carefree, open-hearted student again.

Through supper I wondered whether to raise the unpleasant topic of my attempt to seduce her: after all, part of my reason for coming was to apologise to her, and somehow make amends. It had been weighing on me ever since leaving Joe's. But I was also terrified of raising it; when I looked into my feelings I was deeply ashamed that, after so much kindness, I should repay her with what amounted to attempted rape. What kind of relationship, and what kind of trust, is possible after such abuse? Elaine however appeared quite unscarred by these memories, at least on the surface.

After the meal she suggested we had a tour of the sights. 'We've got some beautiful old buildings, as well as the ruins of a ruined castle. There's also a stone circle, though there's not much left of it. But I often go up there to remember what I'm supposed to be doing down here.'

Nicola stayed in to watch a TV programme. Elaine said:

'You could do your music practice while we're out, couldn't you?'

'Yes Mummy,' she muttered curtly. 'Goodbye.'

We walked up the hill out of the village and then turned off the road onto a steep earth track which ran directly up the hillside. The sun was setting and a ground-mist was folding itself into the shadows below us. We entered a small stand of fir trees, Elaine pausing frequently for me to catch up. Her hair had unravelled in the breeze, making her look even more seductive.

'Not much further,' she called; 'It's worth the effort, I promise you.'

We emerged from the trees and I immediately saw the stones a few metres above us. They were quite small: only about a metre high, and the passage of time had long since deprived them of any visible order: they all leaned dizzyingly from the vertical, and had large pieces broken off them. We stood together looking out at the almost vanquished sun.

Without turning to me, Elaine said: 'I feel connected with everything up here. Sometimes I can sense the presence of the people who must have stood exactly where we're standing three thousand years ago, singing and doing their ceremonies. It's very healing. Time and space mean very little when you get into that state.'

'I know. I've often thought we create time by our need to be continually doing things. Life would be so amazing if we could simply stop and be totally content in this moment.' Almost subliminally I felt myself lean towards her, and was startled to feel her body suddenly pressed against mine. Our fingers touched, and I felt her fine apple-scented hair floating against my cheek.

She whispered: 'I want you to sleep with me tonight.'

For a few seconds I was speechless; I thought it must be happening to someone else, but as we were quite alone, I concluded her words had indeed been addressed to me.

'Elaine, I have to say, I feel so awful about my behaviour at the cottage. It was totally inexcusable. I feel I betrayed our friendship.'

There followed a pause, in which I felt all the world's gods were listening in, breathless, to see which way this crucial hinge of the drama would turn. The sun slipped another millimetre into the murk. Shadows down in the village lengthened.

'Well, I don't expect you to be perfect. And I was giving you some very mixed messages. Going away with you to a remote cottage right after I'd split with Jack was kind of pretty naive really. So I have to accept some of the blame. And in a way you woke me up to what was happening: I wanted to have both you and Jack, and I wasn't prepared to sacrifice what I had with him for what I might have with you. So it does take two to tango.'

'I just can't believe how insensitive I was, knowing how you were going through it. You might forgive me, but I can't.'

'Ah well, that's where you have to do the work. "Self-forgiveness is like coming across a fish in the desert," as some philosopher said.

'Did he? Does that mean if you're a vegetarian you can't be forgiven?'

She laughed. 'No, it doesn't, you knucklehead. It means it's very precious.'

I put my arm around her shoulders and gently drew her closer. Then I kissed her, lightly but lingeringly, unwilling to let the moment pass without savouring it to the fullest, convinced that when it ended, my life would revert to its normal routine of longing and feeling at the same time the utter futility of longing.

I tried to think of something to say that wouldn't sound banal or trite, but still nothing would come. We held each other while the breeze blustered around us and the twilight deepened. Rooks wheeled around the trees, calling to each other to establish the right moment for roosting.

I said nothing, but held her more tightly, as the darting breeze strengthened, and the remaining wakeful birds fell silent.

I watched as Elaine took off her skirt and blouse without embarrassment and slid into bed. It felt like a gift just being there with her, not feeling the necessity to speak or fill the silence. Her figure was graceful, full and well-rounded, her skin cool, smooth and delightfully responsive to my touch. We kissed long and deeply, gradually relaxing and opening into each other's desire. To me it felt entirely natural and easy beyond imagining to be intimate with this young mother who I'd known for years as someone else's wife. When she was ready I eased into her and remained still for a suspended blissful moment while we explored the secret reaches of our bodies. Then she began to moan, at first inwardly, as though remembering something precious, then more openly, and we moved together, washed by the waves of the invisible ocean that knew no doubts, and was endless.

The pre-dawn gloom was furring the quiet spaces of the room when I awoke from deep sleep and sat bolt upright.

There was a terrifying grinding noise coming from somewhere below – as though giant earth-moving equipment was trying to gouge a breach into the house. The walls of the ancient cottage seemed on the brink of caving in under the assault. I tugged the light-pull but nothing happened. Elaine sighed, turned over and opened her eyes.

'What's wrong?'

'Didn't you hear that noise?'

It came again: a deep shuddering, like a panicking rhino blundering about in the dark. Then after about twenty seconds, silence.

'Oh no,' she sat on the edge of the bed, suddenly wide awake, and groped around for her nightdress. 'It's happening again'.

'What's happening again?'

She looked scared, and spoke very slowly, as if telling a nightmare. 'About a month ago, there was this awful commotion about three in the morning. I thought it was tanks invading, or something. Then it stopped abruptly. I went downstairs, and there was this huge hole in the kitchen floor, going straight down about twenty feet, and an absolutely nauseating smell like something had died was coming up from it. As if something had tried to tunnel into the house from below, but there was no sign of anything alive.' She screwed up her eyes and stared at me. 'I don't like this, Adam.'

'Stay here. I'll go and have a look. Do you have a good torch?'

'Yes, on top of the cupboard.'

I crept downstairs as quietly as I could manage, as though being silent would somehow give me the advantage over whatever waited down there. But despite Elaine's forewarning I was totally unprepared for the sight revealed by the beam of the torch. Where last night had been a modern varnished pine floor there was now an irregular-shaped pit going vertically down far beyond the limit of the beam. Its sides were jagged cliffs of black rock, wet with some viscous fluid that oozed slowly over the sheared edges. Around the opening the floorboards were blackened, as though the invading object had been hot enough to char the wood all through. There was also a pungent stink of decay that reminded me of the smell I'd faintly detected when I'd first arrived. But of the cause of the irruption there was not the slightest trace.

Elaine's unsteady voice came from halfway up the stairs. 'It's exactly the same.'

'Is Nicola ok?'

'She's fast asleep. She'd sleep through the end of the world. Give thanks for small mercies.'

I crept to the edge. 'I can't see the bottom. It must go down at least thirty feet. The bedrock has been sliced through like butter.'

She came to stand beside me. 'It's horrible. As though something alien had forced itself into the house. Just like last time.'

'But there's nothing here.'

'Nothing visible. Anyway it seems to have finished for now at least. Do you think you might have some material to cover the hole with? Plywood or something?'

'Yes. Outside in the shed. There's plenty.'

I found two strong plywood panels and laid them over the pit, sealed their edges with duct tape, then placed the breakfast table over them.

'We'll have to get that done properly tomorrow.'

'Yes. I know someone who'll do it.'

'How about some coffee? You look pale.'

'I'm just a bit shocked really. If this is going to keep happening I can't stay here. It's not fair on Nicola.'

'I've a feeling it won't. I don't know why. I think it's connected with the Cube. Whole regions of land are becoming unstable. They're messing about with the atomic interactions.'

'They?'

'The people who sent the Cube. They're trying to cure us before we infect the rest of the universe.'

'How come you know so much about it?'

'Oh, I've been eavesdropping on their intergalactic phonecalls.'

'Well next time tell them to leave it out, would you?'

'Ok. Do my best.' I gave her a hug.

I made us both coffee and climbed back to the bedroom. Indigo streaks of dawn were appearing over the woods slumped in the east.

Elaine said, 'Will you stay for a day or two?'

'If you want me to.'

'I'd really appreciate it, with all this going on. I suddenly feel very insecure. It's like living with the monster from your childhood nightmares.'

We kissed again, more hungrily this time, abandoning ourselves to our long-suppressed sensuality. The first sunlight flitted into the room, hitting a crystal pendant suspended from the light fitting and giving birth to a dozen misty-edged rainbows. I felt like someone blind for half a lifetime suddenly given back his sight, or a man at the end of his life being offered the elixir of youth. My paranoia seemed to have dropped away like scales, and I could accept what was given without suspicion of its being a trap. What had enabled this change I'd no idea, since nothing spectacular had taken place since my infantile outburst in the Quantocks (oh yes, apart from my jumping from a second story window while having the nightmare of the century, of course).

I murmured: 'Is it too early to ask you a serious question?'

'That sounds like a serious question,' she smiled.

'Well, mightn't this sleeping together be just a wee bit premature? I mean, what if we're totally incompatible? In all the books I've read you're supposed to get to know each other slowly before satisfying one's passions.'

'You've clearly been reading the wrong books then. Anyway, you shouldn't read books, not about matters of love.'

The moment she mentioned the word 'love' something indescribable occurred inside me: an absolute confidence that this time it was going to go right; that I no longer had to spend every minute fearing I was being taken for a ride, or set up for a spectacular crash, or given condescending explanations for why I wasn't quite up to scratch in the relationship stakes. And it became equally evident, at that same moment, that I'd never experienced love before: not the real multi-dimensional blossoming human thing, as opposed to the thin, desperate scramble for acceptance as a sexual partner that so often passes for that divine faculty in human lives. Love, I thought, yes: how simple it is, when it finally comes; and at the same time what an utter mystery, rendering the tides of recurring misery if not understandable, then at least just about bearable.

'I'm thinking I should go back to Joe's.' I cradled my coffee-mug while the risen sun teased out the rich yellows and oranges of the quilt. 'I've much unfinished business there.'

'It seems to me you've learnt everything you can from Joe. The danger is you could get sucked in to his power fantasies again. It's dangerous territory. Why subject yourself to all that humiliation over again?'

'The thing is, I left in a state of panic and disillusion, which is exactly what I've been doing all my life. I've got to go back if only to break that cycle. Even though my heart plummets at the thought of it.'

'Joe's a kind of wizard, and not entirely a white wizard. So if you do go back – be careful.'

'Of what exactly?'

'Of being seduced into humiliating yourself again. Joe isn't a saint, you know: he has his own agenda. You don't need to put yourself through endless hoops of fire to please him. There comes a point where penance is self-perpetuating: it becomes obsession. Just heal what can be healed, and let go of what can't.'

'Letting go isn't so easy. God knows I've had enough therapy in my life – I should be able to let go of anything. But just when I think I've got over whatever it is, it comes round and knocks me sideways again.'

'But one day it won't. Have faith.'

'Ah yes, faith. I've heard of that stuff. The trouble is I'm virtually a faith-free zone. Except in your case, of course. For some reason that I don't begin to understand I trust you totally and absolutely. I feel a deep acceptance from you. It goes against everything I've ever felt before in the company of others. How do you account for that?'

'As I said – chemistry. The wise pheremones.'

A voice was calling from Nicola's attic bedroom.

'Mummy! Are you coming? I'm hungry!'

'Yes darling. Five minutes.'

'Aren't you afraid she'll find the pit?'

'Oh she'll be fine. She's remarkably positive about untoward events. Much more than I am.' She began dressing.

'It's incredible she slept through all that armageddon.'

'Children are incredible. Provided they have a secure basis of love they can accommodate all kinds of upsets and havoc later on. But breakfast won't wait I'm afraid. Come when you're ready.'

'Are you staying forever?' Nicola paused over her cereal, looking at me with the inevitable "I've sussed out the whole situation and I reckon you'll pass" expression.

'I'm afraid I can't. Not forever. I've got to see some people.'

'What people?' Nicola, on the scent of a half-truth, pursued.

'The people I was staying with before. I left in a bit of a hurry, without saying goodbye.'

'You can say goodbye on the phone. It's easy.' She slurped more milk into her bowl. Elaine smiled knowingly.

'Well, actually I have to say a few more things besides, which are a bit harder to say on the phone.'

'What things?' This last word she pronounced with contemptuous emphasis, like they couldn't possibly be that important.

'Well, things I should have said a long time ago, but I was afraid to. If you don't say things when they should be said they get harder and harder to say. Sometimes they get impossible.'

'If these people really are your friends you should be able to say them anytime. They would understand.'

'That's enough,' Elaine raced to rescue me. 'Adam has to have his breakfast.'

'I know. But he can talk at the same time, like you do.'

'Adam's our guest. You don't batter guests with questions while they're eating.'

'Batter's what you make fish with,' she countered, 'not guests.'

'Finish your breakfast.'

Silence reigned for ten seconds, before Nicola's frustration burst the banks of her patience.

'If you love each other you should live here.'

I wondered that she already seemed to have written Jack out of her script. Something in that scared me.

'That doesn't follow,' Elaine quickly answered. 'Necessarily.'

'I don't want any more.' Nicola abruptly pushed her bowl away.

'Ok. You can go out and play. Don't go far, ok?'

Three days of sun and peace and Elaine's cooking restored me to something resembling equanimity. On the fourth day I came in after an early morning walk and found her fighting off tears.

'Missing Jack?'

She nodded.

I'd known this moment would arrive sooner or later, but I was still hoping it might somehow be tiptoed around. I helped myself to some still-warm coffee.

'Maybe you should go back and try again? Maybe he'll have changed enough for it to work this time?'

'You know Jack, Adam. Can you really imagine him changing that much?'

'He might if he feels you're serious about leaving. Maybe he's just taken you for granted for so long he can't imagine a situation where you'd actually leave. This temporary separation might be the catalyst.'

'The trouble is I think I've changed. I no longer want that kind of life.'

I felt as though several lascivious demons were prodding me from various infernal quarters, urging me to seize my advantage.

'So what is it you do want?'

'It's hard to put into words. Less cerebral. More feeling. More contact. Doing stuff together. Sharing little things like shopping and art. Feeling valued for who I am, not as somebody's support system. Does that make sense?'

'Perfectly. But I can't tell you what to do. All I can say is I want all of those things too.'

'I know. That's why I want to live with you.'

'I can't believe you're saying that. I feel I've taken a wrong turning and stumbled into paradise.'

'Paradise with a hole in it.' She grinned.

I stood up and gazed into the garden. 'You know I will have to go back. I couldn't live with myself just walking out like that. It's what I've done all my life.'

'I understand. But please come back quickly.' She came across and kissed me. Her lips seemed infinitely soft.

'How could I not?'

'And don't try to explain anything to Joe. He won't appreciate you falling into the web of another scheming woman.' She laughed.

As soon as I'd set out on the journey back to Joe's it was obvious that the landscape had suffered more serious deformations. The road had buckled in several places; some buildings had been partially demolished, trees uprooted, fields riven and rucked by fault lines. Yet it wasn't the concentrated destruction of an earthquake: there was no epicentre, and therefore no wholesale focused damage; rather widely separated local disruption with stretches of normality between. But the normality itself now seemed precarious, due to the random nature of the disruption, and every intact structure I passed seemed miraculously preserved from the encroaching chaos. When I came to the bridge I found it mostly unaltered, but the gap between the sections had increased and been spanned with a steel walkway, about two feet wide, so that at least pedestrians could proceed normally. I inspected the edges of the sheared metal: it was as if they had been subjected to enormous heat, and then instantly frozen, so that the surface appeared organic and flowing. The river below seemed not to have been affected at all.

In Kingston the square was largely as I'd left it: people went about their business paying little attention to the anomalies in the landscape. A few children played in clusters, ignoring the protective ropes that had been hastily erected around the skewed pave-stones and irruptions of earth and rock. People seemed to be treating it as a one-off event that could be quickly put right and consigned to history, rather than as the precursor of a radically changed world. While this was understandable, if there was a second wave the general baffled acceptance could change in a very short space to panic and mass migrations to 'safe' areas.

It was fully dark when I arrived at Joe's. All the lights in the house were out, and I began to wonder if Joe and Philippe had gone to earth until the hue and cry had abated. I went to the rear of the house and saw the cabin lights spilling out over the lawn and encircling trees. Something – whether instinct, fear or guilt I don't know – prevented me from disturbing Joe, and I returned to the dark kitchen. I wasn't surprised to discover the house unlocked: Joe's philosophy of not protecting himself demanded it; I found an oil lamp and succeeded in lighting it after several attempts.

There was a note from Joe waiting for me. I had difficulty reading his anarchic handwriting in the unsteady light.

"Dear Adam:

I hope you had a fruitful trip, wherever it led you. We have moved our quarters into the cabin, as we are working intensively and the less distractions the better: the house feels increasingly like occupied territory. You are of course welcome to stay as long as you feel it appropriate. But I warn you to be vigilant: there have been visitors – some human, some less so. I'm afraid the story that we practise unspeakable black-magic and torture children is now unstoppable, and has taken on the mantle of a local legend. The community will not be cheated of its 'justice'. I've locked the sculpture room: it would be seriously bad karma for us if one of those things got into the hands of the marauders. Lastly, I would like not to be disturbed except in extremis. I wish you all the best – Joe."

So there was to be no great reconciliation scene. In my heart I had known this all along: Joe had his new protegé, his alchemical brother, and needed no one else; I'd served my purpose, and the drama had moved on. What had I to complain of? Joe had signed no contract to look after me or protect me from the depredations of the world; I was an adult, free to go where I pleased at any time: emotional bonds were antithetical to the life of the spirit, and if I couldn't take such a teaching I'd better abandon all pretensions to be following it.

Still, I had to admit to feeling rejected: I had come to Joe's in a state of dire need, as a supplicant, and I'd given a large amount of my energy to helping him. By any standards I'd been treated harshly, and even with Elaine's insight I struggled to make sense of Joe's sustained indifference. Maybe, I thought, this was meant as yet another test of my loyalty: a test which could too easily become a path to destruction.

I spent that night in my former garret with the door bolted. A strong wind had got up and I lay for a long time listening to the trees moaning and keening in the moonless dark. I felt certain there was no place for me there anymore; what was the point of challenging Joe's increasingly capricious behaviour, or suffering repeated humiliation? I certainly wasn't going to change him; the only pertinent question was whether such a strategy would help to remedy my own weaknesses, and this I profoundly doubted. It was becoming clearer every minute that I shouldn't have come back; I'd ceased to be of any importance to Joe, and felt my presence was becoming an irritation to him. And yet, I couldn't avoid the opposite thought: who would help him in his stand-off with the local community if I left? I hardly thought an unworldly foreign philosophy student with a rudimentary grasp of English would be of much use in that situation. And Joe unquestionably had unique gifts – even if they were universally misunderstood: he was sensitive, cultured, utterly single-minded in pursuit of his beliefs, had an amazing insight into human psychology, and an unequalled capacity for friendship and generosity – albeit with certain predilections. Part of me – despite my resentment at being sidelined – balked at the idea of such a man being delivered into the hands of a barely educated mob bent on his destruction.

With my mind filled with such arguments I eventually drifted into an uneasy sleep, patterned with the wind's unsettling counterpoint. There was also a distant percussion of voices, never clear enough to be understood, but still sufficiently penetrating to make me conscious of them. At some point I woke and lay listening intently. The voices were still there, and if anything, louder. I sat up, trying to clarify the direction of the sounds; but they seemed to defy location: indeed as I listened, more voices seemed to be added to them from entirely different directions, alternatively diminished and augmented as the wind died and rallied.

Alarmed now, I dressed quickly and crept down the corridor to the far end of the house. There seemed to be a pulsating light at the end where the large window overlooked the garden. When I reached the window I saw what was causing it: the cabin was alight, engulfed in flames which were already encroaching on the roof. For a moment I stood there paralysed, entirely deprived of useful thought. There was no sign of the people whose voices I'd heard, or thought I'd heard. Neither was there any sign of Joe or Philippe. My brain sluggishly grappled with the prospect that they could still be asleep inside, and no-one was going to rescue them if I didn't. For an instant there was the thought that they were probably getting their just desserts – then sanity and humanity reasserted themselves, and I ran down the stairs and out to the blazing cabin.

So much happened in the following few moments that it's impossible now to sort the order of events, or guess how long each lasted. All I recall is a searing chaos of flame biting at the walls and shooting sideways from underneath the floor. I tried rather forlornly to batter the door down with a brick, but couldn't budge it. I remembered a window in the opposite wall, and racing round to smash it found it already shattered, and flames snaking out through the void. Then I saw why Joe and Philippe had not come out: the interior was an opaque wall of smoke bulging and writhing in front of me.

Somehow I found a way to climb through the window avoiding the flames, and immediately caught sight of them, naked and unconscious stretched across the floorboards: they'd clearly been aiming for the door when they'd been overcome by smoke. By now the flames had ripped through the floor and were within inches of the bodies. I grabbed Joe and hauled him towards the door, desperately hoping I wouldn't need to inhale before I got it open. Strangely, the only response I had to touching the bodies was shock at how light they were, and how vulnerable and helpless they seemed in the face of the world's implacable hostility. I couldn't tell in the duplicitous light whether either of them was breathing: either way the priority seemed to get them outside and lay them on the moist earth. But now I realized there was no key in the lock. I cursed myself for not knowing where Joe might have kept the key, never imagining an occasion when being able to find it immediately might divide life from death. I kicked at the door, but it was too well-built to desert its post without permission of the lock.

There was a terrifying crack from above my head as half the roof collapsed. I failed to understand why Joe had taken the key from the lock in the first place: was it to prevent Philippe from leaving? To give himself an extra sense of control? Or to give Philippe one of his special lessons in facing existential dilemmas? I could well believe that, having been on the receiving end of a few of them.

I hunted around in the fickle glow of the flames for a possible hiding place, but time and again the roiling smoke drove me back gasping for breath into the corner. I moved their faces as close as possible to the door, hoping that the small space between floor and door would allow some fresh air to enter; but by now the heat was unbearable, and I knew we only had seconds to get out alive. Then I saw it, lying in the darkest shadows in the corner, barely distinguishable from the surrounding gloom. I grabbed it, fitted it into the lock and managed to turn it, then kicked the door open, gulping down the miraculous night air with indescribable relief.

Neither Joe nor Philippe stirred or made a sound as I laid them in the long grass under the now motionless trees, their thin white bodies smeared alike with ash and irregular livid weals. I became certain at that point that they were dead. With a weary mechanicalness I went into the house to phone the police, then returned with blankets to cover the bodies. It was then that I heard strident voices coming from somewhere in the house. Realizing they were probably expecting to find others inside, I crept into the kitchen and listened, my heart racing with apprehension. The shouts came from the upper floors, and were followed by a sustained battering, as if a door was being attacked; I realized it was probably the sculpture room, the only room Joe had thought worth locking: it was clearly their intention to get inside and either destroy or liberate the contents – depending on what they thought was there; I don't suppose for a moment they imagined it would be full of wonderfully carved animal sculpture.

Strangely, I didn't much care if they carried off the artworks, or even destroyed them. With Joe dead, the whole enterprise was history, and I felt no further involvement with it; furthermore Joe himself would have been against trying to preserve the material husk of his vision while ignoring the truth that it had to be re-created afresh each moment. But what I definitely didn't want was to be caught on the one hand by these marauders and considered an accomplice in child abduction and worse crimes; or on the other arrested by the police for arson. My instinct was to melt into the shadows immediately, and put the whole episode of Joe and Philippe behind me for good. It would be so simple: there was nothing to link me with the place; no one but Elaine knew where I was. Yet once again something stopped me; something to do with not abandoning unfinished business, or not delivering your lord's hall into the hands of invaders.

I stood irresolute by the kitchen table, watching the rectangles of moonlight bloom and dissolve on the worn carpet, finally having no idea of the right thing to do, and no very strong motivation for doing it anyway. Then I heard the smashing of glass, and something long held back in my mind shook itself free and howled in anguish.

Chapter Twenty Two

The door of the sculpture room had been rammed off its hinges and small pieces of bright ceramic material lay scattered across the floor like a neo-expressionist installation. Without pausing to think I ran into the room and saw two men near one of the shattered windows in the act of throwing out armfuls of Joe's collection. A third crouched a few yards along the wall closely inspecting one of the glass cabinets. When the two by the window saw me they seemed momentarily to become sculptures themselves. In the gloom I saw I had briefly the advantage of surprise, and grabbed the first heavy object that came to hand – a solid quartz pyramid – and hurled it with all the force of my outrage at the nearest of the intruders. He tried to dodge it but wasn't fast enough, and it knocked him off balance. He fell against the broken window, which cut him badly on his arms and neck. To my surprise instead of groaning or cursing he merely whimpered and slowly lay down against the window frame, bleeding profusely. This equalized the battle considerably: after all there is nothing like scoring a hit in the first moment of a battle to give conviction to one's tactics.

The second man was tall and solidly built, and I sensed the next stage wasn't going to be quite such a pushover. He glanced briefly at his friend on the floor and then stared at me.

'I thought there'd be rats somewhere in this house,' he growled, 'and blow me down now here is one.' He leapt towards me, while his mate by the glass cabinet got to his feet and loped after him. In a flash of inspiration I realized my only chance was to use the power of the sculptures themselves. I backed off, as though making for the door, then at the last moment doubled back towards a cabinet I knew contained Joe's 'special' items. At once I saw one I thought might be suitably potent: a large jade carving in the form of a winged lion. The tricky part would be to get it out of my hands before its energy could trap my mind with whatever 'demon' it embodied. There was a heavy protective cloth covering the top of the cabinet; grabbing this, I used it to pick up the carving, and immediately threw it at the nearest of my pursuers, aiming at his chest so that (I hoped) his instinct would be to catch it like a football. Fortunately he did exactly that. There was a second's pause while he took his eyes off me to see what kind of gift he'd been given; in that second the lion-demon's energy crackled directly into his brain, and he stood transfixed, legs apart, eyes fastened on the deceptively cool liquid green of the creature's face. Then a blood-chilling scream of terror escaped from his throat and rang though the empty house; but his hands were unable to let go of the creature, while I could only guess what horror he was living through in a world where, no matter how much he screamed, none of his friends could reach him.

With that terrible sustained scream still fracturing the air his remaining comrade took the opportunity to hurl another heavy abstract work of art in my general direction before bolting for the door. Clearly this unambiguous demonstration that Joe had indeed been practicing black magic and that I too was party to his secrets, was too much for him; I heard his footsteps echo on the back stairs, and then fainter steps pounding the gravel outside, and finally the sound of a gunning car engine muted by the encircling ranks of fir trees.

I didn't wait to find out how the holder of the lion-demon would return from his unexpected journey: seized with the overwhelming compulsion to get away from the entire domain, I too made for the door. But before I left I pocketed one of the smaller sculptures: a jade toad, one that I'd seen a few times already in my visits, and whose intricate detailing I'd been fascinated by. I imagined for some odd reason it might bring me much needed luck on my imminent journey; and I also thought it might remind me of the better moments in my brief friendship with Joe. Then I leapt down the stairs, crossed the bare unlit kitchen and sprang from the building into the slicks of cool moonlight.

I wanted more than ever to be with Elaine. In those few days I'd become alarmingly close to her, in a way I'd never been with Cora. It was an intuitive, unspoken intimacy that made no demands and made me feel a generosity – an ampleness – towards the world; something, I have to admit, that had been pretty well absent through most of my life. With her I felt I no longer had to make amends for being so self-obsessed and at loggerheads with the world, and more than anything I wanted to remain in that state of shadowless grace.

My timing was fortunate: no sooner was I away from the house than I heard vehicles approaching along the lane; from the cover of the woods I could see two police cars and a fire engine negotiating the track up to the building. I tried to imagine their thoughts when they discovered a burnt out cabin, two naked corpses laid out neatly side by side, and a frozen man grappling with a carving of a winged lion as though in the process of being attacked by it. I waited behind the trees until the police had gone inside, then made my way along a small path beside a sluggish stream that ran south until it crossed the Taunton road, deliberately walking in the water for a while before doubling back on the other side, in case they tried to follow me with dogs.

Dawn was tinting the hills by the time I'd come in sight of the Blackdowns, and I was feeling exhausted and very hungry. Luckily I had chocolate, dates and a couple of apples left in my rucksack. I lay against a fence to eat them, thinking of the peace and simple enjoyments waiting at Elaine's, now only a few easy miles away. Once across the motorway I decided to avoid roads wherever possible: a lone traveller at such an early hour would easily be remembered by anyone I chanced to encounter. Luckily there were many small paths through spinneys and across farmland which in the growing light I followed without too much difficulty. My greatest fear was of dogs, which could quickly set up a hue and cry and alert any nearby community to the presence of a stranger. But the gods were on my side, and I encountered nothing noisier than coveys of rooks arguing in the treetops, and once an owl, dreamily anointing the new day with his haunting notes.

Once on the ridge of the Blackdown Hills I tried to turn east towards South Brockley, but after walking for half an hour I found the path leading me remorselessly downwards and southwards, as though the god in charge of topography was casually re-orientating all the roads and paths out of pique or boredom the moment I set foot on them. Each time I checked myself and climbed a fence or hedge to find an eastbound path, after a few minutes it seemed to decide that no one in his right mind could want to travel east any more, and slyly began to edge south again, convinced I wouldn't notice. After an hour or so of this I gave in and accepted I was probably going to miss Elaine's marvellous breakfast.

After another hour of scrambling and tramping, wistfully glancing at every eastward turning, I found myself on a level heathland, dotted at intervals with stands of pine and larch. Sheep grazed around the trees, and unseen birds roosted and chattered ceaselessly in the emptying canopies. At last the landscape seemed to relent and allowed me to turn east and north towards Brockley. My path began to descend into a shallow wooded combe which seemed unnaturally dark, considering the brightness of the morning. By the time I came to the lowest part of the track the trees were so densely crowded that I could see nothing at all of the sky, and the refreshing breeze that had stayed with me since dawn had dwindled away completely. The path narrowed and became boggy, despite the prolonged drought. I picked my way cautiously between sinuous brambles that flanked the path, hoping I wouldn't sink further into the clinging mud. And as I looked ahead to see how much further the strange hollow extended, I saw it: a twisted creature, about eighteen inches tall, crouching ape-like on its withered haunches in the dead centre of the path, where it began to rise towards the distant daylight. The creature stared directly at me with unflinching pin-hard eyes.

I stopped dead, the mud rapidly engulfing my totally inadequate shoes. I'd seen this thing before, but not while awake: it was the egg-demon from the nightmare at Joe's that I'd tried to consign to the past; but here it was reborn in flesh and blood, defying me to pass it. But there was simply no choice: I had to pass it, or starve on my feet in a perennial mire. My first instinct was to rush forward, and hope to surprise it; then I realised after glancing briefly at its never blinking eyes that this was a naive hope: its concentrated malice was inexhaustible and inexorable. Then I thought of ignoring it and creeping past along the edge of the path like a shadow; but again it seemed vain to imagine it would be fooled by such a specious strategy. The thought of approaching it directly and confronting it made my entire soul shrink with dismay and the blood stall in my veins, so remorseless was the power that emanated from its black stare; but short of taking off and flying out through the shivering treetops I could think of no other way out.

I took a step towards it – a step which seemed like a whole hopeless journey in itself – then stopped, unable to summon the will to take another. The creature had not stirred; it seemed different from how it had appeared in the dream: more earth-textured, more substantial, yet also slightly more in the human realm, more approachable, as one blighted creature might approach another.

Then it shocked me into a new awakeness by uttering a single word: 'Thief.'

If I'd entertained some shred of hope from its appearance, when I heard its voice I at once abandoned it. It was like something from before the beginning of the world: like a fall of rock, icy, without a hint of life in it. Nevertheless I summoned from somewhere the strength to answer it.

'If you mean me, I'm not a thief.'

'The price of what you stole must be paid.'

It raised its left hand, and in it I could see a tiny blade, as slender as a needle and black as deep space, and around its tip dark smoke seemed to cling.

'I didn't steal anything.'

'Liar.' The word seemed to hammer like thunder against all the surrounding trees. The demon raised its arm further, so that the blade now pointed toward my lower body. I could see its tip now, and some searing radiance which I couldn't look at directly issued from it. It was clear I had no chance of prevailing by force against this thing: my only hope lay in convincing it I wasn't guilty.

'I don't know what you mean.'

'Fool.' The word flew from his mouth as if it were an arrow loaded with lethal venom.

The blade now aimed itself directly at my heart. In a moment of panic I tried to turn sideways, thinking perhaps I could scale the rock rearing up fifteen feet on either side of the path. But the demon saw my intention as soon as it entered my mind and without appearing to move suddenly appeared ahead of me.

'Coward.' This time the word was like the ravenous tearing apart of a carcase. Then I saw what it was trying to do: undermine me with my own doubts. There was of course some truth in all its accusations: I had indeed been all of those things at some time or other; what mortal could truthfully claim he had never once stolen anything, or lied, or acted foolishly or cowardly? Suddenly I saw I wasn't entirely abandoned: there was something on my side, even though at times it could be very hard to discern.

I faced the creature, our eyes meeting without evasion.

'You are right: I have been all those things. But I've changed.'

'What proof?' The tiny lance glowed sullenly, and I thought there came into the demon's eyes something akin to interest.

'I rescued Joe and Philippe from a fire, and fought off three intruders.'

'True.'

'I learned not to fall for deceptions.'

'Also true.'

'I learned just now that truth is my protector.'

'You did.'

The lance remained locked onto my heart, as though its own will was giving it strength. I could say no more.

'But a thief you remain.'

Then I realized what he was thinking of: the jade toad I'd snatched at the last moment from Joe's house. I had to admit then that I had stolen it. I took it from my pocket and held it high in the air.

'Is this what you want?'

'You must give it up before you may pass.'

'Why?'

Instead of replying, he advanced towards me, while the lance seemed to spring alive like some implacable dragon's head. 'I answer no questions.'

I fingered the toad in my hand, half-intending to throw it at the demon and make a run for it; but I quickly judged he would be far too quick for me, and I saw no good reason why I should give it up: my debt, if I still had one, was to Joe, not to this sub-human horror-movie travesty of a man, and I reckoned Joe owed me this in token of rescuing him from the burning cabin.

'I won't give it to you, or anyone else save its maker.'

'Then I must give you my gift.' With astonishing speed he jumped towards me, the tip of the lance burning brighter as it came closer. I made a huge effort to extract my foot from the mud, but it sucked at my shoes like some blind, voracious earth serpent. After what felt like an interminable stretch of time I reached dry ground and immediately fell forward, feeling a sharp tingling in my side, as though my flesh had been instantly drained of its blood; followed by a spreading numbness. I collapsed on the ground, trembling uncontrollably, one single thought drumming in my mind: once again I'd failed the test, and this time I'd pay with my life.

When I regained consciousness the sun was gently warming my body and there was no sign of the demon. The tree-shaded path stretched ahead eastwards; a slight breeze stirred the turning leaves in the high canopies. It seemed to be late afternoon or early evening, but I'd no idea how much time had passed in reality; it could easily have been the next day for all I knew.

My left side throbbed where the lance had seared it, although when I examined myself there was no more than a livid patch of skin a couple of inches across: there seemed to be no actual wound. I got a little unsteadily to my feet, and peered around for signs of the demon's return. Maybe, I thought, I'd escaped the full effect of the demon's weapon because I'd refused to give up the toad carving: maybe in some way it had protected me. In any case, I felt unaccountably glad I hadn't surrendered it on the demon's demand.

It occurred to me that I ought to seize the unexpected reprieve and put some clear space between me and the creature's stamping ground as quickly as possible; the daylight was ebbing, and I was still set on reaching Elaine's before dark. But when I emerged from the shade of the trees I found the sun already gliding down the sky on my right, and saw the path was once more fixated on heading south.

The sun was grazing the horizon when I reached the next town. I was no longer anywhere near the Blackdowns, whose unreachable outlines could now be seen as a purplish shadow low on the northern horizon. I imagined Elaine in her kitchen surrounded by baking tins and cake mix and heaps of dried fruit, glancing up from her work and gazing worriedly at the darkening window. I thought perhaps now that I'd escaped the egg-demon's trap I'd be allowed to continue unhindered to my preferred destination, but it seemed this was not going to be the way of it.

There was no name-sign to identify this town: only a lane leading to a tarmac street flanked by unremarkable red-brick buildings from the 50s and 60s. I was struck by the absence of people, but assumed it must be some kind of public holiday. Only as I approached the centre did I begin to realize that something untoward had happened: the buildings had shrunk progressively as they neared the centre, until by the time I reached what by rights should have been the market square there was nothing but a vertical pit some ten metres across, going down further that I could see, its sides alarmingly similar to the smaller version in Elaine's kitchen. I stopped as near to its edge as I dared and tried to make out the cause of the strange texturing that became finer as it approached the brink, until at the very edge of the pit the surface resembled lava – jet black, diamond hard and mirror smooth. I ran my fingers across the surface, willing my brain to understand what I was seeing. Then it hit me: I was looking at exactly what had been there all the time, but massively reduced in scale; when I bent down to look closely I could make out the streets and occasionally even the individual buildings of the original community, but compressed by many orders of magnitude. The implications of this took a while for my brain to absorb: what had happened to the inhabitants in the central zone? Had any survived? Or had the change been fatal? There would have been massive changes to atomic structure and chemical reactions in the body; it seemed impossible that anything like normal functions could have been maintained over such a huge change of scale. Yet there must have been a point at which life had continued: maybe at that point nobody had noticed anything different, or they noticed only gradually.

There were so many unanswerable questions. I thought of back-tracking to see if I could find any survivors, but before I could move a disturbingly familiar voice called my name from a few metres behind me.

'Adam? Is that you?'

I swung round and saw a young woman resembling Rachel to the life. But of course it couldn't have been. My confusion must have been evident, because she stopped where she was and said: 'It's ok. I'm not dangerous.'

She still had Rachel's beautiful east Fife accent, but she had changed considerably in other respects since our last fateful meeting in my days of madness. She'd lost her innocent virginal look, her femme fatale appeal so seductive to testosterone fuelled predators; and she'd changed her dress philosophy accordingly: she now wore a dark ankle-length woolen skirt and a loose-woven baggy jersey that covered her neck so well I couldn't tell if she was still wearing the silver lapis lazuli pendant I'd sent her in a fit of remorse shortly after the Magnus debacle, a few weeks before I strangled her to death.

Her presence more than a year after this terrible accident presented me with a bit of a conundrum. When I first met her she was unquestionably alive; then I went a bit overboard in my efforts to stop her escaping and buried her (not very deeply because I was intending to move her somewhere else after the pigs had taken their snouts out of my affairs). Then I did that weird underground journey, emerged back in my kitchen and found her still alive and blissfully innocent of the act of being strangled. Yet, despite her spectacular return to life, I had never been able to rid myself of the unmanning conviction that I'd still murdered her in the searing heat of that moment of long accumulated rage. But now here she was again, calling me as though we were long-lost playmates strayed from an unfallen world.

'Rachel?'

'What a bizarre place to meet you've chosen! On the edge of a time-pit!'

'A what?'

'That's what you're standing next to. I wouldn't get any nearer unless you fancy being dumped in the tenth century and taking the long way back.'

I stepped back a little and gazed at Rachel's image like someone who'd abandoned hope of ever catching a glimpse of their own kind again.

'I'd resigned myself to never seeing you again in this life!'

She glided closer with an oddly rigid motion and looked at me with eyes that recalled unruffled valley mist before dawn.

'What life are we talking about?' There was an impassive seriousness in her expression. A deep doubt rippled through me then, and I felt like turning from her and walking straight into the pit.

'Well, the one we are living. You know: eating, drinking, sleeping, telling jokes, that sort of thing.'

'Oh, I see. Yes, of course. You still think you're alive.' Her voice was low, as if she were allowing me to overhear a thought that had just occurred to her.

'It isn't a question of thinking. I know I'm alive, just as you are. My heart beats, I can hear birdsong. I can talk to you.'

'I'm dead.'

'I'm sorry?'

'I'm not alive. You killed me. Remember?'

A second pit – much bigger than the one I was standing by – then opened up in my heart. I scrutinized Rachel from top to bottom, looking for the tell-tale hazy bits at the edges, or the star-filled sky blossoming between her shoulder blades. But she seemed as solid as I was.

'Do you think we could go to a cafe or something?' I asked, feeling suddenly extremely shaky. 'There are quite a few things I need to ask you, and this rat-hole is making me very nervous.'

'I doubt very much you'll find any cafes still operating,' Rachel said. 'Everyone who wasn't killed outright by the distortion has fled to the country. But we can try if you like. Try not to step on the buildings, just in case there are survivors'.

'Who could survive being compressed to a millimetre in height?'

'I don't know. But better safe than sorry. There are green areas that are probably Ok to walk on. It'll soon be obvious as we get away from the singularity.'

We picked our way southwards with extreme care. The moon had risen, making progress marginally easier. I began to feel I knew what Gulliver had felt like: each footprint covered acres of human habitation.

'Rachel, will you please explain what you mean about being dead? I mean, we're walking and talking with each other right? That must mean breathing, energy metabolism, oxygen conversion, blood pumping round the body – which isn't really my idea of being dead.'

'But none of it's really happening Adam. It's all a great big virtual reality show that never stops, and you can't take off the headgear because the headgear is – well, it's your head. But I assure you, ever since your encounter with the swamp demon, you've been as dead as the Tasmanian tiger.'

'How did you know about that?'

'The simplest answer is because I'm dead.'

'Try me with a complicated answer.'

'You'll see it yourself quite soon, when you get out of the habit of thinking in concepts'.

'Rachel, you'll appreciate that I'm having difficulty with this novel approach to making conversation. You'll have to give me time. Brain's not as receptive as it used to be.'

'Look out!' Her arm was suddenly in front of me.

I'd been about to collide with a nine-inch high supermarket fronting onto the main street. I peered inside. A few bodies were lying spread-eagled like insect specimens in the darkened aisles. I hated to think what their last moments must have been like.

'Jesus Christ! This is awful. A massacre. And where are the rescue services?'

'They've probably made this a prohibited area. The military will get here soon, I expect.'

'But what's causing it? This could be happening everywhere. Surely the government can do something?'

'Governments usually move too slowly to do anything but mop up the mess when it's all over. I wouldn't expect too much from any of the authorities, frankly. This is unknown territory for everyone. Anyway, I think you already know the cause, don't you?'

The truth was I was frantically trying not to imagine what was causing it. Les was the world's saviour, I reminded myself whenever I thought about him; he was the one who was finally going to beam us up and out of the terminal mess we've created out of the paradise we inherited; he couldn't be allowed to fuck it up, at least not on this scale. He may have got some of his numbers slightly out when programming the Cube, but one had to trust his heart was basically in the right place. Heart, did I say? Trust? What quaintly obsolete human concepts! Whatever was I thinking of?

'I have a strong suspicion, yes. I just didn't want to believe he could make such a cock-up of it. I thought that was a uniquely human prerogative.'

The streets were by now wide enough for us to walk along in single file, and we made better progress. Everywhere was the evidence of ordinary people suddenly finding themselves in greatly reduced circumstances: a school I discovered was particularly shocking: classrooms crammed with puppet-sized pupils frozen into positions of surprise and terror while in the act of playing or speaking; it was impossible to be indifferent to their instantly terminated lives, so full of energy and possibility did they seem. I couldn't but wonder how the end had come to them: slowly, with increasing pain, bewilderment and fear; or summarily, the world of light and movement blanking out in mid-gesture without the slightest intimation that anything was amiss.

As the scale of the town reverted to normal there were suddenly no bodies visible; the entire place was deserted, as though word had got round and everyone had dropped what they were doing and high-tailed it for the countryside. There was an unnatural silence too: it seems the birds and animals had also been part of the general flight.

'How is it,' I asked Rachel, 'that you can be alive and dead at the same time?'

'No. I'm dead, Adam. What you're seeing is what you want to see. The Cube has eliminated the distinction between physical forms and imagined ones. The whole world is fiction now. So please be careful what you imagine.'

I glanced at her: exactly the same look of imperturbable seriousness. If I hadn't been before, I now began to feel very nervous regarding my life-death balance.

'This is totally mad; I know for a fact I'm not fiction. It's self-evident.'

'Don't worry about it Adam. In the end everything's rearranged and we just start over again. Eventually the penny drops and it all makes perfect sense.'

'That's the last phrase I'd apply to all this.'

'Nevertheless it's all the consequence of altering a few fundamental constants very slightly.'

'So if I had killed you – not that I'm admitting it – how was it possible we had that dinner party and you left my flat in perfect health to go to your brother's wedding, exactly as you planned?'

'Oh that's simple: even then the Cube was performing its tricks: you wanted me to be alive, so it generated a world in which I was alive. And it did it exceptionally well. It took me quite a while to realize the truth.'

'But if your theory is correct, there would be two truths: a "Rachel alive" truth, and a "Rachel dead" truth, both equally, er, true.'

'True. I suppose the dominant truth at any given moment would be the one you perceive.'

It was at that moment that I realized with a wonderful clarity that Rachel had simply gone mad. It was clear as a bus that she was as fully alive as I was; but something very painful had happened to her that had caused her to take flight from reality. Suddenly I saw a way to help her.

'Listen. I was on my way to a friend's house in the Blackdown Hills when I was detained by a horrific demon. Why don't you come with me? You could have a good rest there and we could talk properly. I know Elaine would be delighted to put you up as long as you wanted. There wouldn't be a problem. There's tons of space. And she's a fantastic cook. You should taste her gooseberry pies! Up there with the gods. What do you say?'

There was a long pause while she considered her reply. Her large soulful grey eyes looked like she was struggling against the urge to console me.

'It wouldn't be a good idea. It would distress Elaine to sense you and not be able to see you or talk to you.'

'But she would. She's extremely sensitive. She has long conversations with her cat. Really, it wouldn't be a problem. You and she would get on marvellously.'

A desperation was welling up inside me. The nonsense about being dead had unsettled me, in a place that hadn't been properly unsettled before, and it made me want to run through every proof of being alive I knew of, from reciting alternate letters of the alphabet backwards to kicking boulders and observing the ensuing agony. Rachel's impassivity and unsmiling sympathy was also disturbing, because it was not how the mad were supposed to behave.

'I'm sure we would. But if we went now it would just drive her crazy. And it would drive you crazy because you couldn't do anything about it.'

'Rachel, will you please for God's sake stop talking like this! Neither of us is dead! This is reality, no matter how bizarre it seems. It's the only reality we have, so it behoves us to live in it as fully as possible and try to help people while we're here. And I really do need to see Elaine. She'll be going frantic not hearing from me.'

Then I had the obvious idea of phoning her. I asked Rachel if that would work.

'It might. The voice seems to persist for quite a while after the physical form has gone. You've probably noticed dogs and cats prick their ears and stare into space for no reason. But it wouldn't be a good idea. Really.'

'Why not? It would stop her worrying.'

'It would lead her to believe you were still alive.'

I didn't rise to the bait. There was a row of public phones outside a post-office but all of them were dead, which upped my sense of unreality by several notches.

'We'll have to go further out. There'll be a better chance of normal service away from the centre.'

We walked another half mile and found a normal-sized deserted cafe with its lights still blazing. Luckily it had an old wall-phone which miraculously was working. I fumbled for my address book and dialled Elaine's number.

'Hello Elaine. It's Adam.'

Her voice was sharp with tension. 'Did you say Adam?'

'Yes.'

'Oh. It's good to hear you. You sound like you're on Mars.'

'No. Only Dorset. How are you?'

'I'm fine. But you sound strange. Sort of scratchy and wavery.'

'There's been a weird event here, that's seriously affected communications. One of your pits has appeared in the centre of a town. The whole place is deserted.'

'You keep disappearing. I'm having trouble following you.'

'Elaine, Listen. I'm on my way. But I may be some time. The roads are confused. But don't worry, I'll get there.'

'That sounds ominous. Are you alright? I've been missing you.'

'Yes. I'm absolutely fine. I'm missing you too. A couple of small diversions happened is all. I'll see you tomorrow sometime.'

'I didn't catch that. Your voice keeps falling sideways.'

'I'll see you tomorrow, providing I can persuade the roads to go in your direction.'

'Oh, I forgot to say. I've got some people coming to inspect the hole in the kitchen. It may be slightly chaotic here for a while. Just to warn you.'

'Elaine, don't let anyone go into it. You may never see them again.'

'That sounds rather dramatic!'

'I'll explain later. Just keep away from it. Especially Nicola. It's important, ok?'

'I'll try. But these are government people. They may have their own ideas about it.'

'Have you noticed anything else strange in the house? In the kitchen particularly?'

'Not especially. Only that Nicola won't eat in the kitchen any more. She says her tummy feels squashed.'

'She's probably right. Keep her away.'

'What did you say?'

'Keep Nicola away from the pit.'

'Your voice has gone wonky again.'

210

'Never mind. I'll see you soon. Love you.'

Feeling apprehensive, I replaced the phone and returned to the street. Rachel was sitting on a bench. On an impulse I took her hand, and was reassured to find it warm.

'She's ok. It's a good thing I phoned though: some government officials are going to inspect the hole in her kitchen.'

'It won't make any difference,' Rachel said. 'If they try to close it it'll just appear somewhere else. It's space-time itself that's altered, not matter.'

'I still can't understand how Les and his crew managed to make such a gigantic cock-up of the whole business. You'd think with their infinite computing power they'd have managed to get their figures right, wouldn't you?'

'But didn't you say they had no concept of the irrational?'

'Yes.'

'So there you are. That's why they're not God. And why they need us.'

'Trouble is they didn't do their homework. They should've known sending a thing like the Cube would set the cat among the owls. No one likes to be lectured on his own doorstep by something that resembles a piece of over-budget Startrek scenery.'

'So they need a public relations manager.'

'It's not me. I don't do relations, public or private. As you may have noticed.'

'What I have noticed is you're extremely good at giving yourself a hard time, and very bad at understanding why you do that. Break that cycle and you'll be unstoppable.'

'Explain please.'

'Well, you killed me out of sexual jealousy. Very understandable, given how much I provoked you—.'

'Hang on there, Rachel. I murdered you and you say you understand?'

'Of course! Being dead is a great releaser from partiality. I'm no longer attached to the person I was then, any more than anyone else I might have been. I acted very foolishly with Magnus. I can forgive myself for that now, just as I can forgive you for what you did in the heat of the moment. That's not to say it was a good thing to do of course. But understandable.'

In the moonlight her grey eyes had turned impenetrable as tourmalines. They were looking at me now with an intentness that demanded attention, as though we'd arrived at a moment of high seriousness. I was deeply moved by her words, and said so.

'It's hard to believe you really don't bear a grudge, to say the least. I deprived you of your life after all.'

'And gave me this death. Freedom from time and space and an infinitely variable point of view! Not a bad exchange. Anyway we have millions of lives Adam. Most of which we waste and fritter away. I've learnt a great deal from you actually.'

'Such as?'

'Oh. Not to project my unconscious needs onto men who are just playing a power role. Not to try to rescue people who seem vulnerable. To value true qualities rather than appearances.'

'I must say I feel you've freed me from a huge burden by not blaming me. It's like I can now begin the process of healing without being weighed down by having to constantly punish myself at the same time.'

'Yes. you've been putting yourself through the mill, certainly. But there's still something you keep backing away from, that keeps dogging your steps and which will continue to do so until you face it with complete honesty.'

'How do you know all this? I mean, we've known each other barely a year, and most of that time you avoided me.'

'As I say, being dead probably had something to do with it.' Even now there was no trace of a smile, or touch of resentment in her voice. She simply mirrored what was happening.

'Can I just say one thing? You are not dead. You're warm and breathing. I can feel the life in you. You can put words together as cogently as anyone I've known. Therefore you are thinking. You're also beautiful – not generally considered an attribute of a corpse. So could we just lay that, em, ghost to rest? Please?'

'You will understand very soon now, Adam. I can't convince you because it goes against your deepest beliefs about how the world works. But there's no way out of your hell unless you can come to accept what you did and what caused you to do it.'

Then the all-too-familiar gulf opened in the trackless dark, and I broke down and wept my heart out.

Chapter Twenty Three

I was surprised to find Rachel still sitting there when I eventually returned to my senses. Unmoving in the moonlight, her hands extended on her knees, she was like an Egyptian deity, gazing serenely upon past and future. Despite her irritating insistence on my being dead, I felt immeasurably glad she was there.

'It was the worst mistake of my life, Rachel. I regret it more than I can say. But I've always held out the hope that it had been some kind of hallucination – particularly as my last sight of you was your figure walking – a touch inebriated if I recall correctly – out of my flat after an enjoyable dinner party. I've been holding onto that memory ever since to preserve my sanity.'

'But you didn't really believe it, in your heart, did you?'

That must have been kite-flying, but she'd hit the spot.

'I suppose not. But you can understand my wanting to, can't you?'

'Of course. Perfectly.'

'I suppose it was another of the Cube's tricks to make us feel better.'

'Very likely.'

'I'd give anything now for it not to have happened.'

'It happened in your mind and your will at that moment. That's what counts in this new world.'

'I don't understand. You're saying it doesn't matter whether I actually killed you or not, if I wanted it to happen?'

'No. I'm saying if you wanted it to happen strongly enough – and you must have done at that moment – the Cube would create the narrative of it happening. Conversely, if you wanted it not to happen, it would create an appropriate narrative for that too. The only difference now is it has the capacity to render the barrier between imagination and objective reality transparent.'

'"There's nothing real but thinking makes it so." My god! And it wants me to be its global marketing manager!'

'Forget what it wants, Adam. Follow your own conscience. You had some really good qualities, once you stop this pernicious habit of denying your past. In the end all we ever change is our own heart.'

Where had Rachel acquired all her wisdom, I wondered? Dundee University must be quite a place. I should have had her as my therapist instead of the thousand-pounds-an-ounce Clare who didn't even offer me tea. Bit of a shame I murdered her, I thought, if indeed I had, in a moment of long-brewed insanity. I seemed to have ruined two lives in that moment.

I listened to the night busy with its tasks of invisible purification all around us.

'I'm so sick of having all this anger, Rachel. It's like having a demon squatting behind every thought, infecting it with its own limitless hatred. As if someone else has been living my life, instead of me.'

'When you're dead these things are so obvious.'

'I must see Elaine. We've spent so little time together. And after all if we've just spoken on the phone I can't be all that dead, can I?'

For answer Rachel took my hand and held it. Instantly I had a sense of a huge unstoppable undertow of dark knowledge flowing through my body, and on, beyond everything human, out into fathomless space.

Then very gently she let it go, and still looking straight ahead, said:

'I think we should move from here. I feel more changes coming.'

There was some kind of commotion up ahead. Men in military uniform, searchlights on poles, chain-link barriers, orange police tape stretching as far as I could see. And a huddle of people shouting and gesticulating towards the town. It occurred to me that by now this could be a common sight throughout the country.

'Maybe they won't let us through,' I thought as we got nearer.

'Don't worry. Just keep walking. They won't notice us.'

'How can you be sure?'

'Trust me.'

We walked on, directly towards the check-point. My heart began to pound as the lights faced directly in our path. Off to one side I could see two military policemen holding off an angry group of residents.

'The danger's over!' one of the men was saying. 'What harm is there in us going back? This is nothing but damn stupid bureaucracy!' There was a general surge towards the barrier.

'No one's allowed in,' one of the uniforms announced, not very confidently.

'Try and stop us!' someone said.

There was a scuffle, and another voice cried: 'You bastards! This is our home!' Then a shot was fired, and a figure crumpled to the ground. There was an instant silence, before more uniforms began to appear out of the shadows.

'Just walk across,' Rachel said. 'Don't speak.'

A dog barked at us, but no human took any notice. I shut my eyes tight and walked. We were out. I suppressed a strong urge to run for cover. None of the guards had so much as glanced in our direction.

We made towards a small wood a hundred yards or so from the barrier.

'That was an amazing bit of luck,' I said when we reached cover.

'You'll find you have quite a bit of that sort of luck from now on,' Rachel replied. I imagined I saw a smile on her face, but put it down to the deceptive light.

'I'm going to get back to Elaine's. You sure you won't come?'

'No, thank you. I think two ghosts would be too much for her. Go safely.'

She turned away and before I could stop her she'd merged completely with the shadows. Without thinking I shouted her name. The trees rustled, but there was no response. Suddenly I felt very alone and shocked that she could vanish so unceremoniously.

I had no sense of time or direction, and began walking away from the town, hoping to discover a path that would lead me north again. At all costs I had to get rid of this fury that was slowly eating me alive. The very last thing I wanted to do was dump it all on Elaine. And you could bet your bottom euro that's exactly what I'd end up doing if I moved in with her, exactly as I'd done with Cora and Rachel. Cora had got out in time, but Rachel had made the mistake of feeling sorry for me, rather than trusting her first intuition.

Suddenly I heard the familiar scratching sound in my head, which was the signal that Les was once again desirous of hearing my opinion on some topic of deep significance to him. The scratching gradually resolved itself into words of immaculate English.

'Hello Adam. I trust you are keeping well?'

'Considering I've just been pronounced dead, I'm feeling remarkably well, thank you Les. Though a touch more paranoid than when we last spoke, having been ambushed by one of your little helpers who had a rather low opinion of me. Still, that's a small detail considering the weighty matters that you deal with every nanosecond of your existence.'

Les, as I think I've remarked before, is totally impervious to irony, so all this was water off a trilobite's back. He regarded such gambits as semantic lubricants that these intriguing little humans seemed to find essential for serious discourse.

'You may have noticed some peripheral disruption to the surface structure of your planet,' he said in his best pilot's passenger-calming voice.

'Sounds like you're learning how to do English understatement at last!' I replied. 'Congratulations.'

He ignored my sarcasm completely.

'We anticipated this in our calculations,' he went on, 'and there is no need to be concerned. It will not impact seriously on your civilization.'

'Les, can you cut the crap, please? I know you didn't anticipate anything of the sort, and I know you also know it's already impacting, as you so diplomatically put it, on the lives of thousands, if not millions, of people here. Some are already putting two and two together and reprogramming their nuclear warheads to target the Cube. It can only be a matter of time before someone's patience snaps.'

'You must prevent it, Adam. That is your new task. Number one priority. We will of course assist you in every way possible.'

'And I've already told you I'm the worst possible person in the world to do it. Why don't you make contact with someone who has influence? A rock star, or a top-drawer footballer or film actor? Any of those would be infinitely more suitable than me for the job.'

'Naturally we've done extensive tests on this matter Adam. Unfortunately none of the types you mention have the required openness to our ideas. They are locked within their primitive belief systems. In particular they deeply distrust voices appearing in their minds with no obvious cause. They can only think of being 'cured' of the illness, as they perceive it. So we have reluctantly abandoned such an approach. You alone possess the right temperament and mind-set for this work. If you refuse, you will imperil not only your world but the galaxy you inhabit and, eventually, beyond it. Your race's insanity will at some point inevitably reach us. We cannot allow it.'

All this time I'd been walking along a slowly rising mud-track through a straggle of beechwoods, and now I'd reached a padlocked metal gate that seemed to mark a boundary of some sort. I leant on the gate and considered. The wind had dropped completely. A scatter of early stars high overhead. I could almost hear Les holding his breath a thousand light years away.

And then the proverbial hundred watt light bulb flashed several times above my head. I realized I'd nothing to lose. My single remaining asset was Elaine. In fact my single remaining reason for not slurping a tub full of whisky-flavoured paracetamol was also Elaine. For the first time in my life I felt something like complete trust in another human being. That fact alone was worth losing a fat chunk of the world for. But what if I lost more than that? What if the price of saving the Cube was saying goodbye to everything? What if I succeeded, and then woke up the next morning to a planet where the human race was only a slow infra-red pulsation in Les's infinite databank?

And the combination of saving humanity and walking through the moonlit English countryside suddenly invoked a memory of my father on one of his hikes in his beloved Lake District. I forget now where exactly we were heading, but we were in a piece of deserted woodland with a pot-holed track winding through it very similar to the one I'd just reached the end of. As so often, we'd been talking politics, with me trying, as ever, to tempt him from the arid uplands of socialist ideology into the lush, wildflower-scented water meadows of human feelings. It was never easy; I'd frequently suspected his socialism was a decoy to lead possible persecutors away from his vulnerability.

'The trouble with all that,' I remember saying as we negotiated the flooded wheel-ruts, 'is that you can't regulate the human spirit: it will always rebel. People are very complex. They need freedom. You know the saying, 'if you want to tame a rebellious horse, put him in a large field'? Well, socialism puts man in a tiny backyard where he can barely turn round, and tells him it's all in the cause of a better society. At the end of the day, it's just plain bad psychology.'

Without breaking step, or even, I suspect, really taking on board the gist of what I'd said, he came back with a defence of his elders.

'You've misunderstood what Socialism's about Adam. It's not about taming or controlling. It's about giving people a chance who've never had one before. Not just the privileged and wealthy, but everyone, regardless of circumstances. True equality. Everyone is born with equal potential; so tell me why so few actually have a chance to improve themselves? It's the arrogance and self-interest of the upper classes. Whatever anybody tells you, the bottom line is, despite their claptrap about wealth trickling down to the underprivileged, none of them really believes that: and they don't care a fig either, so long as their own privileges aren't threatened.'

It was always hard to argue with him because deep down I needed him to win: he was my Dad, after all, and no one likes to see his own father exposed to ridicule. But in my heart I knew his heart wasn't in his argument; it was what he'd always believed, of course; but what he believed was a result of what his times believed, which in turn was a reaction against what the preceding times had believed, and so on. I realized there was a further layer beneath mere belief, which might be called gut-feeling. And his gut-feeling mistrusted socialism as much as I did, and for the same reasons: for all its rhetoric it didn't respect the human spirit and therefore desired to replace it with a system, like a perfect clock that always delivered the precise time, but never thought to ask why we need to measure it in the first place.

'Maybe that's what it was about in the beginning, but it soon descended into fanaticism, didn't it? Surely you're not going to try to defend Stalin and his horrific brood?'

'No. That was a madness. An aberration. It shouldn't have happened. It had nothing at all to do with socialism. True socialism has hardly existed so far: perhaps the nearest we've yet come to it were the kibbutzes: that's where it got practiced on the ground, day by day, in humane conditions. You know, that proved to me that human beings really could work and live together for the good of the whole, provided their individuality is respected. Soviet socialism forgot that bit, and went for control and regulation. That's where the rot set in.'

I chewed on that for a while. 'The thing that always worries me is that the free individual is always seen as a threat to the system. The assumption behind this is the individual can't be trusted to act altruistically; left to himself he will always act to the detriment of the whole. That belief is the fundamental flaw in all ideologies: it inevitably leads to social engineering. And then you get resentment, rebellion, revolution, and counter-revolution. The crucial vision is lost.'

'Well it doesn't negate the original premise: men can live for the good of the whole, given the chance. But so far it's been bungled by leaders with limited knowledge of human psychology. One day we'll get it right.'

'We won't ever get it right if we ignore what individuals actually want from their lives. For instance, what do you want? For yourself, I mean, not for humanity.'

I don't think anyone had ever asked him that before. He stood still and glanced nervously at me as though he was terrified we'd be caught by the telescreen.

'I don't know,' he eventually confessed. 'It's not a question I've ever asked myself.'

'Perhaps you should.'

Much later – maybe as much as a year later – we resumed that conversation when we were on a birding holiday on the north Norfolk coast. Ever since his youth he'd been a keen birdwatcher, and would slink off by himself at a moment's notice if there was some rumour of a rare sighting somewhere. In later life he was more organised, and had taken me with him to a large, sprawling wilderness on the North Sea's margin with mile upon mile of squelchy mud track where on a wet November morning you could virtually guarantee to encounter no other human soul – or at least not one who wanted to talk to you.

'This is what you really, love, isn't it?' I said, raising my voice above the sirening of the wind. 'Solitude. Nature. The wild. Isn't it?' I turned to see his reaction, but he didn't answer. Instead his silence was laden with eloquence more than any words he might have spoken. If only I'd had the nous then to simply shut up and let it be heard. But no: being the son of a true socialist that was something I couldn't find it in myself to do. I pursued my quarry.

'How does this sit with your socialism? What would headquarters think of your being here at the end of the world, when there are so many iniquities to put right?'

'You're talking about communism, not socialism. I never was a party man. Never will be either. Communism is where it all went horribly wrong. A disaster from the start. Please don't mix socialism up with that.'

'Actually I'm talking about feelings. What people like you and me actually want. And I don't think you really want to put the world to rights. Not in your heart of hearts. You want – well, this: solitude, space. The great noble rhythms of nature. And there's nothing wrong with that. Socialism represents the crowd mentality, and people are sick of it. It's anathema to the human spirit.'

Again he said nothing, but slowly raised his binoculars to a distant sand bar which was crowded to the waterline with the ragged shapes of sea birds vying to claim squatters rights on their four-inch patch of mud. And even then I pursued him mercilessly rather than keeping quiet and sharing what he loved.

'That's ultimately what I have against socialism – not the aim, but the mentality it breeds. There's no space for doubting. No space for just being who one is. No negative capability. It's all imperatives and threats.'

The cold rain drove in from the North Sea and we turned to retrace our steps to the steamy shelter of a cafe. I'd won the battle, but when you're young there are some battles you need to lose. It wasn't until years later, after his death, that I discovered how bitter some victories can taste.

It was almost dawn and I'd absolutely no idea where I was. The moon had set behind the still not quite bare limes and sycamores a hundred yards to the south. And I was neither tired nor hungry despite walking through the night. As for being dead – well, as the man said, it's not over till the fat lady sings – and as yet the fat lady hadn't even appeared on the stage.

I dropped from the gate and landed in knee-high lush grass, then set out across an open field to what I hoped was a second gate in the far corner, with the single objective of finding a road that would lead me to Elaine, where I could feel her delightful human body against mine, and worry about nothing more serious that the wretched rabbits eating her winter carrots. I wasn't a world-saver; dammit, I couldn't even save the lives of my friends when they finally depended on me. With a great deal of luck and vigilance I might just manage to be a good friend to Elaine, and avoid buggering up her life with my legacy of intricate paranoias. That, at least, was my ardent hope.

Another meadow lay ahead of me: this one rose steeply towards a wooded crest that blocked my view of the landscape beyond. The sky was brightening behind it, and I hoped I'd be able to find a path that would at least lead me eastwards. But when I reached the crest I was astounded to see the land falling sharply away to a town, still shrouded in shadow and moonlit mist, and beyond it what appeared to be the sea. All this time, despite my persistent attempts to go east, I must have been traveling more or less due south, directly away from Elaine's.

I stood looking down at the sleeping town, while a cold breeze from the east rattled the remaining leaves and stung my face. I'd had enough of my willful solitude; winter was ahead and I wanted nothing better than shelter and friendship and lashings of TLC. But something didn't want me to have it, and I was beginning to suspect the something was not a million miles from the Owl Nebula. I decided to call up Les and try to get a straight answer from him. At least then I'd know what kind of force I was up against. But even before I could form my question his crow-cold voice was filling my brain with calm and perfectly weighed language.

'Adam, we've received information that has made us all very sad indeed. One of your militant groups has launched missiles towards the Cube. They are due to reach it in nine minutes. We will of course be forced to withdraw it before impact. This means your response to our earlier request is now irrelevant. It also means our mission to reform your world must be postponed temporarily.'

I struggled to take on board the huge implications of his message. Militant groups could only mean – in the circumstances – a Middle Eastern, anti-American coalition. The US was bound to retaliate. It probably meant a third global conflict.

'What kind of weapons are in the missiles?'

'Our most recent probe indicates the technology is nuclear fission.'

My heart instantly began to prepare for a futile flight. A nuclear strike on Cumbria by an Islamist alliance: the news really couldn't be worse. Without question at this moment a counter strike was in progress on the suspected culprits. In nine minutes the first global war of the twenty-first century would begin.

Unless, of course, this was yet another ploy of Les's to get me to take up the post of his publicity manager. I had no way of finding out, lacking a mobile phone or hot-line to the military. I needed reliable information, and the only place I'd find it was the peacefully slumbering town below.

All my father had been asking for was love, I reflected ruefully, as I found a well-worn path leading down from the ridge through scrubby boulder-strewn pasture. And I hadn't been able to give it. Instead, I had to complete with him for a system for saving the world. If only some alert angel had taken me quietly to one side and and told me that people tell you their deepest needs in code.

It was eight a.m. and everyone was gaping open-mouthed at the TV set on its high pulpit over the counter. Its screen showed an image that formed a large part of the West's perennial nightmare: a wide ragged cylinder of black smoke rising high into the atmosphere, then bulging out into a shallow hemispherical cap. When the camera pulled back to show the landscape around the base of the column, there was no sign of a town or oil-depot or industrial centre: whatever had been there had simple been vaporized, broken into its original elements, so that what remained was now less than dust; maybe even less that molecules. What the picture revealed was a blackened crater, surrounded by charred structures that might once have been dwellings for humans. The commentator was visibly struggling with shock and disbelief. "There is simply nothing left standing within a two kilometre radius of the point of impact," he was saying. "This once thriving Yorkshire town of Althorpe has been simply razed to the ground. It is premature to spin theories of course, but it seems generally accepted that the intended target was the alien artifact popularly known as the Cube. There is considerable confusion here as to whether or not the artifact was destroyed, because no debris of any kind is visible on the site it occupied. It seems the Cube simply dematerialized at the instant of impact. This morning the town had a population of eighty thousand people. It is estimated that ninety per cent of this population has been killed outright..."

A crescendo of outraged voices made it difficult to hear any more. I sat on a tall stool by the window and tried to gather my thoughts. I wanted to get far away from this madness; take refuge in the sanity and peace of Elaine's world. The trouble was, Elaine's world also had a hole in it, which at any moment could open and take everything she possessed into its maw. I edged round to the counter and tried to order coffee, but couldn't make myself heard above the incensed cacophony. I turned to a thin, unshaven man on my left and asked him if he'd heard anything about reprisals, but he seemed neither to hear or see me, but carried on staring at the incessantly repeated images of smoke and rubble on the screen.

It was only then, in the smouldering late November dawn in that sleepless cafe on the south coast of England, crushed on all sides by outraged or terrified or terminally weary men and women taking refuge from the first cold wind of winter, that I faced the brute fact that I was truly dead.

Chapter Twenty Four

After crossing the river Axe I'd finally come out onto a deserted cliff top a couple of miles west of Lyme Regis. A bitter easterly wind had arisen, making me shiver in my ancient overcoat; but my compulsion to continue walking south did not abate.

As I neared the edge of the grass, where it gave way to rubble and chalk, panic began to assert itself, like a freezing hand sliding inside my guts. Strange there was no fence here, not that fences had any deterrent effect whatever when it came down to it. What fence ever deterred the envisioned explorer? The chill wind swooped up to meet me, like a spirit summoned from the farthest circle of the world.

Now I had left the grass verge behind and was standing on bare chalk, kept from crumbling by a frail web of thin, wind-blackened roots. Far below the foam-headed waves growled and hissed in their cage of gravity. It seemed a very long way down. Yet what did it matter? Everything I'd imagined as worth working for was revealed nakedly now: success, friends, lovers, ideals, career, self-respect; from my new perspective the tiny gap between life and death seemed of little consequence.

The wind's upsurge abated momentarily, and I felt myself sway slightly forward, dislodging a few more clods of earth and chalk. I became exhilarated: I was about to become Icarus for the twenty-first century, to discover what lay just over that slender ledge of time and space…

And then, glancing vertiginously down at the threshing white-capped waters, something caught my eye: a tiny intense spot of opalescent light, seeming to come for the very rocks around which the green water swirled. It seemed to flicker, as though someone were signaling with a mirror, sending pulses of blinding light up the cliff-face. I watched it, mesmerized, wondering if there really could be someone down there, trying to communicate. Something snapped sharply underfoot, and I lost my balance, and there was nothing beneath me but cold air and a grey motionless cloud of suspended chalk and small pebbles. Despite being dead, the long habit of fear dissolved my guts into a churning sea of terror.

Only one desperate thought filled my mind as I gathered speed, glancing off outcrops of unforgiving rock every second or so, and that was William Blake. My one huge regret was that I'd not managed to meet him again, after that single bizarre long-ago encounter in Marylebone. My heart suddenly opened and depths of grief flooded into it, as though this one omission in my life was the source of all the other errors and disasters. He was my true father, my mentor, protector, guide, exemplar – and I'd never managed even to speak to him. He embodied every value I held meaningful in existence, and I'd not made the effort to emulate him, or even properly understand his art. And now I'd summarily left the human realm and committed myself to who knows how many ages of unconscious drifting among disconsolate ghosts. I'd cut off all chance of redemption, of redressing the chaos I'd created through my persistent forgetfulness. I could, at the very least, have helped people, done a little good to those I'd met who were in a worse state than myself; or at least tried not to create more ill than there had been at the start of my earthly career. But it seemed even that little was beyond me.

I opened my eyes and saw the toothed rocks looming below, and the notched blades of wild water reaching up towards me like the fangs of Charybdis. The strange flickering light had blossomed into a large disk that seemed to hover in space between my falling body and the rocks, and now there seemed to be shimmering colours mixed in with the white, like a little circular mirage beating in the air. I thought for a moment there was someone standing in it, like a tiny demon trapped inside a pentagram. But now a state of remorse mixed with terror entirely gripped my mind. I could think of nothing at all but the imminent destruction of my body and consciousness, and what I wouldn't give to undo that last act of apathy and self-pity. Images spontaneously formed themselves in my mind: making love with Cora for the first time, her caressing fingers exploring my body; my father at the kitchen table one Christmas making a model boat out of balsa wood and glue; the face of my mother on her deathbed, seeing the heavenly effulgence of daffodils for the last time; Rachel's delicate breasts and lustrous hair like fine gold-leaf; a clear hill stream dipped in pristine sunlight from childhood; and Blake's face, orioled in sky-blue brilliance...

Blake's face? My eyes were wide open; this was no final memory before blackness claimed me: this was a present image, fully formed before me. And not only his face, but his whole body was there, standing on nothing, cradling a sketchbook under one arm, as though I'd interrupted his work by my reckless descent. And I seemed no longer to be falling: my nemesis was still some fifty feet below; the rush of icy wind had stopped; and now that I looked more closely, the waters themselves had freeze-framed into a green and white backdrop, a rhythmic procession of spots and streaks of vivid colour which reminded me – absurdly for one in my position – of a late Howard Hodgkin oil painting.

'So we meet one more time,' Blake said, his marvellous unafraid gaze calmly resting upon me.

He addressed me from within a kind of patterned ring formed out of ancient devices: compasses, pentagrams, mason's marks, an engraver's knife, an eye in a circle, a triangle with flames in it, a crescent moon, an eagle, a raven, a hammer, a flaming sun, the whole encinctured in many shimmering gold and silver stars. His clothes too were richly emblazoned with similar symbols.

'I'm truly sorry,' he went on, like a loved uncle addressing a headstrong nephew – 'that we couldn't have contrived to meet in better circumstances. In fact, if you had kept your mind on your intended mission the night you stayed in my house, we would almost certainly have met then. We were very close to meeting.'

'You were there after all?' I heard myself cry out.

'Of course. If you had managed to slow your mind down a little you would certainly have seen me. But I can understand that there were distracting influences.' He gave me a smile that was at once complicit and slightly reproving. 'But no matter. Here we are. And you can still learn something. Who knows? You may be lucky in your re-birth, and remember this encounter.' He sat down on something I could not see, crossed his ankles, and laughed. 'You have the same expression on your face as when we met in that orchard at Marybone. A newborn babe could not express more amazement!'

'Am I not dead then?'

'You are in death's antechamber, where he appraises you for dwelling with him. With some souls, this can be a long sojourn. But the laws of heaven are not mechanical. In fact, I have already made some small adjustments to them, which normally would not be permitted.'

'Adjustments?' My voice insisted on perching like an insane parrot high in my skull, far out of reach of control.

'As you see, you are no longer in headlong descent. Time is in a state of suspension while we converse.'

'Why have you done this?'

'Let us say a combination of your genuine remorse for your past wrongs, and an overwhelming heart-longing to meet me. That touched me deeply. Such desires may occasionally sway the laws of the universe, momentarily, enough to open doorways and passageways we'd never normally suspect were there. This universe is, after all, a work of art, not a mechanical construction.'

I could not find any words to meet these revelations. The truth of what was happening to me was sinking in: I was, against all odds, talking to Blake – and maybe, beyond all hope, certainly beyond deserving, I was being offered a way out of my misconceived exit from the world.'

Blake went on: 'So I want to help you. As you've come part way to meet me, so to speak, this may be possible. I know what it is to despair. I have known many years of it, when I doubted not only the world's interest, but my own vision. Then I crawled to work each dawn like a worm, and home again at dusk like a serpent, angry and sullen, swollen with spoiled energies and hope abandoned. No one knew me, or cared to know me: only Catherine sustained me by her love and friendship in all weathers, and her lowly practical devotion when I was too deeply mired in despair to protect myself.'

'So how did you survive? I mean, what gave you the courage to go on with your art?'

'My angels spoke to me, as I am speaking to you now. They persuaded me that the only crime in the eyes of God is to abandon one's work. In my case that meant my spiritual effort. My quest to embody reality in paint and copper and ink, so that others may know what kind of world we travail in, and to what end. I saw that everything else must pay tribute to this quest, no matter how dark that path is. I saw that strength will be given at the time one needs it, provided one keeps faith with one's work. Art is work. Work is spiritual travail: casting away shadows to reveal the fire. As soon as I saw that truth, my life was renewed, and I cast aside all self-doubt. And I thank my angels in eternity for showing this to me.'

'How do you know which are angels? I presume they don't have wings and long white dresses?'

'No. They look exactly like ordinary things. Flowers. Pots. Candles. Insects. Sometimes birds. The difference is in their energy. Through that they are able to look back and be aware of me. Their visible form is only a deception. Thus the spiritual world is a fire enclosed by cold forms, and nothing is outside it.'

'I believe I am outside it. For me the world was a trap with nothing but cinders at its heart. And I never found angels in it, apart from Dr. Johnson, who I mistreated terribly. I suppose now I'm a damned soul at the gate of Hell.'

Blake inclined himself forward and fixed his clear eyes on mine. 'No. Not damned. Maybe at the gate of Hell, but not damned. For consider that the gate may not open to you. Adam, let me tell you a story. Like you I was once cast down after my first exhibition of paintings was entirely ridiculed by those misformed souls who appoint themselves as judges upon artists. This was nothing to me: I had no expectations of them, being the mere outward shells of human beings. But my friends chose to follow them in their estimate of my work, and that I took cruelly. So I betook myself away, and wandered a day or more in Wapping and Limehouse, among the brickmakers' fires, meditating my state of exile. I decided to give up art, and be a journeyman, taking work wherever I may, having no family, or fixed home, or expectation of success or fame. So I set out at daybreak, and quickly found myself in a land of smoke and perpetual dusk, where people wandered blinded by the thickness of the air, unable to greet each other for the dust and ash constantly swirling between them. And such sights of terror greeted me that I was convinced I had left the world of men and was already in Hell: two men fighting with daggers for want of the shrunken carcase of an ox; another, with bulging red eyes, moaning constantly and scratching like a rat among stinking garbage; a woman heavy with child and weeping with hunger and thirst; a naked child covered in the pox and screaming for its mother who was nowhere visible. And a stench of burned flesh and rottenness everywhere, as though the earth itself were sick to death and lost to the memory of joy. And all this so near to the seat of profit and luxury, where men grow fat on others' labours, and want nothing. And I reflected that I was not in Hell, but on Earth, and in London, the very city of my birth and nurture. So in weariness

I sat down on a rock, and ate some of the bread I had brought with me, and drank some clean water I had in a bottle, and watched this bursting vale of sorrow, and asked of myself why the people did not rise up and with one voice demand justice. And I saw that it was because they were so long parted from human discourse that they had forgotten what they were, and were so weighed down with need and suffering that they had no strength to stir themselves spiritually. So they lived in perpetual twilight believing it was full morning, and that the fire and soot around them was sunlight, and that there could be no other state possible. And I then asked of myself, what do these people need of art? They need justice, bread, milk, freedom from disease, and the strong sunlight of education. But not art. Therefore I should abandon art, and become a healer, an agitator for release from unjust laws made only for those who wish to preserve their stolen prosperity. I should be a thorn in the side of tyrants and a trumpet to the ear of those who sleep the fat sleep of luxury. Thus I debated with my angel all the long morning.

But my angel – who was then a sleek crow sat on a nearby ash-heap – raised his voice against my stubbornness.

"Art is the method by which God spreads understanding, by means of signs and figures and harmonies. Take art away and you take away the tools men need to do their true work, which is the work on the heart's atonement, and you leave them with only work on the shadow world, which does not sustain them. Without work on the heart there is eternal strife, fear, want, envy and the pursuit of the mere shadows of their heart's desire. This is the world of single vision, which has no end, and yet never begins." Thus my angel spoke from his palace of ashes, while I marveled that such beings could come into this world of night and converse with men about the things beyond night.

And so I thanked him and wandered on, and came to a derelict place where the world bore no mark of man, but abounded in creatures with scales and hair and fur, and worms and other low creeping things. Here there seemed even less hope for joy or release from woe, as each one was either consuming his neighbour or being consumed, or fleeing the prospect of being so. There was no moment set aside for repose or reflection, but every inch of time was a ferment in which each creature wallowed hopelessly. What hope for art here, I asked again, when there is no rest and no means of hearing or seeing beauty?

But my Angel had followed me here too, and was now a pale yellow moth lit on a broken willow stem. And he refuted my despair thus:

"The creatures you see here may be blind in the human sense, but they are by no means insensible. If you emanate anger they will know it, and if you emanate love they will know that too. They may not hear music, but they know kindness. So let your art be love and kindness. Create works of gentleness, forms of sympathy. Even though the cat and the tiger have their killing natures that you cannot change, still you can plant a seed in them which will come to term in the world that your art creates. For there is a golden web, invisible to mortal eyes but visible to ours, which spans all minds, from the lowliest leaf or creeping creature to the angels and archangels, whereby no virtue is lost, but travels to all worlds and all times. Therefore practise your art, and do not waste yourself in doubt, for you will see, in the right time, that what I tell you is no less than the great Way of Heaven." Having thus delivered himself of this speech, he opened his wings and flew away silently southward, and was quickly lost in the murk of another dusk.

After that, I was at once restored, for I knew by an instinct that he was an angel come down to that spot in space and time for my education, and that he spoke no less than the truth as it is rarely heard on this globe.

I made my way back home, and in the afternoon found Catherine at her needlework, in the spot of sunshine she loved to sit in beneath the hollyhocks. And she jumped up and demanded why I'd been away so long, without word, and when I replied that it was barely a day, she informed me I'd been gone seven whole days and nights, and she had feared I had fallen among cut-throats or soldiers, and she would never see me alive again. Which made me conclude that I had been away not only from my own home, but also from my own time, and had dwelt somewhat in angelic time, which is compared to ours like an oak tree to a daisy. And I marveled again, thinking in whose company I had been, and went upstairs and wrote some little verses about it, by way of telling Catherine with whom I had conversed, and in what place.'

'That's a fantastic story,' I said.

'No,' said Blake emphatically. 'It is entirely the truth. I would not burden the precious hours with falseness.'

'No, I meant it is a great story. A wonderful story. Truly inspiring. And I must confess there have been moments when I felt the presence of something angelic, in those fragments of the day which don't seem to belong anywhere, when there seem to be tiny cracks in the minutes and seconds where bits of another world might push through. I think if I were a writer I'd write about those moments, because they seem to have infinite possibilities.'

'Then you should do so at once, without delay.'

'How can I? My life has been extinguished.'

'As I told you, I have the power to change the laws of time, for nothing is fixed irredeemably, as Newton from his Shadow insists on telling us. And the more out of the vegetable world we climb, the more plastic and malleable the laws become.'

'So you could reverse my death?'

'Not quite. Listen carefully to my proposal and weigh it in the balance before you decide. For the choice will be yours. You may embark on any project of art, in any form and upon whatever theme you wish. You may have as much time as you please to finish it. You may go wherever you wish and take as long or as short a time as you desire. In that time I will not meet you or exhort you. But the moment you complete the task you will find yourself here again, at this exact spot, falling onto the rocks down there. For the consequences of your act cannot be cancelled, but only postponed. In the end you must eat the fruit of the seed you have planted. But your life will not have been in vain, and what you produce henceforth will not die with you, but live on to nurture others." I looked at his face, and he was perfectly serious, and I had no doubt he could do what he promised.

What I did doubt was whether I had the skill and the energy to undertake what he asked. I had never completed anything before; maybe I was incapable of completing a book, of whatever length. And this made me think that there might be an escape clause in Blake's proposal.

'What if I abandon the work, and leave it unfinished? Will I then still have to return here?'

He smiled benignly, as though indulging a child's transparent party trick. 'You will not return here until you finish it. But neither will you be able to live your life until you finish it. When you are not working you will be like a wraith, wandering the wild heath in quest of its true home. You will not have peace until you deliver the child fully formed into this world.'

'But what if I made it endless, knowing what will befall me at its conclusion?'

'You will not know. You will forget this meeting as soon as you are released back into life. You will remember only your task until it is brought to term. And then, of course, you will remember everything until your death reaches you, which will take – excuse me while I calculate these broken crumbs of time – three and a half seconds.'

It was the strangest bargain I'd ever been offered, and I could see that I would be a fool to refuse it: three and a half seconds of life – with not too many options available during it: basically falling helplessly to an irrevocable death – set against as much time as I needed to work on any project I wanted: good works, painting, sculpture, a poem, play, philosophy, or the novel to end all novels, maybe the novel of my life. But I would know nothing of this bargain; what if I produced it very quickly, and completed it within a few days? Or even hours? Would I realize my predicament before reaching the final full stop?

I thought deeply for maybe a minute, then turning to Blake, said:

'If I accept the bargain, will you ensure it will be a good work, and worthy of who I am? It would be terrible to spend twenty years on a task, only to realize at the final moment it had been a mistake?'

'Only you can ensure that. I can offer you only your life and time in which to complete your work.'

Suddenly the decision was before me, bright and inescapable as death itself.

'Alright, I accept.'

'Then let us begin. Be firm. Doubt not your skill. Remember the angels! Fare well.'

And with those words, as novelists say, ringing in my ears, he became again a shrinking disk of brilliant light dancing in the void, and I felt my world dimming, my consciousness fading to a grey limbo, and then to nothing.